Messiah

Love, music and malice
at the time of Handel

T0159450

Messiah

Love, music and malice
at the time of Handel

Sheena Vernon

**TOP HAT
BOOKS**

Winchester, UK
Washington, USA

First published by Top Hat Books, 2014
Top Hat Books is an imprint of John Hunt Publishing Ltd., Laurel House, Station Approach,
Alresford, Hants, SO24 9JH, UK
office1@jhpbooks.net
www.johnhuntpublishing.com

For distributor details and how to order please visit the 'Ordering' section on our website.

Text copyright: Sheena Vernon 2014

ISBN: 978 1 78279 768 5

A CIP catalogue record for this book is available from the British Library.

Design: Stuart Davies

Printed and bound by CPI Group (UK) Ltd, Croydon, CR0 4YY

We operate a distinctive and ethical publishing philosophy in all
areas of our business, from our global network of authors to
production and worldwide distribution.

Acknowledgements

My thanks to friends who were kind enough to make helpful comments during the writing of this book, particularly to the author, Jane Myles, who was so encouraging.

Biographical note

Sheena Vernon divides her time between Sussex and Dublin. When she is not walking her dog, designing people's gardens, watching operas or wasting time on social media, she is much afflicted by a desire to weave stories for both young and old. Her career suggests an early and continuing fascination with words but the name of her website, www.yourexpertwriter.com, should be taken as ironic since, to her regret, she is not an expert on anything.

The Beginning

1. The Charterhouse School

In the candlelight of the German Chapel the night before, their singing, thinks Harry, had been all of a piece with the gleam of rounded pew ends, the shadowy relief of the tracery and the sombre faces of the congregation. From his position in the choir stalls he could see the king, sitting in the front row, his face a mask of stoicism for the poor man suffered from piles. Beside him was a brace of crones, their sagging cheeks betraying the Hanoverian droop. Behind them sat the younger princesses, giggling and fidgeting, until shocked into silence by the clump and clatter of a falling prayer book.

Harry's reverie manages to blot out the torpor of the classroom and the grind and groan of Mr Beaker, the master who taught the boys Greek. The alto, he recollects, how exquisite it had been as it lingered on a single note before taking off like a bird. Mr Gates, the choirmaster, liked their Tallis to be steady and slow, and that's how it had been, like a cart carving tracks through soft ground. The dreamlike way in which the tenors came in is so vivid that Harry hardly notices Mr Beaker coming to a halt by his desk. Chalky fingers yank his ear to make him stand. Momentarily, the master looks disconcerted, for now his pupil is looking down on him.

'Mr Walsh, my apologies for disturbing you.' Exaggerated politeness by a bum brusher, Harry realises, never bodes well. 'Please be so good as to go to the warden's study. Explain to him, if you will, why you find it so disagreeable to pay attention in class.' Harry sighs. Now he will be a trial, yet again, to his dearest Papa. As he approaches the warden's forbidding doorway, he does not know that, in time, he will look back on this day in February, 1732, as one of the happiest of his life.

'Doctor Walsh, we have tried every means to educate your son but the only resort left to us is prayer.' Harry's father has been hauled in from across the square for it is his misfortune that the rectory resides almost next to the school. 'My advice to you is to take him home and give him a thorough beating.'

'What have you to say, my son?' asks the reverend. His tone is weary for these interviews have become increasingly frequent.

'I try, Sir, I really do, but when I read or write, the words, they jump around the page so.'

'What utter nonsense, Walsh, you simply lack application.'

'But it don't happen with a sheet of music.'

'Ah music, yes, in that you excel. You must be proud of the fact that he sings for the Chapel Royal, Doctor Walsh.' Like his faith, the reverend's pride in his son is full of doubt. In any case, manifestations of boastfulness he regards as a sin. His need to temporise, however, is allayed by the warden's next words.

'Sadly, in every other respect, your son is a nincompoop and a dunce. We are going to have to ask him to leave the Charterhouse School.'

Harry looks down at the floor with an abject expression. He thinks he has just been expelled. The opening chord of one of Mr Gates's organ voluntaries reverberates between one ear, which is red and sore still, and the other, then climbs to a thrilling crescendo. He is overcome with a desire to tear off his cap and gown, reach up to the gothic casement and cast them out. Why, he might even throw his arms round the warden and plant a kiss on the bristles that fur his pallid cheeks.

'I think I must heed the warden's words,' says Doctor Walsh as they make their short journey home.

'You mean beat me?'

'No, my son, to do anything so barbaric would be impossible. Resort to prayer, I mean.'

'Tell me, what will you pray for?'

2

He thinks awhile.

'That you'll make a success of yourself, I suppose. That you'll always be loyal to your friends, yes loyalty, that is most important. And that one day, I pray, you will bring home a good and gentle woman to be your wife.'

'I promise you, Papa, I will make sure your prayers are answered. I intend to become a famous singer.' Harry links his arm through his father's and laughs. All he can think of is that he has been expelled and that he is free. For good measure he adds, 'And when I'm older I will bring home a wife.'

His father smiles at his callowness. The reverend is bookish, stooped and old beyond his years, such a contrast to his sturdy, straight-backed boy with his billowing brown curls and rosy bloom. Harry meets his smile; he knows that the promise he has made is fantastical and absurd. How to start? After all, he is only sixteen and as green as the weeds that sprout beneath the horse trough to the front of the house.

This notwithstanding, the good Lord, often so deaf to Doctor Walsh's prayerful entreaties, on this occasion, hears him, and decides to reach out an unseen hand. It will barely be felt amidst the venerable pillars of St Bartholomew's church in Smithfield, where the reverend presides. But its force will be more apparent at the choir of the Chapel Royal for it will positively propel them towards an unexpected destination. They will find themselves, not under the high vaults of a cathedral's roof, or in the intimacy of the court chapel, but at the King's Theatre, the epitome of elegance, home to the Italian opera.

Their journey starts with a chance encounter at the Philharmonic Society's music rooms. Much to the regret of Mr Gates, at his choristers' modest performance of a little-known oratorio by the name of Esther, the composer of this work will happen to be present. He is delighted; the music, after all these years, still so fresh, so full of memories of when he wrote it. An idea forms in his mind; he will stage it at London's opera house where he is Director of Music. His play bills will promise a spectacle of massed choirs round his company of Italian singers. His ambition is to recreate the pomp and grandeur, no less, of King George's coronation. Sacred music as entertainment. What a capital idea! It means that young Harry Walsh will find himself singing for the greatest musician of the age, George Frederick Handel.

2. The King's Theatre, Haymarket

The clock on the tower of St Martin's chimes the hour which tells Harry he is going to be late. It is his first day and the maestro is known to explode at the slightest provocation. As he runs, panting, through the doors of the theatre, the first person he sees is a blond fellow, Peter, Handel's assistant. He remembers him from the coronation, even though he, like Harry, was a boy then and half the height he is now. Regrettably the choristers had enjoyed a joke at the assistant's expense. He'd managed to tip Handel's music bag between the choir stalls at the Abbey, shedding score sheets all over the floor. This welcome diversion from the tedium of rehearsing had caused the boys to laugh. Soon they'd all been snorting behind their hands, virtually peeing in their britches.

'Hello, we've met before,' says Harry as he tries to get his breath back. 'Has Mr Handel started? I gather he gets awfully cross if one's late.'

Peter doesn't say a word. Instead he puts his head down and hurries past, out into the cold. Harry is surprised. Surely the paper-skulled ninny couldn't be holding a grudge about what happened at the Abbey five years ago? Mr Gates emerges from the auditorium and looks relieved and harassed at the same time.

'Ah, Walsh, you have arrived. Such problems with Bishop Gibson. He says the choristers can appear on stage so long as they stand still and do not act. To be frank, I'm surprised we've got this far, he and Handel, as you know, don't get on. The only

person the bishop hates more is the manager here.'

'What about the Italian singers?' Harry asks.

'His restrictions apply to everyone, the Italian soloists included. You and John Beard, by the way, have solos, small ones, of course, and don't worry, they'll be in English.'

'It's exciting, Sir.'

'Yes,' he sighs. 'Everyone is talking about Handel's oratorio.'

It is little surprise that the bottle-headed bishop thinks he's being taken for a gudgeon, Harry muses; when he and Handel used to clash during preparations for the coronation, it was always the composer who won.

'Herr Handel,' he would mew, 'why such a large orchestra? So many singers; this is a place of worship, not a concert hall.' Then he would brandish his Bible like a firearm. 'Texts, sacred texts, I have chosen those that will serve well for your anthems.'

'I have chosen my own,' the composer would reply, pushing out his stomach and puffing up his wig. His secret weapon was always at hand - royalty - how they loved him. Harry remembers the mint new king, another George, followed by a line of stiffs, converging on the great man after the first run through of Zadok the Priest. His face, always red, was redder than ever, flushed with delight. Queen Caroline trilled, "c'était magnifique, solennel si magestrale"; the little princesses, Handel's pupils, grabbed his hands; the young dumpling, Cumberland, tried to ignore the choir boys who had started to snigger. All you could see, amidst the silk waistcoats and hooped skirts, was a halo of powder from the maestro's wig, lit up by a shaft of light slanting down through the stained glass. To a young boy he seemed so grand. There was the added fascination that his 'w's sounded like 'v's, his 'th's like 'z'.

Mr Gates guides Harry into the auditorium and for a moment all he wants is to stand still and take in his surroundings. Carved pilasters climb upwards, like vines, searching out the domed light of the roof; gold painted boxes look down on the pit, one

layer stacked onto the next like orderly Roman catacombs; gilt candelabra repeat a hundred times in the mirrors; on each side of the stage are the royal boxes. What must it be like when the candles are lit and the place crowded with people?

For the present time it echoes with the chatter of musicians who sit around in groups, their music cases strewn across the wooden benches of the pit. To one side a gorger with a fat stomach warms his voice, grunting and growling as if trying to eject a hard stool. Two women babble in Italian to each other, a maid in their wake. Without drawing breath, they remove their capelines, gloves and boissons; one then replaces her boots with dainty, high heeled slippers, the other dons a diaphanous buffon and pats her powdered hair. Their dress is so immaculate you would think they were going to a ball. The plumper of the two starts to flap her hands, to loosen the wrists, tilts her head from left to right, to release her neck, and gets into voice by panting like a dog. The other pulls out a mirror, contorts her face, then pinches her cheeks.

To the front of the pit sits a tall and beautifully coiffured man, his rouged face looking pained as he sips from a silver flask. An attendant is buffing his nails. At any moment Harry expects him to unfurl a set of wings and, with a flash of colour and an echoing screech, fly up to the gallery. He can only be Senesino, the most celebrated castrato in London.

In the centre of all this activity is the magisterial figure of Handel. He is doing no more than leaning over a score with a portly companion by the harpsichord, yet invisible strings connect him to everyone who is present; he it is who has pulled the company present together. He is dressed in green velvet with a flowing wig that would have been the fashion some time before Harry was born.

'Come, we will start.' he calls out, clapping his hands. The 'we' is 've', the 'will' is 'vill'.

Harry finds his place next to close friend, Jonny Beard, and

they grin at each other. The maestro takes the choir through the choruses then has Jonny sing his solo. When it comes to Harry's turn he stops him mid-sentence.

'Are you sight reading, Valsh?'

'I am, Sir.' It is a skill that all in the choir must master.

'Your last note was wrong, read it correctly.'

They try again and this time the composer thumps the harpsichord. The chatter in the pit ceases; the two sopranos stop fussing over their toilette, their maid looks frightened; the plump gorger stops grunting; the nail buffer pauses and turns his head. Only Senesino remains oblivious.

'Valsh, you are a semi-tone out.' Mr Gates rushes up to him.

'His score, it has an error,' he explains.

'Let me see, pass that to me.' Handel glowers as the offending sheet is passed to him.

'Why yes, it is Johann's fault, my apologies.' He smiles, then chuckles and shakes his head. 'Fancy, the score, it has an error. We will try again.' The background noise resumes.

Harry's cheeks burn and blush and as soon as they are dismissed he whispers to Jonny that he cannot stay, for he needs to get home to the rectory. He makes for the stage door, not wishing to mingle in the foyer, and soon finds himself hopelessly lost in a maze of stone floored corridors. A large Roman pediment ambles towards him, followed by two, equally large, pillars and an ornamented balustrade.

'Watch where you're going, half-wit, you'll be in the suds if I drop this,' says a voice from behind the pediment.

Harry hears banging and timidly looks into what turns out to be a workshop. A beetle-browed man, hideous growths sprouting from his cheeks and forehead, is looking over panels depicting maidens and shepherds. One has a spillage of paint across it.

'You,' he shouts. 'Come in. Are you the one who do this? I dock your pay, you realise that?'

'Leave him be,' says a man with a carpenter's leather apron on. 'He don't even work for me.'

'It was one of them screaming Italian buffoons you're so fond of what did that. He said you bobbed him,' says the carpenter's mate.

'I cheat no-one. He say he do screens by last week but no, he is late, then he ask more money, this I not pay, tell one of the men to make repair on this.'

'Don't you worry, Swissman, we'll do your bidding.'

'We'll get it repaired, Mr Heidegger. Why you employ them bobtails, I dunno.'

Harry creeps away down the corridor. He has no wish to make his way back up to the stage for he knows that the Italian singers are rehearsing. Besides, he will probably get just as lost if he does. Instead, he puts his ear to each door and gently opens every one in turn, only to find empty dressing rooms. When he hears scuffling behind one of them he feels emboldened, by fear, to knock in the hope of being given instruction on the whereabouts of the stage door. There is no reply so he quietly pushes down the handle and inches the door open. A man's buttocks, unclothed, are rhythmically moving up and down; only the naked thigh of the woman underneath him is visible, the rest of her is camouflaged by fabric. The man is a violinist, judging by the shape of the instrument case propped up against a chair. Behind the couch a mirror reflects back Harry's solitary form, ghost like, afraid, peeping through the door. Both protagonists are groaning and the groans are getting louder and more urgent. Harry has never seen an act of intercourse before and would like very much to continue watching, but the corridor starts to echo with the sound of footsteps and a sort of low howling.

'Barbaro, tiranno, mostro.' Senesino lumbers into sight, his cheeks wet with tears, his form looking somewhat comic with the knees facing inward and the hips unusually wide.

'Boy,' he says on seeing Harry, 'get me a glass of Modena. John

Swiney, at the Three Crows, he keep a bottle for me under the counter.'

'I will, Sir, if you indicate the way to the stage door.'

'How can I work for him, he understands nothing, I cannot be subjected to humiliation day after day. Dio mi protegge da questo mostro. The stage door? Down there, to the right, keep going to the right. My special wine, not any wine, John Swiney, he will know.'

'Mio caro, mio caro. Così terribile, non piangere.'

One of his compatriots has joined him and hugs and pats him as if he were a pet dog. He has his black hair slicked down and a tiny moustache running along his upper lip. When he sees Harry, watching, he waves him away with a flick of the hand.

At last he finds it, the door to the street. A ragged doorman, with a row of brown stumps where his teeth once were, looks out of a box.

'What have we here? A gentry cove? Speak your business then.'

'Mr Senesino, he needs refreshment. If I fetch it from across the road, will you give it to him?'

'That rather depends on what I get ourovit.' The doorman has a coughing fit, a miasma of noxious fumes fills the air. He leans over so the stumps are unpleasantly close to Harry's ear.

'The man-bitch. He may look like a French capon but women can't keep away from 'im.' He narrows his eyes, the better to impress upon the boy, who is leaning back from him, the wisdom of his words. 'Women,' he concludes, 'they likes an odd dog.'

'If I get his wine, you must give it to him. I'll check on that tomorrow,' says Harry.

'So yus really is a gentry cull. Move yer kicksies, then, I'll give it to him.' His malodorous laugh manages to wash over Harry's face before he escapes on his errand.

'So Senesino's had another little outburst,' says the fellow behind the bar at the Three Crows, presumably John Swiney.

'You're new, aren't you, lad? Welcome to the opera.' His eyes twinkle and he smiles.

As Harry makes his way home he starts to remember the endless hours that they'd spent at the Abbey, rehearsing for the coronation. The cove with girly blond hair, Peter, had probably just started to work for Handel at the time. He would have been, like Harry, ten or eleven. He is filled with regret now at having been unkind to him. It had started because his chum, Jonny, sitting opposite, had been yawning his silly fat head off; what sport, Harry had thought, if he screwed up the cover of his score and threw it into his open gob. When it had landed, instead, on Peter, the young assistant had smiled shyly but then the incident with the music bag had happened.

'What are you doing?' his master had asked sharply, in the tone Harry had heard him use today. Peter's face had gone red. He'd looked mortified then started to run, winding his way through the orchestra, which had yet to be banished to the organ loft, then down the nave. What toads he and Jonny had been. They had asked if they should go and fetch him back, mainly because doing so seemed more fun than sitting still. But when they'd opened the heavy west doors, all they could see, on that grey October day, was a collection of sedans, the bishop's coach and the dismal hovels of Westminster.

'Handel's slave has found freedom at last,' Jonny intoned which, for some reason, caused them great amusement at the time. As they walked back, up a side aisle, two bassoonists, like them, seeking escape from the tedium, were arguing.

'You tap monger,' one snarled, throwing a pair of dice across the floor, 'give me back my rag.'

'Me bung's empty,' said the other, holding his purse upside down.

'Don't bilk me.'

'I ain't, you fat cull, go on then, hit me, I can flash a rare handle.'

Harry had taken a pew nearby, hoping they'd start to fight. But also because he was thinking of the yellow haired boy. Before his scrolled up paper had landed on his head he was looking down and seemed to be counting the floor tiles. Why, he'd wondered? Then, before making his exit, he'd turned to look back at the choir and Harry could see he was crying. It'd made him feel queer because he hadn't meant to upset the ninny.

As Harry trudges past the coachmakers' on Long Acre he thinks how helpful it would have been, today, to have had Peter as a friend. Just at this moment he never wants to sing again.

At supper, his father sits across the dining room table while Samuel serves the soup. A young girl with bare feet, yet another stray from the village in Essex where his aunt lives, serves bread.

'I cannot believe that my beloved son is to appear in a theatre like the King's. What was your first day like?' he asks.

Harry cannot bring himself to tell him that it was absolutely miserable.

3. Brook Street, Mayfair

Peter is waiting in the foyer for Mr Gates the next morning with a message to say that the choristers will not be wanted. But instead of disappearing and giving Harry the cut he catches his eye and smiles. It helps Harry's courage which is sorely wanting; he is so relieved not to be singing. Peter comes over.

'Do you want to join me upstairs and watch the soloists rehearse from one of the boxes?'

Once they are seated, and looking down on the scene below, Harry says, 'Tell me who these people are. The pretty fellow Handel's greeting, I came across him yesterday - what's his name?'

'That's Heidegger, the manager of the theatre. The growths on his face, they're lovely, aren't they? He's a rum bite on all matters to do with money. The man by the harpsichord, that's Johann Christoph Schmidt. Handel calls him Johann. He copies all the maestro's music.'

'He got me into trouble yesterday.'

'I know. I watched you rehearse.'

Harry can feel his cheeks getting red in the darkness.

'I wish you hadn't, my singing was awful. Don't say anything about it, will you?'

'It wasn't awful. I think your voice is nice.'

'Handel, he's worse than a bum brusher, he can be so fierce.'

'It's his way of preserving order and decorum. He finds it's often amiss in the society of musicians.'

'The soprano Handel's bowing to? She looks like one of Cinderella's ugly sisters.'

'La Strada. She's known as "The Pig" for reasons that become clear when she starts to sing. Handel likes her because she's a good set of bellows on her. Also, she's less quarrelsome than his last prima donna, the lovely Cuzzoni.'

Handel is bowing to the gorger with the fat stomach.

'Montagnana, the bass. Senesino's missing, I see. Surprise, surprise.'

'I believe he had an argument with Handel yesterday.'

'He has an argument with him nearly every day. The maestro can be explosive at times. The Italians love that.' Peter pauses then sighs. 'I suppose I better be going. Errands, errands, there are always errands.'

'Please don't.' Harry stammers. 'There's something I want to say. I owe you an apology, about what happened in the Abbey all those years ago. I felt awful about it afterwards it but I never saw you again.'

'I stayed outside with the coachmen, I didn't want to be seen.' Peter looks at Harry with china blue eyes and a half smile, the same one he can remember from the coronation. After what seems like a moment of indecision he says, 'I promised Sid and

Nell an extra walk today.'

'Sid and Nell, are they Handel's children?'

'Heavens, no, he's not married. Sid and Nell are dachshunds; they come from Germany and are utterly and totally adorable. He would never marry.'

'But he loves dogs?'

'No, hates them, they belong to a neighbour, I'm the one who looks after them.'

'Not married?'

'He needs to leave himself free for his music.' Peter raises his eyebrows and shrugs.

'He sounds very particular.'

'He won't even have more than one maid in the house in case they quarrel; says it'll be like being back at the theatre.'

'He's lucky to be able to choose; there are no women in our house because my mother's dead.'

'I'm sorry.' Peter looks across the theatre then adds, 'My mother's still alive, but, in truth, I wouldn't be too sad if she wasn't.' At that they both laugh and, for the first time, feel that the awkwardness between them has been broken.

'I'll walk back with you. I'd like to meet Sid and Nell, to take them for their extra walk.'

First Peter has to call by the stage door. Harry's toothless friend leans out of his box.

'Well if it ain't Mrs Twaddle Poop trolling out with her gentry cove. A flat from the pricklouse left a suit for yer, says th' maister needed it altering.'

'Give it over then, bird-wit.'

He leans towards Peter and lowers his voice.

'La Strada. Wouldn't mind a bit of rantum scantum with a dell like that.'

'To be sure, she harbours a great passion for you.'

The doorman guffaws. 'Mort's tits are nice. I'd lay a bet she enjoys being wapt.' There is more choking and spluttering followed by a stench like a waste heap.

'Never leave a note or anything with the doorman,' says Peter once they are down the alley. 'He's one of Heidegger's little spies.'

Peter leads the way to Hanover Square, a part of London that Harry has never been to before. There are wide pavements to either side of the thoroughfare, trees line them that are just coming into blossom, the façades of the houses are flat, and so neat and uniform. The streets bear signs that name them, and the house fronts are numbered. The place is a wonder.

'You ought to see the houses near Charterhouse Square, they're all so old. They lean into the road, bits of them fall off overnight. It's smelly too; on a killing day at Smithfield the stench travels east to the City and far beyond and you can hear the animals cry out.' A look of horror crosses Peter's face and he begins to tap each set of railings as they pass. 'This all looks so spacious, it's quiet. There are no hucksters plying their wares.'

'Handel was one of the first residents of Brook Street. The dust from the builders drove Betsy mad. She's the housekeeper. She likes cleanliness and order. We all do.' There is more tapping of railings.

'There isn't a jot of order in my home, just piles of dusty books belonging to Papa which he hopes one day I will open. We have an old barn one side of the courtyard in front of our house and every day, it seems, some country booby, looking for work, finds shelter there. My father, his heart is soft.'

Their conversation pauses as Peter leads them round to the kitchen door of one of the newer houses on Brook Street. Sid and Nell, who belong to a Mrs Pendleton, hurtle towards him, yapping their heads off. He kneels down and they dance around him like a pair of hop merchants. Once the maid has tied a dainty collar round each of them and taken charge of the altered suit, they follow the boys happily as they cut south down the side streets. In no time at all the houses give way to building plots and market gardens until the sward of Green Park appears. The boys step out across it to St James' Park and trig along the canal, under the trees, prattling like a pair of buffleheads. Harry tells Peter about the warden, and Mr Beaker, and how he'll never be a gentleman because he can speak neither Latin nor Greek. Peter reels off the names of the titled families that have taken leases in the new houses going up at the end of Brook Street. Because his companion looks impressed, he boasts that Lord Grosvenor's square will be the mightiest in London.

'Does Handel know all these people with titles?' Harry asks.

'He knows a good many.'

'He's so eminent, he frightens me.'

'In a way he's grand and in a way he isn't. His manners are formal. He keeps his distance from all but a select few. I think it's because he knows he's a genius.'

'Does it help the singers, knowing he's a genius?'

'Probably not which is why they don't get on. Johann Christoph is more his sort. They were at the university together in Halle. You can just imagine it - "Come Johann, to ze Domkirk, and listen to zis fugue I just compose." That's students for you.' Peter is bang up with the accent.

'Have you always worked for him?'

'I was bought up by my mother in a troupe of travelling entertainers.'

'How splendid. A troupe of entertainers, that is exotic. You're French, aren't you?'

'Huguenot. It was my uncle who secured a position for me with Handel. I write with a fair hand. He allows me to do his letters now.'

'Did you live in a painted caravan like a gypsy before moving to Brook Street? Did Handel find you at the May Fair?' Harry is laughing; he has a fund of questions to ply him with, about his father, his uncle, his mother. But Peter has begun to go quiet and look anxious. He hadn't planned to walk the dogs at all, he tells

Harry; he has neglected his duties.

'Does that worry you?'

'Just a little. I must pick up some proofs from the printers, then a wig that's waiting on the maker's block.' He reprimands the dogs for chasing ducks, then asks Harry how many ducks he thinks there are and starts counting them. Harry, uninterested in this pointless game, joshes him and smiles. Peter fixes him with his blue eyes. He is not used to the foolery of boys. Harry shoves him again and gets the smile he wants. They both snigger. After the two exhausted dogs have been returned they walk together as far as Denmark Street which is where their ways part.

'Will I see you again?' Peter asks. It must be a change for him having performers at the theatre of his own age.

'Of course.'

As Harry walks home he feels happy, for when he goes to the theatre the next day he will have a friend.

4. Music and Malice

'Where did you go yesterday? I searched for you.' Jonny Beard looks cross.

'I met Handel's assistant, you know, we came across him years ago at the Abbey. He knows everyone and everything, you'll like him.'

'Mm.' Jonny is doubtful.

Handel and Peter have just come through the door and are joined by the man who Harry saw comforting Senesino two days earlier. Voices are raised, the composer throws up his hands and stomps towards the auditorium.

'Who's the rum gagger who upset Handel?' Harry asks once he's introduced Peter to Jonny.

'Another of the Italians. An oily little paillard called Paolo Rolli. If Handel changes a single word of his libretto he says the entire work is ruined. As if we'd notice, the plots are all nonsense anyway. He was a friend of the other composer they had here,

Bononcini. They were drawn together in mutual hatred of Handel.'

'Hatred?' Jonny looks shocked, being the good natured, amiable fellow he is.

'Yes, it's the clay from which life is formed in music circles.'

'That's stupid,' Harry says.

'It's just something about music. It makes everyone so competitive. They're either wracked with jealousy or denigrating each other with infamy and slander. Talking of which,' Peter says as he glances up at the tall, lumbering figure coming through the door. 'Don't look now but someone has deigned to turn up. Now he's the most spiteful of the lot. What he enjoys more than anything is a really good sulk.'

'Is Senesino not a friend of Handel's?' Jonny looks shocked all over again.

'Handel tolerates him because he can sing but, no, he's not a friend. Look, I better go. Sit in the pit and I'll join you.'

'Do you like him?' Harry whispers to his friend.

'I think he's a bit of a know-all,' he sniffs.

Just as they enter the auditorium Handel raises his eyes and sees his castrato.

'We are most honoured by your presence, Signor. Why, you are only a day late.'

Senesino is holding a handkerchief to his nose. He brings a chair onto the stage.

'Go pick up my tonic,' he calls out to Peter, 'this climate is barbaric. I am succumbing to the cold.'

'Peter, you will stay where you are. We will start at the second act.'

After this declaration of war, Peter hastens forward with the leather bag and pulls out the music with a flourish. He pats and prods it into shape so the sheets form a perfect line on the top of the harpsichord. Handel waits patiently, while he fusses and rechecks each one, then nods to a cove who stands in front of the orchestra. The cove nods to the strings so that every violinist lifts his bow in readiness. The maestro then nods to his page-turner who takes his place by the harpsichord, surreptitiously winking at Peter. Slowly, the composer raises a hand, takes a last look round to make sure that everyone's eyes are trained on his, then brings it down. The music starts.

Senesino, who so far has ignored the activity going on below him, puts his handkerchief away and rises, reluctantly, from his chair. He straightens his coat, opens his mouth, pulls his lips around as if something is caught in his teeth, and looks into the distance. As the music goes quiet, his notes come out, clear and effortless, like a bird's. His voice has the volume of a man's and the clarity of a young boy's; he improvises and ornaments while the harpsichord and oboe wind round his trills like silk ribbons. In the half-light Harry glances at Jonny Beard. His mouth is open, his concentration complete.

'Will we ever be as good as that?' he sighs after Senesino's aria comes to an end. He feels almost stunned by what he has heard.

'Even if we were it wouldn't do us any good,' says his friend. 'The maestro is in love with the castrato voice.'

By the time Peter joins them they are sunk in gloomy intro-spection.

'Ah yes, the castrato voice,' he says. 'Did you notice how Handel knows just how to tease his audiences with it? Don't believe that guff about it sounding like the voice of angels. The man-boy sound is a titillation, that's the truth of it.'

'You seem to know a lot about it,' Jonny sniffs.

'I watch the audiences,' he says. 'Even the language, it titil-lates, it inflames people's senses. When he composes in Italian, he's Cupid, shooting darts through the thick skins of Society. They may be hardened and worldly but he manages to rouse them.'

'Even when the conquering hero sings like a woman?' Harry's tone is sarcastic.

'The aristocracy believe that to care about such trivia as what sex a person represents would mean looking like a tradesman.' Peter sighs as if what he is saying is almost too obvious to mention. 'Let's face it, we're all over the place, here at the opera, what with women playing boys and boys playing men. The nobs really like it. That titillates them as well.'

'Are the band all foreigners like the singers?' Harry feels depressed because Esther is an exotic departure for Handel, for the mere fact that much of it is in English.

'Pretty well. The strings are both German and Italian, the strummer-in-chief, Carlucci, a good sort, is Italian. Horn players are always from Romania. His page-turner, that's John Christopher, son of his friend, he's one hundred per cent German though he sounds English.'

'I thought I wanted to be a singer, I'm not so sure now,' Harry says to Jonny as they leave. In three hours they must return for the first performance of Esther.

'I crept into the footman's gallery the other night and watched Flavio,' he replies. 'When Handel entered you should have heard the cheering and stamping. The applause, it was so ardent. He feeds on the glitter, the crowds, the fine company, the chatter and activity going on all around him.'

'Maybe that's why people become part of this circus and put up with all the back-biting and spite that goes with it. They need the adulation.'

'Yes, maybe. Can you remain personable, and still be a singer?' wonders Jonny. 'It's not just the conflicts that worry me, it's the agitation at the thought of being on stage. At this moment I feel sick with fear.'

'Me too,' says Harry.

'Why on earth, are we doing this?'

'Because we vant to titillate.' They start to laugh. Soon they are so helpless that they only just avoid falling into a pothole fashioned by the rain outside the theatre. They caper across the street, causing a calèche to swerve and nearly pitch the elderly article, sitting in it, out into the mud.

'Valsh, you are semi tone out, read it again,' shouts Jonny.

'Signor, you are only a day late for your rehearsal.'

'Madame Strada, you vant I titillate you?'

'Next week I turn seventeen,' says Harry, 'then I will start to titillate, I will titillate everyone and everything.'

'You'll have to do something first if you're serious about it.'

'What's that, get myself docked?'

'No, you numbskull. Learn Italian.'

1732 (continued)

5. The Three Crows, Haymarket

It takes Harry a few moments to work out that Signor Rolli has just called Handel the Teuton Cabbage. This is his first Italian conversation lesson that his beloved father has agreed to pay for and it is taking place in the Three Crows.

'So despite the maestro's little excursion into English, this new oratorio, Esther - such a success, I am surprised - you want to learn Italian?'

'I do, Sir, very much.'

'I understand. It is, after all, the real language of song, the only one I should say.'

Harry thinks hard about what he can manage with his limited vocabulary.

'Have you known Signor Handel long?' he asks.

'My dear Harry, I call you that, yes? I first met him when he was twelve, yes twelve, at the court of the Prussian king.' Rolli intersperses what he says with a paraphrased version in English. 'I was with my dear friend, Bononcini, who was a composer here, once, at the Academy Opera. He was destroyed by the forces ranged against him. Oh yes, destroyed would not be too strong a word, by the machinations of a certain party. Handel turned the king against him, made sure that he loved only his Teuton, his Cabbage, and ignored Bononcini. I am not talking about the current king for I have no contact with him. As you must know I am tutor in all things Italian to our dear Prince of Wales and he and his father, well, let us say, they do not consort. No, I am talking about the old king, the first of your Georges, a barbarian in every way except one. He loved the Italian opera.'

'How was he destroyed?' Harry asks although he has already heard gossip that Bononcini was forced into exile after claiming other people's music as his own.

'How? By libel and title-tattle, his confidence was undermined. Poor man. "My pretty tunes, they are so lacking in substance and depth," he would moan. Sometimes, of course, he would go too far. "Just think," he'd say, "there was a time when I was the genius, the wonder of the age." I, for one, had no recollection of him ever being the wonder of the age, but in Potsdam, there is no doubt, he was a man of substance.'

'And that's when you and he met Signor Handel for the first time?'

'Yes,' sighs Rolli. 'The boy, he had such a precocious talent. Bononcini, he was cruel, he set him a complex piece of music in an effort to undo him in front of King Frederick, but the ploy didn't work, the young Handel played it effortlessly. Bononcini felt that his unkind act had come back to haunt him, that il Sassone was like, what you call here, a "bad penny", always turning up. First it was at the mansion of the Duke of Chandos, then as Director of Music at the Academy.'

Swiney, the proprietor, chooses this moment to come by laden with plates of food.

'Now, gentlemen, a treat for you, some steak and kidney pudding.'

To Harry, it looks delicious, but Rolli scowls at the brown gravy, oozing from pastry, and waves it away.

'Don't believe all he says, he's a right bucheen,' Swiney murmurs in Harry's ear.

'Poor Bononcini, he had to endure the caresses of a dreadful duchess in order to enjoy the hospitality of her London home. It was the one place, he always felt, where he would not bump into il Sassone.'

'There must be some good to live in London.'

'Living, not "live". Yes, Harry, there must be. But what, I have always to ask myself? A free press? So they can write lies about us? So they can claim that we at the opera unman John Bull? That we are spies? Emissaries of the Pope? No, it cannot be this freedom that everyone talks about. Honesty, a lack of corruption? Certainly not, look at the Duke of Chandos. He paid for his mansion and his artists by creaming off supplies from the British army. Eh eh?' Harry tries to compose some sort of a response but Rolli has not finished.

'No, Harry, we Italians, Senesino and the like, we have a mission. It is to civilise the savages of this island.' He takes a sip of wine, nodding at the sagacity of his words. 'At times, how it makes us suffer.' Then he looks wounded and stares out of the window. The heaviness of the duties resting on his shoulders seems to have upset him.

'Who is that gentleman staring at you?' Harry asks. Rolli looks in the direction indicated while his companion gestures to John Swiney to fill Rolli's glass.

'Oh him, he's a seedy little bookworm called Pepusch. He's of the same Lutheran stock as the Cabbage. He's full of himself because of his success with the Beggar's Opera, a vulgar burlesque he wrote with a popinjay called John Gay. Gay's comedy is full of cheap jibes against the Italian opera and as to the man himself, he is quite insufferable. Pepusch, my dear friend, what a delight to see you. This is Harry Walsh, a singer with Handel.'

'I gather that Senesino, amazingly, is still one of his singers as well,' says Pepusch.

'Yes, amazing indeed, for while Signor Handel has lofty ideas of the office and dignity of a composer he has a very low estimate of the office and dignity of singers.'

'I take it you are not a castrato, Mr Walsh. The truth is that most Englishmen find the castrato voice funny, their sensibilities, you see, are crude. Is that not right, Rolli?'

'I think it is beautiful,' says Harry. Rolli simpers.

'Signor Rolli, here, cannot forgive your compatriot, Gay, for making fun of them. As for the theatre owner who instigated the Beggar's Opera, John Rich, as I keep explaining, he just wanted to make money, it was a commercial exercise, not a phrase you could apply to the opera.'

'No, opera is not a commercial exercise, it is Art,' says Rolli.

'Although helpfully remunerative for the singers,' adds Pepusch.

'Do the Italian singers get paid well?' Harry asks.

'The sums are legendary,' Pepusch assures him. 'But the Beggar's Opera certainly made Rich gay and Gay rich as the wits put it. So amusing. I, of course, just scribbled off an overture and picked the songs, it was a bit of fun, not what I normally do. I am, Sir, a serious musician, a founder no less of the Academy of Ancient Music.'

'You must know Mr Gates, my chorus master.'

'Yes, of course, a most honourable gentleman.'

Rolli interjects. 'You are now so famous, Pepusch, you will, for ever, be associated with the Beggar's Opera.'

Pepusch flushes. Just a little too archly, he says, 'I hope I will be better remembered for the twelve cantatas that I wrote while with the Duke of Chandos.'

'They were good days, were they not? At least, then, you composed works in Italian. Those wonderful gardens, with the peacocks and sphinxes, it was like being at Versailles.'

'That is the past, it's better to live in the present.'

'Fine words for a founder of the Academy of Ancient Music.'

Across the road Harry catches sight of Handel entering the theatre in the company of Heidegger.

'Signor Rolli, our performance of Esther tonight is our last. I must go for the show will start in an hour. Thank you for your patience, I hope that one day I will be fluent in your beautiful language. Mr Pepusch, I bid you goodbye.'

He hurries across the road to the King's, intoning, 'Italiana, la lingua della canzone'. Handel is in the foyer with his ugly friend, looking at a model of one of the sets. He calls Harry over and Heidegger glowers at him.

'Ah, Valsh, our last night.'

'I am sad, Sir, for I love singing here. I am trying to learn Italian. I've been in the Three Crows with Signor Rolli.'

'Our dear friend, Rolli; how did you find him?'

'He is bitter, Sir, as a bag of lemons.'

'Malice is a language you must become fluent in if you are to be a musician.'

'I am sorry to hear you say so.'

'Your amiability is attractive, young man, it has a personality that comes through in your voice. But for your singing to develop character you must suffer. Conflict, torn emotions, doubt, fear, those are good for the voice. Am I right, Heidegger?'

'He put paint on my screens,' growls his companion.

'I have a task for you, Valsh, the idea for another work in English is forming in my mind.' The maestro is in the best of humours. His words open a hope in Harry's heart that maybe he will be able to return to the King's. 'Two young upstarts, Thomas Arne and John Lampe, are putting on a masque I wrote many years ago while with the Duke of Chandos.'

'They are pirates, it shouldn't be allowed, especially since they make money,' says Heidegger.

'I want you go to the Little Theatre across the road and see it, then report back to me, tell me what the singers are like. Can I repeat the success we have had with Esther?'

'Yes, Esther, it make a profit. We must try more shows like it.' Heidegger is certainly in this business for the plate, thinks Harry, he'd frisk your purse if he heard it clink.

'What is the audience's reaction? You can be my spy.'

'I would be honoured to be your spy, Sir.' His next words are particularly pleasing.

'Peter can accompany you if you like.'

'We can both be your spies.'

'No, I don't trust his judgement; he is a little in love with the soprano, Susanna Arne.'

'Is it your wish to stage this show?'

'Possibly, if the Bishop does not ban me from using his choristers. He is sure that Heidegger and I, we are corrupting their morals. Alas,' he chuckles, 'for most, such a precaution is too late.'

The image of pounding buttocks plays in Harry's head as it does almost every hour. His morals are more than ready to be corrupted.

'Stay away from the paint,' Heidegger mutters as he leaves. One of his facial growths looks inflamed and sore. Me and him, thinks Harry, we will never be friends.

6. The Little Theatre, Haymarket

Everything about the Little Theatre is seedy. It has no license to stage musical entertainments and the wooden staircase up to the higher galleries is an invitation to fire. The smell of sweat, once Peter and Harry find seats, is almost unbearable, and the press of bodies around them makes it hard for anyone to sit in comfort. They are near the ceiling, so few people hold candles, but smoke from the lower floors fills the air. The evening is still light outside but, inside, it is dark for there are no windows. The show seems to be wondrously popular, the place is packed. Within minutes it is not hard to see why. On the stage there is all manner of horsing around and lewd gestures. Handel's story of virtue in peril has been transformed into a bawdy romp.

Polyphemus, the Cyclops, is suitably evil and has a good strong bass voice; Galatea, a very innocent looking Susanna Arne, is suitably naive; Harry is relieved to find that Acis is most decidedly a man. He swoons and sighs against a crude backdrop of such arcane prettiness that at any minute Harry expects a herd of singing sheep and a chorus of shepherd boys to burst onto the stage. When Susanna Arne starts to sing, the audience, who had been whooping and egging on the leering Polyphemus, becomes silent. Many, no doubt, are imagining enfolding her in their arms.

The voice, simple and untutored, and the airs she sings, are most certainly an exercise in titillation.

Harry wants to lean over to his companion and point this out but, in the darkness, Peter's features look ill at ease. His friend, he has found, is a martyr to sudden changes of mood; one minute he is full of wit, a positive chatterbox, the next he is silent. He can feel Peter's leg being pressed into his and after a while can think of little else. He is conscious of sweat forming on his brow and his hands becoming moist and wonders if the pressure of Peter's leg is, perhaps, intentional. He glances sideways; how fine Peter's cheekbones are, and the nose, so neat.

Behind the two of them there is scuffling and a knee presses into Harry's back. He turns to remonstrate with the uncouth nick ninny who is pushing him forwards and finds that an act of copulation is being enacted within inches of where they sit. The second time in only a few weeks, he thinks, envious that he can't join in. The scuffling sets up an ache in Harry's loins. At the same time he is puzzled and disturbed by the longing he has to grasp Peter's hand. Susanna Arne, he says to himself, keep singing your beautiful song.

When the show ends many of the inhabitants of the gallery are reluctant to leave. A few are so drunk that they are slumped across their seats and the boys have to climb over them. It takes them a while to reach the staircase and, when they do, progress is slow because of the crowd. At least it is less smoky than the auditorium; air rushes up the staircase from the street. Peter stands above those around him so Harry can see him; he can tell by the angle of Peter's head that he is not happy.

'All those mutton mongers enjoying themselves, it was amusing, was it not?' They are walking up the Haymarket, ignoring the beggars who hold out their hands, as they pass, with pitiful laments.

No answer.

'At least I can report back to the maestro that the audience reaction was positive.' Harry expects the hint of a smile but gets nothing but a prudish purse of the lips.

'The show, did you like it?'

'No.'

'You're a maggot.'

'Perhaps.'

'Shall I walk back with you, to Brook Street?'

'Probably best not to.' Harry tries to hide his disappointment.

'Why do you not cut down here? It's the shortest way, isn't it?'

'I have my own route. It's the one I always take.' Peter sounds irritated.

'Oh look, I'll leave you.' Peter taps a railing. 'You're sulking, just like Senesino.'

When they come to the next alley, Peter says, 'This is my route. Good night.' He starts to run, leaving Harry annoyed at suddenly finding himself alone. Light spills out ahead of him from the Three Crows and the sound of merriment seeps from the doors. Once Harry makes his way to the bar John Swiney greets him.

'Harry, boy, it looks like you need a glass of something.'

He has never touched alcohol before but intends to do so now. Swiney takes charge and places a small glass of golden liquid in front of him.

'Irish whiskey, I gets it sent over from home, there's none of Walpole's duties paid on this.' He winks as Harry gulps down the entire glass. He does his best not to choke even though steam is about to issue from his throat and a line of fire is tearing a hole in his gut. A bellicose party to his left, looking dishevelled, bumps up against him.

'That's Gay, one of my regulars,' says Swiney, sotto voce. 'A regular troublemaker I should say, part of my "literary clientele". Careful now, John.' He stops the party from falling over. He presses his face to Harry's ear. 'He keeps company with Pope, the poet, he's standing over there.'

Harry looks across the room to a small, dapper man with a

hunched back.

'He's a touchy fellow with a sharp tongue, but he's made a hod of money with his classical translations. He dresses well, you'll notice, while Gay gives the impression of someone who's slept in a ditch.' Swiney raises his voice again. 'Whoa, John, easy now,' then turns back to Harry and explains. 'His appearance declined once he lost his all in the South Seas debacle.'

Harry by this time feels lushey. The South Sea bubble - he was a child then. Too much greed, too much greed, that's what Papa always said.

'Was John Gay greedy like the rest of them?' he asks.

'No, he was just an eegit. Excuse me, Harry, it's busy tonight. Mr Truelove, Lord M, what can I get you? Been to the opera tonight?'

Once the two newcomers have been served, the man addressed as Truelove, who is fat and jowly, raises his brandy and says in a loud voice.

'To our great leader, Walpole, and death to all Jacobites.' His tall, distinguished-looking companion smiles benignly. Gay raises his glass.

'To our great leader,' he slurs. 'And to his love nest in Twickenham and his little maid, Maria. To hell with abandoned wives, for our dear, fat-arsed member of Parliament here obviously supports adultery.'

Truelove glowers.

'Your biting wit may amuse others but it don't amuse me, Gay.'

'It don't amuse the Lord Chamberlain either. He has done me a good service in banning Polly. Now no fashionable household can be seen without a print of it.'

'Flush in the fob are you, you reprobate, raking it in? You don't deserve to be.'

Gay at this point takes notice of his companion, the man Swiney called Lord M.

'If it isn't Filch, Macheath's loyal servant. Or is it Jemmy Twitcher, Crook-Fingered Jack or Matt of the Mint? '

Lord M throws his head back and laughs.

'Excellent names, Gay, excellent names. I enjoyed the Beggar's Opera.'

'Been attending one of the great German's masterpieces?' asks the playwright. 'He and I, we've worked together, you know, as guests of the good duke whose hospitality we all enjoyed. What a coven of artists we were. I'll tell you something, gentlemen,' he says, holding the bar to stop himself from stumbling. 'Handel, he expresses... what it means... to be British.' Those around him wait to hear him out. He tilts sideways and rights himself again. 'Because that's what we all are now, isn't it, though you might not think it if you come from Scotland or Ireland, am I right, John?'

'Jaysus, Gay, keep me out of this, I just pour the drinks.'

'He expresses the sense we have of our own greatness, our command of the High Seas, our burgeoning trade, our expanding Empire.'

'Very eloquent, Gay, I'm sure,' says Lord M.

'But I on the other hand.' Gay stops himself from falling over. 'I express another aspect of being British.'

'Jacobite traitor,' sneers Truelove.

'Our shame, our dishonesty, the utter corruptness of those who rule, our amazing tolerance of injustice and inequality, the filthy, stinking midden-house of our great British nation.'

'Quill driver, frig pig,' mutters Truelove.

'You and Handel, Gay, are simply describing two sides of the same coin,' says Lord M.

How graceful his lordship is, his nose, patrician; the cut of his satin jacket, elegant. Harry admires him while, like Gay, he clutches the bar for support. He looks down at his simple black jacket which his father passed down to him; it is uncomfortably tight round the pits of his arms. He stares at Lord M's sallow cheeks and prominent cheekbones, so much more fashionable than his cheeks which are as pink as a country clod pate's. The hair is pulled back in a simple queue; Harry's tumbles, unruly, to his shoulders.

As he lurches homeward, towards the City, he keeps his distance from the bundles of human filth groaning in the doorways, for should they choose to leap out at him he would surely fall over. He tries to picture what a hod of money might look like and thinks with envy of Pope's literary prowess. So many years in the classroom and, still, he can barely write. He feels troubled by Peter's surliness but more than that, he feels shame. What does it mean, this desire he has to touch him? He feels the soft report of his boot sinking into a pile of steaming horse manure. Once home he opens the heavy door of the rectory and gropes in the dark for the banister, spreading horse muck with every tread. Lord M, he thinks, he wasn't wearing dirt spattered boots, like me, but shoes that shone, they had heels on them and large silver buckles. His bedroom door creaks open and he fumbles for the pot. He makes himself a promise as he pisses. One day, I will earn enough to get myself some shoes like that.

7. Button's Coffee Shop

As Harry makes his way to Covent Garden, holding his breath as he passes the rotting remains of vegetables and ordure that have set up a stink in the Piazza, the atmosphere is hot and clammy. How understandable it is that the Town leaves London for the months of July and August to take in the country air or to find diversion at a spa. The choir's success with Acis and Galatea at the King's has emboldened Harry to ask Peter if he would write to him from Bath. Nothing was ever said about what happened outside the Little Theatre and soon Harry banished the memory of it, for it would not be in his nature to fret about what is past. Peter's a prude, he thought, also a slave to his own routines, to counting railings and straightening things. Yet, despite these oddities, he would find himself thinking of him, looking out for him when at the theatre, longing for his company. Sometimes he would watch as he talked to Handel, deep in their own private affairs, then catch sight of Jonny looking, in turn, at him. If this happened he would laugh nonchalantly and shrug.

With the summer, the theatre is in recess and he finds he misses his Italian lessons. He misses sitting in the pit with Jonny, listening to Senesino and the other Italians rehearse, for Handel's new version of Acis was part-sung in Italian. He even misses Senesino. Sometimes he would join Rolli at the Three Crows, and sit in on his Italian lessons. He would clap like a child when Harry managed a long sentence and tease him for his youth.

'Harree,' he would say, 'you are good looking boy. I give you one of my duchesses to fuck, you like that? I have so many, maybe we make threesome.' Harry would blush and just wish that his Italian could master, 'A threesome, what excellent sport, Sir, I accept your kind offer.' He finds that he is falling in love with all things Italian. Peter was right, the language, Handel's music, they are certainly an exercise in titillation. So too is Rolli and Senesino's crude jockeying. At the same time a different sort of passion brews inside him.

In Harry's pocket is Peter's letter from Bath. It is full of satiric comment on his master's grand friends and his liking for the steam room. Harry knows every word by heart for he has read it several times a day. Shortly after he received it he even walked across town to Brook Street, with no other purpose than to look at the front door and dream of the life that went on behind it. Afterwards he had made a sketch for Peter, for drawing came easily to him and he was good at it. He drew grotesque characters queuing up to kiss Handel's hand; the stomach and wig were enormous, a roll of music stuck out from under his arm; a harassed Peter, stooping over his employer, his hair a mass of artistic curls, sought to keep the crowds at bay and shooed away a pastry cook carrying a tray of rich confections. If he likes my sketch, he will write again, thought Harry.

When he reaches Button's he joins Jonny Beard who sits opposite two young composers, Thomas Arne and John Frederick Lampe, instigators of the pirated version of Acis and Galatea whose success so affronted Heidegger. Jonny is hoping they will give them both work. Their latest venture is to be a masque, called The Maid's Merry Tale, which they plan to stage at another seedy playhouse, John Rich's theatre at the Lincoln's Inn Fields. Harry needs to find employment, not least in order to escape his father's continuing attempts to interest him in books.

The two young composers entertain them with reminiscences of their staging of Acis; John Frederick was the one who rearranged Handel's music, Tom's father staged the show and Tom, himself, led the orchestra. Harry tells them about the embracing couples in the upper gallery, suggesting in his rendition that he too might have had some female company. Then Jonny embarks on their antics as young choristers at the Chapel Royal.

'The coronation, a wondrous occasion. When Gatesy's hand came down we made our Zadok-the-priest shoot round the Abbey like the blasts from a musket, our God-save-the-king echo and boom like a cannon. You should have been there,' he says.

'You forget, Jonny, I am a Catholic,' replies Arne.

'I see them now, your horns.' All of them laugh, except Arne. He has a doleful face, like an undertaker's.

'While you sang in the Abbey I had my nose pressed into a law book. My father hated the idea of me being a musician, he said I'd end up like his father, in the Marshalsea.'

'A place we all live in dread of,' says Lampe. A German accent is vaguely discernible, he is smooth faced and sensitive looking and slightly older than the rest of them.

Harry beckons to an unmannerly ruffian who approaches their table.

'Yeh, what?' The service at Button's is famous for being unfailingly monstrous. He exchanges a smile with his old friend. The pair of them order chocolate, for fear that the Arabica will injure their voices, and the others order coffee. Harry cannot help noticing the predatory way in which Arne stares at the women working in the kitchen; to help keep the place cool the doors to the back are open as is the door to the street. Button's is pleasingly empty which is why they all look up when John Swiney can be seen hovering outside, then, on spying them near the open door, comes in.

'So you have met up, my musical gentlemen, that's how I thinks of you.' One day, Harry thinks, I will be like John Swiney; wherever I go I will come across people I know; my acquaintances, like his, will be wide and varied.

'We were talking about the coronation,' says Jonny.

'A demonstration to all and sundry of the king's taste for pomp and ceremony, I remember it well.'

'The king's taste or Handel's? You couldn't have a public occasion without him setting it to music.' Arne's comment is said with sarcasm. It suggests he is overshadowed by the older man, by his greatness. It cannot be easy to compete with someone like Handel.

'No, indeed.' Swiney's bony features are wreathed in a smile.

'The Maid's Merry Tale, you'll find, is nothing like the coronation,' says Lampe. 'It's part of our English Opera Project, isn't that right, Tom?'

'Yes it is,' says Arne, leaning back while the gummy waiter slops coffee across the table. 'We're reviving the old works of England. Lost masterpieces.'

'If they was masterpieces, surely someone would have remembered where they left them,' says Swiney. Arne glares.

'We intend to create our own style, one that is closer to our own traditions.'

Swiney shakes his head and continues to tease.

'You'd have us all dancing round a maypole, if you could,

with daisy chains in our hair.'

'Very amusing. But we need serious music that is sung in English. Something better than Gay's burlesques, less foreign than the Italian opera.'

'I, for one, will support you,' declares Jonny, 'and I think Harry will, too.'

'A most worthy enterprise,' Harry murmurs, thinking how tedious it is. He is happy to sing both in Italian or English, although his preference would be Italian, for, as shallow as he knows it is, he seeks glamour. What must it be like to stand on the stage at the King's with the audience, silent and entranced, listening to you, as they do with Senesino? His dreams, he thinks, even as a child, they had music in them. But now the orchestral sounds that sing in his head each night are louder, more urgent. Sometimes they seem more real than the life around him.

The group return to the subject of the proposed masque. They laugh and talk among themselves until John Swiney gets up to go.

'I must get back to the Three Crows. Join me there, lads, we'll drink to the English Opera Project. We can't leave the field wide open to a lot of simpering Macaronis.' They wish him goodbye and get up as well. Harry is singing that evening in the choir at St Bartholomew's. The coolness of the church interior on summer nights, and the echo of the plainchant off the ancient pillars, soothe his troubled spirits.

As he leaves, Harry's hand touches his coat pocket. For a full hour he forgot the letter. Some heady infatuation has gripped him, a most unwise one, but soon it will be over and he'll be free. For what? To visit one of the bawdy houses of Covent Garden? The idea does not appeal.

8. Batson's on Cornhill

'Monsieur has a fine physique.' The hands of the young tailor's assistant rest a moment longer than they should at the top of Harry's inner thigh. 'This suit, I'll make you look like a proper swell, a flashman.'

'And the brocade waistcoat, is it ready?' he asks.

The blue changes with the light as the tailor's assistant holds it up then helps him put it on. The fruit of his earnings. He admires his reflection in the mirror, agrees with the comment about his physique, then remembers his father's admonitions about vanity.

'I'll take it today for I am meeting soon with a friend, Lord M, round the corner.' He is, of course, not a personal friend, but Handel's introduction has proved useful. He wishes for Harry to sing at a soirée to be held in honour of his daughter's birthday. Harry is anticipating, when they meet, improving his understanding of the Rules of Polite Conversation.

'I can see you are a gentry cove, Sir. This Lord M, an older man, is he?'

'Old and decrepit but he looks after me.' The pricklouse does not realise he jests. He is emboldened to tell Harry that he has a room upstairs, that he's there every night and how alone he feels. For one moment Harry is tempted by his offer because of his own loneliness and the physical longing that grips him every waking hour. Now that Handel and Peter have returned to London his foolish infatuation, he's learnt, is far from over.

As he approaches Batson's he can see Lord M through the window. It is the haunt of medical men, who sometimes consult with patients there, and of City bankers and the like. Lord M stands out because his black coat is edged with gold thread and pink trim which makes him look, as Harry does in his blue waistcoat, as bedaubed and bedecked as a Frenchman. In contrast to the expansive girths all round him, only partially obscured by good tailoring, Lord M is elegantly thin.

'Harry, m'boy, sit down.' His long legs are stretched out, uncomfortably, under the table. In front of him is a copy of The

Craftsman.

'Ever read this?' he asks. 'It's full of splenetic, Jacobite nonsense by the likes of Gay and Swift. How they hate Walpole.'

Harry accepts his offer of coffee, a drink he dislikes, and tries not to grimace when a small pipe is pulled from his lordship's pocket. His throat will most surely be annihilated.

'Mary won't countenance these at home.'

'How is Lady Mary?'

'Sadly, in the best of health.'

As a pot of the Turkish beverage is put on the table, Harry can almost feel his throat contract. As a singer, he thinks, one is surrounded by danger.

'So, you must see their majesties at the Chapel Royal each week. Do you ever get to talk to them?'

'No, My Lord. Besides, the king is often away; he spends many months of the year on his family estate in Hanover.'

'Herrenhausen, intolerable place. I spent time there as a diplomat when the Elector Georg Ludwig was being courted by our Parliament.'

'I have heard, My Lord, that Handel worked for the Elector before he became our king.'

'Had to teach the children of his ghastly mistresses among other things. No wonder he hied off to London at the first opportunity. We were the pot of gold, you see, sitting at the end of the rainbow.'

'Do you mean that Handel came to London simply to make his fortune?'

'Nothing as crude as that. I don't as a habit delve into motives. All I would say is that if you grow a crop you need the right type of soil. The same applies to a creative talent.' Harry looks puzzled. 'People with money and so forth, you're an artist, you should know. The atmosphere at Herrenhausen, it was stifling, still is. There's a lot of creeping round mirrored corridors, bowing at those above you in station and sneering at those below. Then there's the hordes of liveried flunkies with ears pressed to the keyhole.'

Lord M exhales and a puff of smoke travels in a straight line to Harry's nostrils.

'For Handel, these chaps here represented freedom. We're surrounded by alchemists, do you realise that?' He waves a hand to indicate the patrons of Batson's. Harry has no idea what he is talking about. He leans across the table. 'They create gold from clinker. They devise ways of using capital to make money. You are sitting here, Harry, in the fulcrum of a revolution.'

He sits back, pleased with his observation. Harry looks round at the scurrying waiters and earnest knots of men, deep in conversation, anticipating, no doubt, a generous dinner. The inhabitants look wonderfully at peace with the status quo. Lord M decides to elaborate.

'Harry, on my family estate in Tyrone, we grow corn and flax. Wealth, my father always taught me, rested with land and with the making and exchange of goods. The money men you see around us, they don't go along with that.'

'I see.'

'What the City men have taught us is that you do not have to own land in order to get rich. You don't even have to make things, you can use your capital instead - invest, lend, under-write. Can't you see, m'boy, the separation of wealth from land, it changes attitudes and so forth, creates more of a free for all.' Lord M takes another puff of his pipe. 'Yes, Harry, London provided the right type of soil from which Handel's talent could grow.'

Harry tries to ignore the medical man at the next door table who is asking his patient in a carrying whisper what colour his stools are.

'This talk of soil and freedom, the growing of flax and what have you, has me confused, My Lord.' It strikes him that he should really take an interest in newspapers, pamphlets, polemics and so forth, to make up for his lost years in the classroom and become familiar with the topics of the day.

'That's because you are a musician, Harry. Now, tell me, Euphemia's birthday, can you manage a few airs in Italian? My daughter is like her mother, her views are very fixed. She wishes for airs from the opera.'

'I would be delighted.' Harry's cheeks flush with pleasure. His progress in Italian, according to Rolli, is prodigious, so much so that he is frustrated that Handel will not invite him to sing in his operas. The Maid's Merry Tale is doing well but the theatre at the Lincoln's Inn Fields is old fashioned and the audiences are devoid of the panache that so dazzles him at the King's. He throws out a few suggestions, Lord M agrees to all of them for he cannot tell one Italian air from another.

'I'm sure Euphemia will be charmed, whatever you do, you're a good looking young man; handsome waistcoat too.' He drains his second cup then greets one of his City friends who comes and stands over them. The two men talk about a debate coming up in the Parliament. Harry clears his throat of the phlegm that the smoke has caused and wonders if it would be rude to say he is leaving. The ashen-faced patient next to him, who has just concluded his medical consultation, comes to his rescue by trying to pass. Harry rises then thanks Lord M for his company.

All around him, City men are filling the tables, leaning close to each other, wheeling and dealing, or should he say, digging and sowing. His tutorial in Polite Conversation has served merely to emphasise that he is a greenhorn. But the company of Lord M, how congenial it is, how much he can learn from it; moreover, his words have been reassuring. If one no longer has to own land in order to be wealthy, well then one day, perhaps, he too can become rich.

9. An Afternoon at the Rectory
Peter comes round to Charterhouse Square one afternoon in November with a message from Handel asking if Harry will sing

in his revival of Acis and Galatea. On several occasions the two boys have walked the dogs or met at Button's but this is Peter's first visit to the rectory. Harry's father is impressed by the presence in his house of Handel's secretary and is delighted when told that Peter loves books. Immediately he ushers him into his study and lets him hold an ancient copy of the Ephemeris. Then he presses on him the plays of Dryden, Wycherley and Etherege. Peter flicks through the delicate pages with his long fingers and Doctor Walsh entreats him to borrow them.

'I teach a young neighbour, Lucy, how to read. We will look at them together,' Peter says.

'Peter,' the reverend replies. 'Pray, help me do something with Harry, his writing is like a child's.'

'I think I am a good teacher, Doctor Walsh, but your son, is he a good student?'

'No, I am a lost cause.' The pair of them seem quite insensible to his feelings. His father immediately brings forth an extra chair and a copy of Pope's lengthy poem, the Dunciad, and bids Harry write a few lines from it. Then he consults his pocket watch and explains that he must hurry away. He has a meeting to attend at the Church Rooms behind St Paul's, after which, he and his fellow clerics will enjoy a modest supper at one of the ordinaries on Cheapside.

Harry starts to write but he feels humiliated. He can sense Peter straightening the rug, then fidgeting with his chair so it is parallel to the desk. His fingers reach for the Dunciad and adjust its position, so Harry has to put his head to one side to read it. His heart goes out to the young neighbour, Lucy, his student. After a single sentence he gives up.

'I cannot work when you will not stay still.'

'Why, Harry,' Peter says as he looks over the one line. 'Your father is right, your letters slant backwards, you swap one around for another, and the beginning of this word has been put at the end.'

Harry tears up the page.

'So, I am a chuckle-head. You have no need to tell me, I learnt that at school.'

When Peter sees the pain on Harry's face, his hand goes up to it. For a moment he looks shocked at what he has just done and makes to draw back. In that fleeting second they both have a choice, to return to the time that has just past or to cross a threshold. His head comes forward, Harry's hand reaches for Peter's cheek. Their lips brush against each other. They kiss. Harry pushes his chair back, knocking Peter's which has been so carefully straightened; he pushes the Dunciad aside, which has been lined up with the edge of the desk; he rucks up the rug below them.

'I missed you when you were away, I'm so glad I'll be coming back to the King's.' His voice sounds unfamiliar to him.

'I've missed you too.'

'Will you come upstairs?'

The house is empty, save for Samuel who is rattling pans somewhere down in the bowels of the kitchen. They go up to Harry's bedroom where they take off their garments and start to embrace, first frantically, then slowly. How pleasurable it is, Harry thinks, to lie naked as the day one was born in the presence of another. How trusting we are to allow our hands to reach to wherever they will. How natural it seems for our faces to be so near, for our eyes to look into the other's. Their lovemaking is fumbling and inexpert. Afterwards, Harry whispers hoarsely.

'Were you expecting this?'

'I've thought about it, since that night at the Little Theatre, sort of hoped and hoped not. I don't think it can be right. It is most definitely a sin.'

The idea of sinning, Harry finds most pleasing. He sits up on his elbow and strokes the yellow strands that lie across his pillow. Can it be normal, he wonders, to love another man? He recalls schoolboy sniggering about one of the masters. He and Peter will have to be discreet, for their own safety if nothing else.

'I feel so happy,' he says to his companion. 'I think you are...' he pauses, trying to find the right words. 'I think you are special... graceful... and so, so beautiful.'

'No I'm not, but that's what you are. Your cheeks, they glow, like a peach. When you smile, your teeth, they're so even. I wish I was untroubled, like you.'

'But lots of things trouble me.'

'I don't think so. You're uncomplicated.'

Perhaps once, Harry thinks, but not now. Will Handel hear a difference in his voice? Does the jumble of emotions he now feels amount to the doubt, fear, and conflict that the maestro told him he must experience in order to be a proper singer? He is not sure. When the time comes for Peter to go, tears wet his cheeks which makes Peter cry as well. But underneath the tears, he feels complete. He has been corrupted, he feels alive.

1733

10. Drama Off-stage

Handel is being charmed by the fragile actress sitting next to him at his harpsichord. She has dove-grey eyes and long chestnut coloured hair. Lord M is admiring her openly even though Lady Mary is sitting next to him on the chaise longue surveying the graceful lines of her rival's neck through her lorgnette.

'Ah, Miss Arne, your voice, it is so beautiful. Why is it you don't learn to read music?'

'Why would I when I have you to teach me note by note?' Her eyes flutter and the composer beams back at her. She is quite his little favourite.

They are preparing for his new oratorio, Deborah. Harry, predictably, has but a minor part, but at least he has been honoured with an invitation to Brook Street. He feels a great joy at the thought of working at the King's again. Several times, over the last few months, he has crept up to the footman's gallery from which he can breathe in the excitement and noise of the King's auditorium below. Not only can he enjoy the opera from there, he can sit in the dark with his love, holding his hand, getting lost in his dreams. To Peter's disapproval, he also topes with Senesino, visiting him his dressing room, prompting him as he learns his lines for Harry finds it helps his understanding of Italian. Even La Strada knows him by name and sends him out sometimes on little errands.

The two singers are being taken through their arias in front of Lord M, Lady Mary, Mrs Pendleton, Sid and Nell, who pant by her feat, and a man of the cloth, by the name of Trebeck, who is also accompanied by his wife. The company are sitting in the upstairs sitting room at Brook Street, which would be spacious but for two harpsichords and an organ. Peter fusses over refreshments and Harry has to stop himself from catching his eye. It is nearly a month since he last spent a night at the rectory for, during the music season, he is rarely free. The Reverend Trebeck is standing near a panelled wall, eyeing the paintings and commenting now and then.

'Ah, a view of the River Tiber, I thought as much. A conversation piece by Watteau, a Frenchman if I am not mistaken, very fine. Handel, you have been busy at the auction rooms.' Mrs Trebeck, who is the mother of six children according to Mrs Pendleton, whose distaste is evident when she whispers it in Harry's ear, is dressed with almost Puritan plainness.

'Mr Walsh, your singing was most affecting although I do not pretend to know anything in the musical line. Do you ever give lessons?' she asks.

'I'm sure I could,' he stammers, for the possibility of being a teacher has never struck him before.

'Ambrose, I think I have found someone to tutor Emily. We live round the corner in Hanover Square, just next to the church where my husband is rector.'

'A most fashionable establishment, I gather.'

'It is indeed, the aristocracy choose it as a place in which to celebrate the nuptials of their young. They may be looking for singers. Ambrose can put your name forward.'

'How kind, Mrs Trebeck, I'm sure I could oblige. I can sing airs in Italian as well as in English now.' Harry avoids meeting the maestro's eye.

'Yes he can,' says Lord M. 'Euphemia is fairly in love with the young blade.' Harry would be with her if she wasn't tall and masculine, like her father, and devoid of humour like her mother.

'The language matters not, so long as the airs be light.'

'I understand,' says Harry, 'nothing that will tax the musical palettes of the congregation.' He is all too keen for his voice to accompany well-born young ladies, as they tie themselves to some chinless cove with a title, so long as there be profit in it.

'Do you know, I think I have met your father. He is a most

charitable man. He runs a soup kitchen does he not? He and Ambrose meet at times in the Church Rooms.' Mrs Trebeck's manner has an unrelenting quality.

'Yes, when the weather is cold he mixes a flummery for the poor. They would starve otherwise.'

'How they depend on our philanthropy. I expect you help out as well.'

'Most certainly,' Harry lies.

'Hush now, I present to you, Ladies and Gentlemen, the lovely Miss Arne, singing the part of the wicked Jael from the Book of Judges.'

Susanna's voice is thread-like but pure and affecting. Lord M looks at her hungrily; no form of wickedness would be too much for him. Harry feels at ease although it is his belief that underneath the bonhomie, the plump form sitting at the harpsichord is restless and out of sorts.

Before the aria comes to an end the dogs start to yap and Handel thumps the keys.

'The dogs, they must be removed, Amelia. Besides they are shedding on my rugs.'

'Someone is at the door, that's why they're barking,' says Mrs Pendleton. At that moment the repose of the gathering is destroyed by the entrance of a large-nosed, pink cheeked lady with an ungainly manner who is dressed in the very latest style. The plumes issuing from her head seem to have a life of their own.

'Anthony, brandy, quickly, I feel quite faint,' she announces to Handel's long faced steward, Peter's uncle. 'Thank goodness you are all here, quite dreadful news, I heard it from Jan the Dutchman, he brings his vegetable cart round on Thursdays.'

'Sit, Anne, you seem distressed,' says Mrs Pendleton, having conveniently forgotten the order regarding her dogs.

'Yes, sit here, Ambrose has no need of his seat,' adds Mrs Trebeck.

'Thank you, Rachel, I am sure I will do quite well standing,' she sniffs. 'The news I have to tell you is that Lucy, the workhouse orphan whom you entrusted, Rachel, to the service of General Plunket when his wife died, is with child.' The speaker pauses so that the impact of what she has said can take effect.

'I'm hardly surprised,' announces Lady Mary.

'Are you not? Well I am, but sadly it is beyond dispute. Jan saw her washing dishes in the area to the front of their house and her condition was very clear to be seen.'

'He will send her back to the workhouse, I suppose, Mrs Donovan,' sighs Handel. Peter's face goes red.

'He will do no such thing,' the newcomer replies. 'Can't you see, the old goat has tupped her. He must marry her at once.'

'You are mistaken, Anne, I'm sure of it,' says Mrs Pendleton.

'General Plunket is a member of my congregation, a very decent type,' interjects the Reverend.

'Little jade was probably after his money,' says Lady Mary.

'Hush wife,' says her husband.

'She is no jade, but as to General Plunket, do not be taken in by outward appearances,' says Mrs Donovan. 'Of course he gives the impression of being too old and unsteady to do anything but it seems he's fully in the saddle when he wants to be.'

'I think he is innocent,' says Handel. 'Besides, his children would never let him marry Lucy.'

'You have to be realistic, Anne,' adds Lord M.

'It is because I am realistic that I went round to General Plunket's house and gave him a piece of my mind,' she says. 'I can now announce that he agreed less than an hour ago to make Lucy an honest woman.'

The room becomes silent as the company digests this news.

Handel pats Susanna's hand and mutters. 'She is younger even than you, my dear, merely a child.' Lord M would like to pat her hand as well.

But the soloist has not finished. She turns to Rachel Trebeck.

'This is all your doing, Rachel, you will meddle so. First you wanted Handel to take her, but Betsy refused to allow her in, so you put a young, innocent girl into a house on her own with a widowed man. What were you thinking?'

'She was too bright to eke out her days at Mount Street. I wanted to help her.'

'Mrs Donovan, do not blame Mrs Trebeck. We know very little about Lucy or who her parents were.' Handel is trying to act the conciliator. His female neighbours, it strikes Harry, are a trouble to him.

'Judging by the colour of her skin I would say her parents were both in service, there are blackamoors in some of the grander houses,' interjects the Lady Mary in an acid tone.

'I am sorry to have to tell the company this,' Handel sighs, 'but I have seen her walking up and down the Haymarket late at night.'

'I've seen her too, after the theatres close, but let us not speak of it,' says Lord M.

'You see, Anne.' Lady Mary looks pleased.

'We can only surmise at what she was doing there.' Handel shakes his head thoughtfully; Peter stares at his master but says nothing. Handel looks up at him. 'Peter, I know you were teaching Lucy to read and write and that you are fond of her; this revelation must be distressing for you.' Peter remains silent.

'The trouble is, Handel, yes I do blame Rachel. After all, it is not the first time. Before that it was the case of Rosengarve and Miss Beverage. And now look at St George's, it no longer has an organist.'

'I was simply finding him a pupil to give music lessons to.'

'No you weren't, Rachel, you thought to find him a wife. You had a lot more than music in mind. Then, when he fell in love with Miss Beverage, and her father rejected him, poor man, he went mad.'

'That's musicians for you, so sensitive,' murmurs Mrs

Pendleton.

'He didn't go mad exactly.' Rachel Trebeck looks wretched. 'He lives happily with his brother in Dublin now.'

'I hardly think being found by you, thumping the organ when stark naked, is normal,' says Mrs Pendleton.

'Ladies, ladies, let us leave the matter to rest. We will all pull together to help young Lucy in her hour of need. I must repair to the theatre now with my singers. I am sorry to ask you, but you must leave.'

'I had to help her, she reminded me so much of myself at an earlier age,' Mrs Donovan explains to her friend as they go down the stairs.

'You cannot compare Lucy's situation with your husband running off to France with an actress,' says Mrs Pendleton.

'And leaving you with all the money,' are Lady Mary's last words as she climbs into her coach.

'Get my coat, my boots, my music bag,' says Handel to Peter. 'Now we are late.'

'I can find a sedan for you,' says Susanna.

'No no, my dear, we will walk as a group, the exercise, it is good for me. Anthony, the lady's cape if you please.'

Harry follows Peter to the dressing room, passing the small room next to it where Handel writes his compositions. If they had not been in a hurry, he would have remained standing in the doorway, as if before a shrine, looking at the leather-topped desk, the brass candle-sticks, and the open boxes with brass bindings containing past compositions. It would be Handel's habit to re-use and revise his music endlessly but what sits on his desk this day is a large Bible. On the front of it, in black letters, is Die Bibel, and on the spine it says Castein Bibel Institut, Halle, 1710. On a shelf, nearby, is Playford's book of psalms and hymns, which Harry, as a chorister, is familiar with. A pocket size New Testament, in English, sits on a stool.

While the composition room looks warm and inhabited the dressing room is eerily tidy. The shoes are lined up on shelves and the coats hung in order of length. Peter fusses.

'Don't touch the velvet, it crushes so, or the brocade, your hands, they may mark it.'

'Are these the boots he wants?'

'No, no you mustn't muddle them, they each have their special place. Here, take the Pulvilio, I may have to powder his wig once we get there.'

'Are you unhappy?' Harry asks.

'Yes, of course I am, I haven't seen you for so long.'

'Dearest, I cannot stay up here but meet me, please, come to the rectory again when we can be alone. I miss you too. You're always so busy.'

'Oh it's the theatre. So many horrid things happening there. Senesino, he's such a flat, he troubles Handel. Go downstairs, I'll be with you in a minute.'

'Banished from the dressing room?' Handel chuckles. 'Peter's little empire.'

As they walk down Vigo Street to the Haymarket, he says genially, 'Mrs Trebeck, a tendency she has is to create protégés then something, it goes wrong. I should have warned you this, Valsh.'

As he speaks he walks in front of a horse, causing it to rear up. The rider only just manages to keep his balance but his wig slips sideways, revealing red bristles. Instead of apologising, Handel shouts.

'Ginger-pated blockhead, look where you going.'

'Don't gum me, you nit-squeezer, it was you not looking where you were going.' The rider has a green bag hanging from his saddle, suggesting he is a man of law. Peter smiles up at him and taps his forehead as if to say "mad composer, so sorry". The attorney, unmollified, shakes his fist.

'Get that clouted shoon out of my way. He nearly did himself an injury.'

Peter takes Handel firmly by the arm.

'Why is it you explode in people's faces? You shouldn't be walking anyway, you know it exhausts you.'

Harry takes Miss Arne's arm. She is but a girl and looks slightly shaken by the incident with the horse. Harry has never been so close to a woman before. A nice smell comes off her. Roses? Bergamot? He is not sure.

'I saw you in Acis and Galatea,' he says shyly.

'And I have seen you in The Maid's Merry Tale. John Frederick and my brother, they are earnest, are they not?'

'Do you sing in their shows at times?'

'I do, but my wish is to be a dramatic actress.'

'Maybe you and I will be on stage together one day.'

Harry has half an ear open to what is being said to the front of them.

'How could you say what you did about Lucy?' Peter's tone is querulous. 'Do you want to know the real reason she was on the Haymarket? She was looking for her father. She knew he frequented the theatres there, she wanted to meet him.'

'How do I know these things if you don't tell me?'

'Sometimes you are impossible. How is it, you upset those around you so?'

'How is it I behave like normal person and those around me making so much mischief?'

'Listen to them, kettling like some married couple,' Harry says to his companion.

'They are nothing like my parents,' she answers. 'My father likes to lay down the law.'

She looks disappointed, maybe because Handel is no longer flirting with her. Harry too feels annoyed because he is excluded from the private world which Peter shares with his employer.

11. John Swiney Smells a Plot

'Why did you leave Ireland?'

Harry is toping with John Swiney at the bar of the Three Crows before a performance of Deborah. By the window Rolli is sitting with Senesino and two well-dressed jays, drinking their third bottle of the singer's special Modena wine.

'Why, because, Harry, it's too small. Everyone has to know everyone else's business. It was like a prison.'

'I suppose you can get lost in London.'

'Exactly so. Unless you're a public figure. Our friend Handel is much in the news sheets again.'

'Oh, the uproar about the ticket prices for Deborah, you mean? The papers, they like to create scandal from nothing.'

'It's like the coronation all over again.'

'How so?'

'Let's just say it was mighty convenient, the old king dying when he did.'

'Go on, explain.'

'It gave the news sheets something else to harp on about. You see, when George, poor buffer, blew out the candle in his coach at Osnabrück, it put a stop to the endless chafing and canting about a cat fight at the King's that had closed the theatre down.'

'Actually closed the theatre? Heidegger couldn't have been pleased.'

'It all started because the aristocratic buffoons who ran the King's took it on themselves to add another nightingale to their aviary. The resident songbird, Madame Cuzzoni, was not pleased. Her rival, Madame Faustina, she declared, sounded no better than a crow.'

'I've heard their names but I didn't know they came to blows.'

'They didn't exactly. It was their friends and supporters who came to blows. Behind all the strife, as always, were the Society Ladies, they felt duty bound to take sides. With great energy they fermented an atmosphere of frenzy, as fine-set as a flintlock.

If Lady A flourished her fan in favour of Cuzzoni, Lady B would flourish hers in favour of Faustina. It was during one of Bononcini's shows that the hostile batteries ranged around each Quavering Queen led to a full scale fight between their rival supporters. Poor Bononcini, I never had much time for the fellow but he was mortified.'

'Was it a case of champagne corks at dawn?'

'You have the idea. No doubt a good few wigs went flying and ladies' fans hit the candelabra. Peter told me the theatre looked like a battleground afterwards.' The clumps of freckles on Swiney's face look orange in contrast to the whiteness of his skin, matching his mop of hair. Despite the smile, his eyes dart every now and then towards the party by the window.

'What did Handel do?' Harry asks.

'He retired to the spa at Tunbridge Wells. It was while he was there, getting himself rubbed, scrubbed, steamed and starved, that a message arrived from the archbishop telling him that the poor old king had met his maker while on the way to Herrenhausen. The upshot of it all was that the Prince and Princess of Wales wanted him to organise the music for their coronation.'

'That was lucky, wasn't it?'

'Trouble was, there was already a Head of Royal Music, Maurice Greene, and he rather thought it was him who should be asked to write the music for the coronation.' His eyes veer towards the window again.

'Handel doesn't set out to make enemies but the people around him like to create diversions for themselves,' Harry says.

'He doesn't set out to make enemies but he wouldn't be a great man for making a compromise. Besides that, the world of entertainment, it's full of factions and heightened emotions, just like the opera. Which is why I'm keeping my eye on that gang of rooks by the window.'

'Who are the two milords?'

'Burlington and Edgemont. They're plotting, I know they are.' Senesino gets up for another bottle of wine.

'Harree, Harree. I do not see you here.' He plants a kiss on his cheek and ruffles his hair. He is slightly drunk. He lowers his voice. 'I 'ave a duchess, a new one, this time young, maybe we share.' He giggles before making his way back to the window.

'I wouldn't trust any of their arses with so much as a fart.' John mutters.

'What do you mean by plotting?'

'I'm not sure. But all of them, they have one thing in common. They don't like Handel.'

12. The Vauxhall Gardens

'We don't have to pay a full shilling to get in, if we walk long enough round the side there may be a break in the wall and we can get in through the back.' Harry quickly falls in with Peter's plan and they start to walk. Soon the way becomes filled with shadows, although, being the end of June, it is not yet dark.

They have crossed the Thames from Whitehall Steps in a wherry, a short journey that seemed like a crossing of continents. Much has been spoken of the New Spring Pleasure Gardens but neither of them has ever been before and they were not expecting the entrance fee to be so high. Their walk in the dark seems to take for ever but then they see a place where masonry has crumbled sufficient to allow them to climb over the broken wall. Once on the other side, in the fading light, they see a long avenue and woodland to either side. From the distance music can be heard but closer to it seems like the very bushes are moving.

'I'm not used to trees.' Harry shivers.

'I believe there are lags who wander here, ready to take your bung.'

'I'm not surprised, it would be easy enough.'

Two figures take shape in the gloaming and the pair of them freezes.

'Let's hide,' Peter drags Harry into the darkness among slender trunks that glimmer in the moonlight, their footsteps seem to crash on the carpet of broken twigs. The figures pass. They are a couple of lovers, giggling and talking. Soon they too step off the avenue into the bushes.

'Let's go, it's safe,' Peter whispers.

'No, let's stay here for a while.' Harry's heart has gradually resumed its normal pace. He is enjoying the musty smell, deliciously fresh after the soot and fog of the city, that comes off the ground. He admires the whiteness of Peter's skin in the moonlight, pulls his shirt over his head and runs his fingers over the exposed flesh. He undoes his own shirt.

'Did you tell Handel it was me you were meeting?' he asks.

'Of course not, I said nothing, he simply told me he didn't need me tonight. I'm not a prisoner.'

'Sometimes I feel you are. We see so little of each other.'

'Not a day passes when I don't think of you; you know that, don't you?'

They kiss but cold begins to creep up from the ground. With reluctance they stand and adjust their clothes. As they walk towards the music and lights Harry presses Peter's hand. He wants to hug him and take his arm, because to have all evening alone with him is so special, but, of course, in public they must observe the strictest rules of decorum. They get to a part of the avenue where every tree is lit. What greets their eyes is unlike anything they have seen before.

'Look at the colonnades of the pavilions round the central square,' says Peter. 'Those decorations must be this "Chinese" style that everyone talks of.'

The large space between the pavilions is full of people either walking in groups or sitting at benches waiting to be served. Each waiter wears a blue jacket and has a number pinned to his front. They dash from table to table with their arms stacked with dishes. An orchestra, playing on a tiered bandstand, fills the air with music. Diners look out from a line of balconies, to see and be seen. Every type and class of person seems to be present.

'Look at the paintings in the dining pavilions; village life as you've never known it.'

'Our troupe use to visit the countryside, we were a bit of excitement for the villagers.'

'Did boys really play hopscotch in the dirt and milkmaids tarry with their swains on styles?'

'Not when I was there. You see the man dining in the pavilion that has the Prince of Wales' feathers on it?'

'Yes, do you know him?'

'Mr Tyers, he owns the gardens. He's tiresome, always coming to Brook Street and asking Handel to become a patron.'

'He looks like Montegnana, sounds like him too, with that carrying laugh.'

Harry has some pennies in his pocket and buys overpriced food. Peter starts telling him the news from home: young Lucy has been delivered of a boy, but more exciting than that, Nell has had puppies. Sid has become melancholy because he is no longer the centre of attention; Handel is a brute for not allowing Peter to keep one of the pups; Betsy is making his master fat with her cakes. When it is Harry's turn to come forth with tidbits of conversation, he describes the audiences whooping and shouting during The Maid's Merry Tale. He tells Peter of Emily Trebeck's blushes, now that he gives her lessons, and of the passion he has discovered within himself for teaching. He makes no mention of the plotters at the Three Crows.

It is late when they cross the river again. The water is smooth, and voices can be heard carrying across it as revellers call from one boat to another. A mass of masts can be seen in the distance, behind the roofline of London Bridge, and the dome of St Paul's looms behind a veil of cloud. Once on the other side they say their goodbyes and Peter disappears among the gin shops and hovels, London "pannies", which form a maze around the old hall at Westminster. He promises Harry he will write from Oxford which is where the maestro plans to go soon. Harry begs him to tell his master that he would come up to Oxford if he wished, to sing in his oratorios there. His walk home is over an hour. He keeps his eyes open for footpads and ruffians. When at last he falls into bed, he wishes Peter could be with him and wonders when he'll see him again.

13. Oxford

When the stagecoach arrives at last it is a relief to Harry to stretch his legs after the tilting and jolting along badly made up roads. Only on the last section of the journey to Oxford was the way made smooth by the introduction of a toll road on land owned by one of the colleges. In his pocket is the letter of invitation from Handel, not actually written by him, of course, for the maestro now relied on Peter to turn his imperfect English into a flowing, rather elaborate prose. In it, he asks Harry to sing on the morrow in Deborah.

Arne and his violin teacher, Festing, have been his companions on the journey. One of Arne's annoying traits is that, even though he misses no opportunity to deride the great composer, he cannot resist following in his traces. He passes onto them Peter's warning that the dons stand for tradition and high Tory values and are Jacobites to a man. They invited Handel in order to scorn him for his Whiggish ways, but now he has them crowding round him as if he was the Pied Piper.

'You make the dons sound like rats,' says Tom.

'Come on, even you must admit that the London papers have been lavish in their praise of his concerts here.'

'That's simply because we Londoners expect nothing but respect from those unfortunate enough not to live there.'

As Harry looks around the inn yard where the coach has stopped, it strikes him that even the air feels different. The voices are unfamiliar, so are the houses; as to the people, they could be

Greeks. He bids goodbye to his companions because he is sure that the gaunt, bookish youth who approaches him is Timothy, Mrs Trebeck's oldest. She has commanded him to have Harry to stay in his rooms. Timothy calls across to an old cuff to take the bags; he touches his cap and says something which sounds to Harry like "Oh, arrgh, aye". He is escorted to a gothic edifice, Balliol College. They are just in time for dinner, Timothy tells him. His tone is so hushed that Harry is determined not to be awed by the sight of the enormous, hammer-beamed dining room.

Before him are row upon row of wooden benches with a lot of bobbish coves togged up in caps and gowns along them. He can see Handel's wig nodding at the high table at the very far end. Menials wander between the tables with bottles of wine. Dishes of roast partridge and woodcock, and platters of steaming vegetables, are being served. They do themselves well, these fellows, thinks Harry. Apart from the gold brocade of his waistcoat there is not an item of colour in sight. Females are completely absent even among the domestics.

Timothy ushers him to a gap in the benches and hisses in his ear.

'Whatever you do, when the port comes, send the bottle in the right direction; people here get into an awful funk if newcomers don't know the rules. By the way, don't converse with the codger at the end of the table unless you're fluent in Latin.' As if this is not enough to rob Harry of his ease, he adds. 'When this is over I'll take you to a brothel, I expect you're dying for a fuck, I know I am.'

Timothy's face is youthful; pimples inhabit his chin like a flock of birds on a field of stubble. He is studying theology, his mother's idea no doubt. If he wishes to live the life of a don it is as well that he familiarise himself with the bawdy houses of the town for he will be forbidden to marry. He winks at Harry, turns to the master and says, with an innocent charm, something about

Rome which sounds to his guest like, 'Numquid quia tu transisti Romam, Domine?'

The master looks delighted.

'Gavisus sum valde Romam.'

For the first time since leaving the Charterhouse School, Harry wishes for Mr Beaker's company.

'Did you visit Le Grand Chevalier while you were there, Sir?' The master glowers at the questioner, Harry's neighbour, a jolly dog with a large face.

'Lapsus linguas, Sturges.' Despite this reprimand, he cannot resist replying. 'Etiam, quidem has altitudo Stuart.'

'The Pretender,' Harry's neighbour murmurs. 'James Francis Stuart. Adipem asinus, qui eam putat thronum calefaciens. He who thinks it should be his fat arse warming the throne. He lives in a palace given to him by the Pope. Each day, when he rises, he holds audiences, just as if he were king, and has to be addressed as His Royal Highness. Makes you laugh, does it not?'

The neighbour turns out to be a good sort. When the port decanters arrive, along with roasted almonds, chocolate fancies, candied fruits, ginger, marzipan and walnuts in their shells, he explains that the decanter must be passed to the left and not allowed to touch the table. Once the master's protruding stomach can be seen moving rhythmically up and down and his head is slumped on his chest, Timothy leans over.

'Hey, Sturges, coming to the brothel later? I'm dying for a fuck, and so is Walsh.'

'Not to my taste, old boy,' says the sensible Sturges.

'Actually, I have to meet with Handel. I'm sorry, I won't be able to come either.'

'You know Handel? What, personally?' Sturges looks interested. 'He's quite a prime mover. The gorgers here didn't approve of him being asked. Thought they were doing him a favour. It's clear he thought he was doing them a favour. Terrific music.'

It is only after the speeches, the delivery of biscuits and cheese with the sherry, the lighting of candles, and the processing of the old cuffs from the high table - Handel, looking irritated, among them - that Harry is able to leave. Timothy is anxious still for his fuck and has found a number of companions who are similarly disposed. Harry is relieved that Sturges does not invite him to tarry awhile but he thanks him for his company and promises to leave a ticket for him for Deborah.

As he makes his way, slightly fuddled and desperately tired, to the young Trebeck's staircase, off a manicured quadrangle, Peter emerges from the shadows. He comes up to Timothy's room where they kiss and hold each other. Peter tells him all about their encounters with the fusty dons and riles at their arrogance and idleness. They undress and lie, side by side, on Timothy's narrow bed, looking up at the gothic tracery and tiny panes of the window. Harry already has in mind the sketches he will make of gown-clad figures, stuffing themselves at the trough, like Norman lords in their medieval halls, their Latin and Greek tomes to one side, their neglected students running riot in the town. Timothy will not be troubling them. Their love-making is slow and passionate. Once they become still, Peter falls asleep in Harry's arms and remains there until the early hours.

The next day, after the performance of Deborah, which takes place in an impressive library of classical proportions, Handel pulls Harry aside.

'Your singing,' he says. 'It's getting better. Yes, I develop quite a liking for the tenor sound. Beard's voice, it is powerful, yours, it has beauty, your range, excellent.'

Musicians, how they love praise, how they need it, constantly, in order to keep doubt from engulfing them. As he sits in the stagecoach on his journey home, Harry glows with pride.

14. Lord M is Troubled

'Just reading the court circular,' says Lord M. 'The Princess Royal plans to marry at the end of the year, I see. Handel no doubt will be preparing the music. It would be unthinkable to ask anyone else.' He is at his usual table at Batson's looking out of the window; his posture is languid and he has his customary half amused look, but Harry is not convinced that he is fully at ease.

'He and the princess are close I believe.'

'I remember her as a little girl, accompanying the old king, her grandfather, to the opera. The royal box at the King's, as you know, Harry, sits in full view of every female's lorgnette. Mary always swept the horizon with hers, like a general surveying the field of battle. Glamorous days those were. The old king virtually lived in the royal box.'

'Was George's wife ever with him?'

'Good Lord no, she'd been imprisoned years before, for adultery. Poor woman never set eyes on England. Word had it that the king connived in the murder of her lover, a Swedish count.'

'Monarchs are above morality, I suppose.'

'They create their own. He was mighty generous when it came to handing out titles to his mistresses and their children. It was just his mother he didn't like. And his wife, of course. Then there was the son, our current king, he absolutely hated him.'

'A man of great warmth, then?'

'And peculiar tastes. The gimlet-eyed Maypole, his mistress, was so thin I couldn't imagine her being bedded by anyone; she was avaricious as well, kept her house in Isleworth stuffed with the nation's treasures. You can be damn sure they disappeared, back with her to Hanover, when she took her leave. The king lavished a string of Irish and English titles on her but round the card table we still thought of Ehrengard Melusina von de Schulenburg as the Maypole.'

Harry cannot suppress the feeling that Lord M is making small talk. His lordship looks round and nods to an acquaintance dressed in the sober black of a banker, then brings the subject back to the opera.

'The quality of music Handel brought to London was unlike anything that we'd ever heard before. He knew how to dig up foreigners who could play an instrument, and he hand-chose the singers and brought them over from Italy. I was an investor in the Royal Academy Opera Company so I know. We were ambitious, we wanted music in London to be the envy of every capital in Europe.'

'I'm sure it was and still is, My Lord,' says Harry with conviction.

'We investors made our mistakes, naturally. We bought in a second soprano for a start and the Town tore itself apart arguing over which one was better, Cuzzoni or Faustina. Harry, you should have heard them, sometimes when they sang I would be so moved that I'd reach out a tender hand to my wife.' Momentarily he closes his eyes. 'At the time I was dreaming of someone else, of course.'

'Was Lady Mary similarly moved?'

'Hers is not an affectionate nature. She'd usually rap my knuckles with her fan.'

An imposing gentleman has just entered, the equal of Lord M in elegance, and comes over to greet him. Lord M smiles.

'Harlow. You know Lord Harlow, do you not, Harry? Like me, he was an investor in the Royal Academy. Come and join us.' Lord Harlow is a royal aide, and like Lord M he is such a bang up cove that he makes Harry feel underdressed. What he would do for an ounce of their style. He nods in a manner that, he hopes, is only moderately deferential.

'I was about to tell Harry that those damned Italian singers, when not on the stage, were an absolute penance.'

'Yes they were,' his companion agrees. 'Handel grew sick of their tantrums; who can blame him?'

'They were as expensive and troublesome as a stable of thoroughbreds. That's why, Harry, the company went bankrupt in the end.'

'Bankrupt? The Royal Academy? I had no idea.' The notion of bankruptcy sounds catastrophic although he is a stranger to what it really means.

'It didn't make much difference to Handel, he just took over the reins with Heidegger, and they set up their own company,' Lord Harlow replies.

'He thought he'd keep a better grip on things than a parcel of titled blockheads as we, the shareholders, surely were,' Lord M explains.

'He was brave but foolhardy, still is.'

'Yes, I'm afraid so. He wasn't aware of the risks he was taking with his own money.'

'The fact is that opera never pays, am I not right, M? A good soprano or castrato voice, well, it's a luxury item, rare and precious, and therefore expensive.'

Inwardly, Harry groans. Matters of economy are hard for him to grasp. The idea of Senesino or La Strada being luxury items seems strange.

'There are limits to what people here will squander on pleasure. It's not a case of unalloyed extravagance as you might find in the court of France, say, or in Dresden. I've been to these places, I know.'

'You're right, M. A nation of money men, that's what we are. We like our wealth.' Lord Harlow leans back, a man very much at his ease in Batson's and, no doubt, very fond of his wealth. 'Besides, we'd already lost the run of ourselves with all that speculation in the South Seas Company. Many of my friends were destroyed by that.'

To Harry's relief this exchange is temporarily halted as their lordships ponder Lord Harlow's friends whose belief in their own avarice led to their destruction. He is familiar with the broad outline of such conversations. Phrases like "scandalous affair", "fraudulent minority of City men", "economy nearly ruined", are usually followed by, "such foolishness", "never again".

'We learnt our lesson all right.' Lord M gives a resigned sigh. 'As to the opera, it's rather like keeping a mistress.'

'How so, My Lord?'

'It's damned expensive and sets up a rivalry with the card table.'

'You should know, old man.'

'Maybe Handel was slow to learn because he never kept a mistress.' Both men laugh at Harry's quip. He hopes that the subject of the opera is now exhausted but Lord M won't let it go.

'The other problem is that audiences are beginning to find alternative attractions. Pleasure gardens, burlesques, English masques. People like Jonathan Tyers know all about it. He may be a bore, going on about his gardens and so forth, but he has the common touch. That's why I wished to talk to you, m'boy.'

'Talk to me? About Mr Tyers?'

'No, about Handel. Someone must warn him not to take further risks.'

'Warn him? You cannot be asking me, My Lord.'

'That's exactly what I'm doing. Let me explain. There's talk of a rival opera company. That could be the ruin of him.'

'A rival company?' Harry looks startled.

'Yes, the Prince of Wales is behind it. We think Rolli and Senesino are too.'

'Trouble is, Handel is so stubborn. This new company could halve his audiences.' It is Lord Harlow who speaks. Harry's thoughts flit back to the group sitting by the window at the Three Crows; it seems like John Swiney's instincts were right. But he's puzzled as to what Lord M expects him to do.

'I have no influence on him,' he points out, fearing for a moment that their lordships are alluding to the fact that he is friends with Peter.

'That's not what I see. You and John Beard, what I call the younger set, you need to encourage him to seek out new audiences. These oratorios that you sing in, they're a great success. You're getting noticed, Harry.' The moment of danger has passed, and such is his relief that he allows himself a hint of criticism against the great man.

'I wish as much as you do that he would write more oratorios for he will not allow his English singers to appear in his operas. But none of us can influence what he writes, or what language it's in.'

'Yes, that's the trouble,' says Lord M gloomily. 'At times he's so bull-headed. I just hope when this company opens, he won't enter into some deadly rivalry.'

As Harry makes his way home, City men in black coats, who are holding their hats against a breeze that comes up from the river, walk by in pairs. A group of clerks, raucous and unmannerly, ideal for employment in Button's, push into him. At the poultry market, beggars are picking up what scraps they can, but he passes with haste, for, even in the cool of autumn, the smell of raw fowl and dried blood is noxious. At Cheapside, the great edifice of St Paul's begins to rise up, ahead, before disappearing again behind tightly packed house fronts. Harry decides to cut across Bread Street but waits for the thudding hooves and tinkling brasses of a coach and four, travelling far too fast, to pass. Just as he reaches a side gate to the cathedral a group of choristers is herded through. Practising for evensong, possibly.

He can feel his spirits sink. This rival opera company, what will it do to Handel's fortunes? Harry knew the great man had enemies, what eminent person doesn't? But his position in Polite Society seemed impregnable. Harry's dreams are so potent: to sing in the opera, or, at the least, to become known as a Handel stalwart, a singer of his English oratorios. What would become of them? He had promised his father, only the previous year, that he would be a success, and that is what he craves. How often he indulges himself with visions of the warden, at Charterhouse, opening the pages of The Spectator and reading about his magnificent concerts; he imagines the malodorous doorman handing him scented notes from titled ladies, leering lewdly as he does so; he pictures Peter, discreet, quiet, but proud to see him do well, even proud that he is so irresistible to women of the highest station. Harry lets out a groan, and pounds his palm with the clenched fist of his other hand. His main fear is this: if Handel sinks, so too will he.

1734

15. The Soup Kitchen

Snow lies on the ground. Doctor Walsh has decided to light a fire in the courtyard to the front of the rectory in order to make flummery for the poor. Already an untidy line of supplicants has formed near the gate. Several women, some with babies strapped to them, are helping to cut turnips which will be added to the boiled oats and marrow bone. Mrs Trebeck has sent a message to say that she intends to come over, from Hanover Square, so Harry has made it his business to volunteer as a helper. Peter has joined him.

Harry feels encouraged that, even though the rival opera company has started at the Lincoln's Inn Fields, they may not last long. Their reviews, so far, have been less than fulsome. Maybe, he thinks, Handel has nothing to fear, and his audiences will stay loyal. When he points this out to Peter his companion goes mute. He looks troubled but shows no desire to talk of it. Harry sighs. He hates Peter's silences, the fact that he will not take him into his confidence, tell him what he's thinking. Beyond this, he has his own frustrations to contend with. He misses the company of the Italian singers who have deserted the maestro en group, and he misses the King's; no oratorios are planned until the April. For the present time he is having to make do, performing in yet another of Arne and Lampe's rediscovered English masterpieces of old.

Every now and then, as the two young men feed the fire and stir the pot, Harry's hand brushes Peter's and a thrill runs up his arm. When Peter's blue eyes turn shyly to his, he is struck by how soft and willowy he is, a contrast to the sturdiness of his own form. How much he would like to comfort him, to make him smile. It was always thus, he thinks, sadly. Peter absorbs the unhappiness of others while I seek to brush it off.

Very soon Mrs Trebeck makes an appearance, accompanied by a large jovial fellow in a wide brimmed velvet tricorn hat who Harry instantly recognises.

'We have been hearing Mr Wesley give a sermon at a Bible meeting, have we not, Mr Tyers?' She beams up at her companion. 'So very inspiring.'

'Inspiring indeed, Mrs Trebeck, my soul feels free already. And my first act of philanthropy will be to undertake to pay all the expenses involved in this worthy enterprise. Doctor Walsh is over there, I believe. I must introduce myself.'

'You know Mr Tyers of the Vauxhall Pleasure Gardens,' Harry says to Mrs Trebeck when he has gone.

'I do,' she replies, 'a very Christian gentleman. Peter, how delightful that you are here as well. Your Master was, as always, in his usual pew at communion this morning. I can stir the pot, so why don't you boys urge those poor, dear people forward, speak to them, make them feel at ease.'

Peter and Harry exchange exasperated looks. Neither of them wishes to get too close to the poor, dear people because most will be crawling with lice and fleas.

'Come,' says Harry, 'the food is ready. Hold out your bowls.'

'Wis Gerry?' a young man asks his companion.

'Slippin. He wapt his mort's bite las night, can't gerrup now.' They laugh lewdly.

'Jer hear abart his brother? Cull was lagged for prigging a peter with several stretch of dobbin from a drag.'

'Werrin the suds too. Ware hawke the bum traps are fly to our panney.' Harry recognises the reference to the sheriff's men, the "bum traps", but that apart, he cannot understand a word. He looks helplessly at Peter who shrugs as if to say, 'Don't ask me. Southwark? Shoreditch? I don't know.'

Their luck prevails when Tyers decides to cut the bread, a task for which he has no aptitude. The loaf before him jumps off the table and the knife slices his thumb. Blood spurts everywhere causing Doctor Walsh, Mrs Trebeck, and three of the female helpers, to rush him into the kitchen to bandage his wound.

'Exit the God-cacklers,' mutters Peter as the two young men return to their rightful position behind the pot and resume doling out with quiet speed and efficiency.

Tyers returns as the fire is being put out and generally gets in the way as the women clean the pots.

'So you are a singer at the King's?' he says. It's not so much a question as an announcement.

'At times, Sir.'

'Then you must come down to my gardens and meet my wife. Any friend of Handel is a friend of ours. He is, Sir, a man I admire beyond all other. He may be famous, Mr Walsh, a particular favourite of the queen's, a man who keeps company with the high and mighty, but do you know what I believe?'

For half a second Harry thinks he is waiting for a reply but his pause is merely rhetorical.

'I believe that one day he will become a man of the people.'

'Do you think then that the Italian opera will become popular?' Harry asks.

'No, Mr Walsh, I do not, its appeal is limited to but a few. It is Mr Handel who will become popular. I am a businessman, you know, some people call me an impresario, I understand markets; my principal trade is in entertainment. When I pursue my ideas I ask not if they be tasteful, not if they be refined or uplifting, but if there be a demand for them. First I ask if that demand already exists, then I ask, could it exist should people be offered something that appeals to them?'

'I do not follow you, Sir.' This is yet another lecture, Harry believes, on the wretched subject of economy.

'Before the Beggar's Opera, would you have thought that people would pay to see a tale about all manner of low-life, set in the back streets and taverns round Newgate?'

'Most certainly not.'

'Until John Gay proved otherwise.' He claps Harry on the back so hard that he almost falls in the embers. 'When that show first opened, way back in '28, I nearly split my sides, I was laughing so heartily; and so were the audience around me. It taught me something. This is what people are looking for, I thought, an expression of both their hopes and fears.'

'Handel's works, they are nothing like the Beggar's Opera. A man of the people, Sir, I do not understand.'

'Just wait, young man, wait and see.'

Peter listens to them while he works calmly and diligently. Harry gives him a surreptitious look and he gives a surreptitious shrug in return, as if to say, if only what Mr Tyers says was right.

'What are you thinking?' Harry asks as they haul the pots back on the shelf in the pantry.

'That I'd like to mace the woodcocks who have formed this second opera company. Now life has become more complicated for us all.'

'Yes, hasn't it?' Peter is referring to the difficulty he has in managing someone who is contrary and fractious. The complications I face, thinks Harry, are of a different order: just as I thought I'd bought my hogs to market, working for the most celebrated composer of the age, his popularity is in decline, and my prospects of success are ebbing away.

16. Paolo Rolli Makes an Offer

The snow has cleared but cold February air blows into the Three Crows every time the door opens, bringing with it dust and soot which the wind has blown towards the Haymarket from the crowded courts and alleys to the east of it. Harry has asked to meet Paolo Rolli, even though his Italian is near fluent, because he wants to hear in person from the maleficent gossip-monger how the rival opera company is faring.

'I gather you are one of the instigators of this new outfit,' he says once they have found a quiet table.

'Why yes, my dear, that is true. Our patron is Prince Frederick, no less.'

'Does the Prince of Wales hate Handel? Is this some act of malice against him?'

'Harry, Prince Frederick is really rather fond of the Saxon Lard Barrel but he hates his parents. This is an act of malice against them. It is important that you understand that.'

'I understood the Prince of Wales to be the most popular man in Britain, so why has he a need to demonstrate a hatred for his family?'

'Harry, your tone makes it sound as if it is you that is under attack. It's the prince's petit faible; he just loves to enrage his father, and it is almost a point of honour to him to oppose everything that his father stands for.'

'But why?'

'Because his feelings have been offended. His parents, they much prefer the younger son, Prince Dumpling, he who at the age of four was made Duke of Cumberland. They deserted him, Harry, left him to be brought up by tutors at Herrenhausen when they followed the old king to England.'

'At least he's cultured. His tutors did a far better job than his father would have, everyone knows that.'

'So true, so true. Your dear monarch, he flies into a rage, quite loses himself, if he sees anyone so much as glance at a book. As to praising his son in his presence, which I did once, he was beside himself, called me a rascal and a liar.'

'What about the queen? Surely Prince Frederick cannot hate her?'

'Oh he loathes her, be assured. That's why setting up a new opera company was a stroke of genius. The queen and the eldest daughter, Anne, as you know, cherish and worship the Fat Cabbage like no other. When they heard that the prince was setting up a new music faction, it was the females of the royal household who were enraged. They refuse to talk to him anymore.'

'Princess Anne will be gone to the Netherlands soon.'

'Ah yes, so she will, with her hunchback Orange Prince. She declared that she would marry a baboon if it got her away from her brother; it looks as if her wish has been granted. Her nuptials were delayed by his illness, I gather. All going well otherwise?' Harry has no wish to be side-tracked on the subject of Handel's lavish masque, written to celebrate the royal marriage, which they will be rehearsing soon.

'How will the prince fund this new venture?' he asks. 'The opera is so expensive.'

'Harry, my dear, you sound like a banker. There are plenty of supporters, they seek to find favour with a man who will be king one day. Handel and Heidegger's little company, I understand, is quite weighed down with debt, so tiresome for them. We, on the other hand, have been promised fulsome support by the prince's companions. There is artistic input, of course, from your very own Paolo Rolli.' He simpers in a way that implies that modesty prevents him from pointing out that he is a master librettist, flautist, poet, composer, and royal tutor on all things Italian.

'How is Senesino?'

'Very happy. Poor man, he couldn't stand being bullocked any longer. We will be joined soon by Cuzzoni, she's coming back from Italy. The real prize is that we have secured the services of the greatest singer of the age, Farinelli.' Harry tries to remain unimpressed but, amongst singers, the name is legendary. 'The younger set, you see, they are bored with Handel, they find him old fashioned.' He waits for his words to sink in then pats Harry's knee. 'Don't look so disconsolate, young man.'

'Isn't the Italian opera itself old fashioned?' Harry is trying to provoke Rolli. 'My friend, Tom Arne, believes that music dramas should be staged in English.'

Rolli's oleaginous features crease with displeasure.

'Everyone, they say, is now going to Handel's oratorios or to pastorals revived by that keyboard thumper, Arne. Believe me, those who do are mere tradesmen, merchants, clerks, apprentices. The Quality knows that to hear real music one must go to the opera and that it should always be in Italian.'

Harry looks down and contemplates an open page of The Spectator which Rolli has been reading. "He thought nothing should oppose his imperious and extravagant Will," it reads. Rolli helpfully pushes the page towards him so that he can read further although, as always, the sentences start to jump around. "No Voices, no Instruments were admitted, but such as flatter'd his ears... He had the impudence to assert that there was no Composer in England but Himself."

'Harry.' The voice is quiet and wheedling. When he looks up, Rolli is attempting to settle his thin black eyebrows and little oiled moustache at an angle that suggests an avuncular concern. 'Join us. We will have the very best singers, the best finances, the best audiences. You will be able to train under the eye of the most famous singer of them all. And one day you too will become famous.'

Harry tries not to impart his excitement at the thought of working alongside the great Farinelli. To be disloyal, surely, is the greatest of sins. But then, how loyal had Handel been in refusing to let him appear in his operas? Then there was his relationship with Peter to consider. The fact that he is tempted by Rolli's offer makes him feel ashamed.

'Give me time. I have to think about this,' says Harry. As he does so, Handel strolls past the window. Will he have looked in? Beside him is his old friend, Johann Christoph; they are probably on their way to Lockets for hot chocolate and pastry. Rolli's lids are hooded and unblinking.

'I would pity him,' he says, 'if he wasn't such a dictator. The sad truth is that he is, well and truly, passé.'

17. Arne's Challenge

As Harry walks down the Haymarket, after rehearsing the anthem for Princess Anne's marriage, Arne emerges from the Little Theatre and walks alongside him. His presence is unwelcome.

'Your mentor is in trouble,' he smirks. 'There is much spirit got up against his dominion.'

'Been reading pamphlets again, Arne?'

'I suggest you do too. The opera is discussed with much warmth. The papers' criticisms and jibes against Handel are the price he pays for being such a public figure.'

'I'm sure it is not his wish to be.'

'Oh no? I gather that there will be over one hundred performers at this grand serenata planned for the eve of the Princess Royal's wedding. The man has a rare taste for spectacle and pomp. Whether you like it or not, Walsh, he relishes being a public figure. If you choose to live by the sword you must be prepared to die by it.'

Arne is bitter because his last revived "masterpiece" has proved to be a three day wonder. But everything the man says is true, and Harry cannot deny it.

'Have you anything further planned for the Little Theatre?' he asks, in order to move to a subject that irks him less.

'Lampe and I, we're reviving Amelia this coming autumn. It was on last year - maybe you saw it.'

Harry has seen it. It was a humourless piece of work about Prince Cazimir of Hungary pining for his love, when at some point or other his country was overrun by the Turks.

'We wondered if you would consider singing the part of the prince?'

All of a sudden Harry realises there are merits to the piece that he has overlooked; after all a singer must find work where he can. He agrees to accompany Arne to Button's, where Lampe and Beard have planned to meet him, and they set off at a lively pace.

By the time they arrive, Harry's collar feels sticky with soot, and damp clings onto the wool of his coat. Lampe is already there, reading The Grub Street Journal, and Jonny Beard arrives as they do. It is twilight and soon the place will filled with actors and actresses. Their habit is to bleat and shout, in what Harry regards as an attention-seeking manner, before disappearing to their dressing rooms at the Covent Garden or Drury Lane. The only other denizens at present are a horse-faced boy, who plays the clown in the intervals at Mr Rich's theatre, and a fop in a plum coloured waistcoat, the clown's companion.

Now that he meets with Lord M, Harry makes it his business to familiarise himself with the news sheets.

'Ah, The Grub Street Journal,' he says with faux authority. 'Its ignorant foisters are snivelling about Heidegger's ticket charges and comparing them to Walpole's tobacco taxes, I see.'

'Walpole's taxes would make an excellent subject for a satire,' Lampe comments.

'They would,' says Harry. He does not add that the subject might hit more with the audience than the Turks overrunning Hungary.

'Come, tell us about your show,' Jonny intervenes, for he has not a jot of interest in the affairs of the day.

'The first thing to tell you is that we have no aristocratic subscribers like they do at the King's or this new company sponsored by the Prince of Wales. What profit we make is from ticket sales alone.' Arne sounds bitter.

'I have an acquaintance,' Harry tells him. 'Mr Tyers. He calls himself an impresario. He says that entertainment is a business like any other. It must respond to what people are seeking, develop a market.'

'You must introduce us to this Mr Tyers, he sounds like a bang up cove with his new-fangled ideas,' says Arne.

'I'm an artist, not a businessman,' says Jonny, amiable and smiling as ever.

'If the music be good, and the performers talented, then surely a show will have appeal,' says Lampe.

'The way Tyers explains it, it is not the quality that matters, it's whether the content chimes with the public. It's confusing because sometimes the audience knows what it wants, sometimes the writer knows better than the audience what they want, but either way, they have to want it.' The others laugh because what he says sounds comical.

'If I was more of a philosopher I would explain it better.'

'Tyers' tutorial on economy is interesting,' says Arne.

'One day I will introduce you,' Harry tells him. 'I think Lord M had him in mind when he described London as a free for all, a place of opportunity.'

'Exciting,' says Beard who reads the news sheets not at all.

'He is right,' says Lampe. 'That's why you and I, Arne, feel able to strike out on our own. I see it because I am not born here, I have the open eyes of a foreigner. There are no Mr Richs where I come from. No Johann Heideggers.'

'No Mr Tyers,' Harry adds.

'No Handels,' says Beard. 'After all, he is both an artist and a businessman.'

'I do not know the answer to your question, Lampe. If the music be good, whether it will appeal. The tastes of the Town, it strikes me, are much affected by fashion.'

Harry is not thinking of Amelia when he says this, for its music is indifferent, but of Handel. He is a great artist yet he appears to be losing his appeal. What Harry cannot predict is whether the new opera company will prove to be a mere fad or if it will last. He looks across the table at his genial friend who he has known for so many years. Life for Jonny, he thinks, is simple. For him, loyalty is everything. For his dearest Papa, loyalty is everything. Yet just at present, for Harry, his ambitions and his loyalty are like a pair of fighting cocks strutting round his brain.

The doors fling open, bringing in a smell from the drains

outside. Actors and actresses tumble over each other, loud and bird-witted. Arne eyes the females. Lampe describes the plans for his show, outlines their parts and explains that Susanna, Arne's sister, will continue as the female lead.

As they rise to go, the clown does too. He has been secretly holding the hand of his companion while listening to his neighbours' conversation.

'What say you, Harlequin?' Harry asks. 'Did our talk of economy put you in humour?'

The clown wipes the expression off his face with his flexible fingers, then pulls his hand up again to reveal an exaggerated smile which he reinforces with a finger describing an upward ark. His mime has them all laughing.

As Harry crosses the Piazza with Arne he is still chuckling at the thought of the clown's smile so he is not anticipating what comes next.

'Come to King Street, visit Mrs Gould's with me, the dells there are cheap. I have such a horn on me that I need a mort's bite right now, this minute.'

'No, I can't, I must get home,' Harry lies.

'What is it, Walsh, do women frighten you? Haven't you ever docked one?'

'To get a venereal bubo on my parts frightens me.' His cheeks flare up, and he feels flustered.

'There are always ointments. It is fear, I know it is. You molly. Good night, Walsh, I'm off to have my fun.'

Harry watches him walk towards King Street. Arne is correct. He eschews intimacy with a woman because of fear. Arne's accusations. Rolli's offer. Which way to turn?

18. A Test of Loyalty

'It's true, he's written a part for Beard in Il Pastor Fido. His voice is stronger than yours. He'll write one for you when he thinks your voice is ready.'

Peter and Harry are lying on a makeshift bed in the basement of the King's, still dressed because of the cold. The excitement of the royal wedding is over and both of them are feeling flat. On top of that, Harry is disappointed. Does Jonny's promotion mean he is being left behind? Peter strokes his hair.

'Have forbearance, Harry, Handel is being pressed from all sides.'

'That's because he chooses to be.'

'Can you blame him, for being determined to fight the new opera company at every turn?'

'He has no need to be so combative. Why compose an opera on the same theme as his rivals? Why open the season early in order to be first?'

Peter sighs.

'Harry, when someone you love is under attack, even when you know what they're doing is mutton-headed, what can you do but remain loyal? That's what we must do now.' His words make Harry recoil. Why, he asks himself, should he assume that I will rope myself to a ship that could be sinking?

'It's always the same,' says Harry, knowing the while that he is being contrary. 'There's you, me and him. You see us as some unholy threesome.'

A silence grows between them then Peter says quietly, 'There's me and you and me and him. I'm the one in the middle.' Harry looks down at the floor. For a moment he is tempted to say he could become a student of Farinelli, if it wasn't for him. Who knows, he might even prove himself to be a man, if it wasn't for him.

'I must go,' is all he says. The light is fading and neither of them has a candle. Harry gets up but Peter doesn't move.

'Are you going to desert him like all the others?'

'Perhaps he's written a part for Jonny because he's run out of Italians who'll work for him.' Peter stares, his eyes blue as ice.

'That I've never heard before. You're being malicious.'

'What's the point of discussing anything with you? You just don't understand.'

Harry runs up the stairs, out past the foul door keeper, down the alley and out onto the Haymarket. He nearly breaks his ankle in the pothole that now sits permanently outside the theatre. Damn Heidegger for not doing anything about it; no-one cares about the state of the roads, Londoners are no better than a colony of Hottentots. Peter's face stays in his mind. What Harry said to him was shameful and without purpose, he knows it. For a moment his instinct is to go back inside and make his peace. Instead, he sets out towards Hanover Square where Miss Trebeck expects him. He has a new piece, a simple air adapted from the opera, Tolomeo, which he wishes her to sing. It is only as he knocks on the Trebeck's front door that he realises he left the music in the basement at the King's.

19. Beard's Snub

With reluctance Harry is meeting Jonny, who has business with Colley Cibber, the manager of the Drury Lane Theatre Company. The music season is still in full swing but the delight the papers take in fermenting discord puts the entire company at the King's much out of sorts. Every day, it seems, they discuss the eagerly awaited arrival of Farinelli. As Harry passes the door to Mrs Gould's nunnery on King Street, Arne's words come back to him. At some point, he thinks, he must overcome the reticence he has about women. Yet, yet, yet, contradiction and indecision torment him; it is the want, he thinks, of someone he can confide in. For nearly a month he has barely spoken with Peter.

All at once, he turns on his heel, stands in front of the door of the bawdy house, then lifts his arm and knocks. The old ewe who greets him has face patches so large that their purpose can only be to cover a venereal pox. The frills of her bodice look yellow with age, her painted lips part to reveal discoloured teeth.

'The hour is early. Monsieur is in a hurry, I see. Is it more than

one you want? Does Monsieur have any particular requirements?'

'No particular requirements,' he says, relieved that her words
suggest that it is not her that he will be coupled with. 'But I wish
for... cleanliness.' She looks up sharply.

'We are all clean here.' She opens an inner door that leads to
an interior that looms, dark and warren-like, with air that is
insufferably stuffy. It looks anything but clean.

'Adele,' she shouts, 'get yourself ready. That's a shilling and
sixpence,' she looks at Harry with hard, beady eyes. He has no
idea if he should try to bargain; the price is the same as a seat in
the pit at Drury Lane.

'When you're ready, Monsieur, go up them stairs, it's the room
in front of you. There's a piss pot by the bed.'

'A clean one I hope.'

'Monsieur can rest assured; my girls are responsible for
cleaning their rooms.'

Harry pushes his way into what is no more than a cubicle with
walls hardly thicker than the frayed wall paper covering them.
The girl, Adele, is just that, a girl. She tries to smile but her eyes
look bleary, and her dress is drawn up above her thighs. Harry
thinks she has been sleeping. He has never seen a woman's bite
before. He sits on the bed and places his hand on her leg. He can
feel it stiffen beneath his touch.

'You are young,' he says.

'It's the bum traps, we're in the suds, me bruvver send me
down 'ere. Git yer business done, Sir, Mrs Gould, she don't like us
to hang abart.' Harry sees a small flask of gin beside the bed.

'Let me look first.' He lifts her dress, opens her legs, tries to
rouse himself but the surroundings revolt him as does her small
bony body and the droop of her bleary eyes.

'I'm clean,' she says eventually.

'I'm sure you are,' he lies.

He sits there, stupid, unwilling to remove his britches. Adele's eyes glaze over, and he is certain she is about to sleep again.

'I'm sorry,' he whispers, 'I must go, I have business to attend to.' She half opens a drugged eye.

'I ain't pleased you, 'ave I?'

Harry is too bent on escape to answer.

As he walks up Bow Street, relieved to be free, he is certain that he sees the portly figure of Handel entering the Covent Garden Theatre. Why, he wonders. What business would he have with John Rich, the manager there? Harry has no wish to bump into him because there has been a coolness between them, possibly because he saw him that time, meeting with Paolo Rolli at the Three Crows.

Harry runs round to the Drury Lane, seeks out Jonny, and tells him who he has just seen.

'Have you not heard?' he says. 'Heidegger's throwing Handel out of the King's. He's leasing it to Senesino's opera group. Such disloyalty, it's sickening. His enemies, their wish is to humiliate him.' Harry is shocked. Handel and Heidegger have worked together for over a decade.

'So, if he moves to Covent Garden, will you move with him?' Harry asks his friend.

Jonny looks at him with eyebrows raised.

'Why wouldn't I? What are you suggesting, Harry?'

'Should we not judge what is in our best interests?'

'Mine is to follow talent, not fashion,' he says. He pushes the score of Amelia into Harry's hand, explaining that he wants him to tell Lampe that he has other engagements.

'Jonny, don't misunderstand me. I'm confused about what to do, that's all.'

'I think I understand you all too well.' Jonny turns away, letting the baize door to the auditorium shut behind him with a gentle thud.

20. Indecision

In the middle of August Doctor Walsh decides to retreat from the rectory, for its environs become filled with thieves and pickpockets in anticipation of St Bartholomew's Fair. They are accompanied by all manner of cloth merchants, wool traders, pewter salesmen and food vendors who come to ply their wares. Soon, vagabonds will knock on the rectory door, day and night, begging for alms and shelter, and musicians and dancers will carouse and drink until all hours in the street.

This summer Harry has no wish to be left alone. The state of discord that exists in his friendship with Jonny hurts him greatly. The fact that Peter is away, and has not written, makes his heart contract. The constant harping of the news sheets on the marvel that is Farinelli, makes him realise that he must make a decision by the end of the summer's recess. To while away his time he agrees to accompany his father to Essex to see his aunt. The prospect of doing so, under normal circumstances, would fill him with dread, but on this occasion it seems better than being abandoned in the mêlée of St Bartholomew's Fair.

Soon after the coach departs from the top of Kingsgate he catches his first glimpse of hedgerows. Behind them are newly built mansions, belonging to the merchants and bankers whose interests are so ably supported by Parliament. Their high metal gate, thinks Harry, have an oppressive discretion to them. In London, wealth serves the purpose of display, why hide it behind leafy avenues?

He is squeezed uncomfortably between the window of the coach and a large dame wearing a straw bonnet. In his head he starts to play the opening bars of Acis and Galatea, which has been enjoying a recent revival. The strings trill and caper round each other, then change tone as the horns break in. He imagines himself in the wings of the King's, looking out at the row of candles on the edge of the stage, hearing the coughs of the audience, his heart beating with anxiety and excitement. He is pleased that, in his English works at least, Handel has been giving him bigger and better parts.

As the coach passes the calico weavers' cottages at Hackney, with their gardens of drying linen, Harry's pleasant reverie comes to a jolting halt. The coachman can be heard shouting at the horses as their steady clip-clopping ceases and a fist bangs on the door of the now stationary wagon. Doctor Walsh opens the door and looks in surprise at a crew of country men and women, holding scythes and pitchforks, demanding that all eight of the passengers get out. The dame to Harry's right starts screeching.

'Bullies, ruffians, they'll take my jewels, my clothes.'

The coachman, who has made no attempt to move from the safety of his perch, joins in.

'Land pirates, royal scamps.'

'What is it you want, my friends?' asks Doctor Walsh in his gentle way.

'We ain't inerested in your plate, nor yer trimmings,' says a man in a grogram smock.

'We wanna know if any o' you be Irish,' explains a red faced matron.

'We've problems enough feeding our young, we don't want no Irish stealing our jobs, getting hay in for half the cost.'

Doctor Walsh assures them that no-one is Irish, saying nothing about the two Welsh girls who are planning to go into service near Norwich. He insists that Harry hands over the loaves they have brought for their journey. If he hoped others might share their provisions he is disappointed. The countrymen, looking dejected, take their leave.

'So much suffering,' says Doctor Walsh as the coach goes on its way. 'I feel for them but then I feel for the labourers from Ireland, who seek to undercut them, for their plight must be desperate.' The dame with the straw hat, back in her seat, and leaving even less room for Harry, opens a basket in which she has thick slices of ham and a wedge of French cheese.

'Reverend,' she says between mouthfuls, 'you would be mindful not to believe everything they say.'

The whole incident puts a pall of sadness round the visit to Essex. Almost from the minute he arrives at his aunt's farm Harry starts to chafe. Life in the country, he learns, is very different from the happy scenes depicted on the walls of Mr Tyers' pavilions. The landscape, for a start, is an essay in tedium: there is a want of company and far too much greenery which seems to grow as you watch it, threatening to climb over anyone unwise enough to stay in one place for too long.

Unlike Doctor Walsh, the aunt is big, with red cheeks. She has an addiction to snuff which she keeps in a wooden box on her mantle and sniffs at after each meal. Her snuffling and sneezing, to Harry, is not unlike the sounds he hears in her stable yard. Late at night he has to endure the constant barking of her gnarlers both of whom lose no time in trying to bite his ankles. What would they make of Sid and Nell with their glossy coats and studded collars? Harry cannot summon an interest in the new breeds of sheep, and novel inventions for the improvement of ploughing, that so engage his aunt. Nor can he rail at the neighbouring farmer who has enclosed his woods and fields, depriving villagers of their grazing land. It strikes him that most villagers would be better off if they upped sticks and moved to the town.

Once they return to London, even the cries of the animals in their pens, wafting across from Smithfield, bring Harry comfort. The church bells chiming deep into the night reassure him, the cries of vendors and night-soil men, first thing in the morning, are no longer a vexation. Two families occupy the straw bales in their tumble down barn and he begins to understand their presence better. He recalls the sad faces of the band who stopped them on their journey east and, for the first time in his life, contemplates how full the world is of suffering. At night he does something he has long since ceased to do: he gets on his knees and prays. Dear God, he implores, make me think of others, fill me with compassion and selflessness like my father. He is disappointed when his prayers have little effect; all he can think of is himself; about the ache in his heart and the decision he has to make.

One day Samuel hands Harry a letter, looking anxious, for letters in his eyes can only bring bad news. It is from Rolli. He is going to Dover to meet Farinelli, he tells him, then they will stay at the mansion of Lord Cowper before giving a private concert at the country seat of the Prince of Wales. Carestini, Handel's new castrato, he says, will be feeble in comparison to the new Adonis. He ends with a question. Next season, will Harry sing for Handel or for Senesino's opera?

21. Senesino at the King's Theatre

In early September Harry starts performing at the Little Theatre and his worst fears for Amelia are confirmed. Even with Susanna's presence this revival seems to have lost the lustre it had on its first showing. He yearns to sing in something better. Walking out of the Little Theatre, one afternoon, he is intrigued to catch sight of Senesino through the open doors of the King's even though there are weeks to go before the start of the opera season. He crosses the road and greets his erstwhile friend. He knows the man is a tiresome fussock, and often obscene, but Harry cannot help holding him in some affection. He is also still awed by the voice and by his elegance. Besides, he thinks, should he end up working for him he must keep on his right side.

'Harree, Harree you will be joining us, I hear, I am so 'appy,' he says in his rapid, high-voiced Italian, giving Harry no chance to reply. 'Come and see my new dressing room, it will be right next to Farinelli's. Cuzzoni, hers will be smaller, she'll complain, I know she will, but that's life, that's what I'll tell her.'

They go through a door beside the royal boxes.

'Look at the gold plasterwork, the plush on the settee. No, that shelf, it must be higher,' he says to a workman. The place is abuzz with toiling and moiling, for Senesino is determined that, when he gets into costume, he is surrounded by luxury.

'My pride and joy,' he screeches, pointing to a niche which houses a painted bust of the Virgin. Wooden tears stand out on her cheeks; one, being scuffed, looks like a wart. Her eyes are wide open, the irises are large, and her lips are apart, giving her an expression of horror.

'Every day I will kneel before her and pray,' he says, genuflecting then giggling with delight. 'Just think, I no longer have to sing like a heathen in Handel's Protestant oratorios.'

'They tell stories from the Old Testament. I don't think he intended them to be Protestant.'

'Yes, they are Old Testament, true enough.' Senesino pouts. 'But a Protestant Old Testament, be assured of that, Harree. How he hates us for our religion.' The source of his vehemence puzzles his visitor for Handel has never evinced anti-Catholic feeling. 'But he will regret how he treated me, yes he will regret it.'

'What do you intend to do?'

'Harree, I intend to destroy him. He is finished. He doesn't realise it yet but soon he will.'

One of the workmen, holding a plank of wood, steps back and thwacks his Madonna, and she wobbles and crashes to the ground. She looks up, horrified, at the lumbering form standing over her.

'Mary, Mother of God, forgive me,' he cries, falling to his knees and kissing her. The workmen, used to his histrionics, ignore him and carry on with their hammering and sawing. While his back is turned, all of a sudden, Harry comes to a decision. He hurries out of the theatre, steps sideways to avoid the pothole, then scurries south down the Haymarket. He can see Jonny's questioning eyebrow in his mind. He recalls Heidegger's glower; who would have thought him capable of disowning his old friend and partner in business? Harry realises he has been foolish, that Rolli's enticements were merely ploys to humiliate

Handel.

As he reaches the Strand, not knowing what to do with himself, he stops in the road, just missing being run over by a cart full of barrels. He is sure he has just caught sight of a portly figure wearing a wig that is so out of fashion that it could only belong to one person. Before he is able to take a closer look, the figure opens the door of Lockets and disappears. He must be mistaken. Handel is surely away still. Nevertheless he waits. Time seems to stand still as no-one either enters or leaves the coffee shop. After a while, a coach and four parks up the street, the horses shaking their heads and snorting.

Harry wonders whether to go inside. A pair of fops pass, actors, who he knows from the Drury Lane, and they greet him. He strides back and forth and nearly collides with two women, hideous enough to work at Mrs Gould's. A vision of Adele's bite passes across his mind but is immediately replaced by the memory of her drugged face. After what seems like a long wait, the doors of the coffee shop open and Handel emerges with Mr Rich at his side. They shake hands and part. Harry approaches the composer, feigning an unexpected pleasure.

'Sir, are you on your way back to Brook Street? May I accompany you? I have an appointment in Hanover Square.'

'Lord Shaftesbury is waiting for me in his carriage,' he says stiffly. He indicates the coach and four.

'Be assured, he can join us,' his Lordship calls out. He will have seen Harry walk up and down the street this past half hour. What will he have made of that?

'So, all go well with Rich?' his lordship asks after they have clambered in. Harry is annoyed that now he will have to go as far as Hanover Square to no purpose; his appointment there is a fiction and he and Handel are not free to talk.

'Most definitely. My next season will be at Covent Garden. His terms, they are reasonable. His new theatre, es ist gut.'

'Heidegger's a money man. I suppose he believes he will

make more money with the other lot,' his friend says.

'And so he will for a while, but not for long.'

Harry feels he should say something.

'The princess,' he stammers, 'gone to the Netherlands, you must be sad she's gone.'

'I am sure she is very happy,' comes the curt reply.

He realises he has committed a faux. He has offered sympathy, an emotion Handel has little time for. He has also encroached on his relationship with royalty, a matter he discusses with no-one.

Harry hurriedly tries another tack.

'Mr Carestini, do you think he will give me lessons, Sir? If you are kind enough to invite me to sing at Covent Garden; I need to work on my legato.'

The great man says nothing but his body relaxes. He looks out of the window. Eventually he says, 'The tenor voice, I like it more and more. Perhaps you are ready soon, Valsh, to sing in Italian. The vowel sounds in Italian are long and open, it's a different type of singing. Yes, Carestini, he will be an excellent teacher for you.'

'I look forward to that.' He feels like getting up and doing a jig. 'But I beg you, do not come to see me in Amelia - it is a sorry mess.'

Lord Shaftesbury smiles. 'Some of Carey's stuff is quite good.'

'And Miss Arne, she is delightful. It is a pity she is to marry Cibber's son, he's a ne'er-do-well and a rotten actor.' Handel is smiling.

'Is Peter at home?' asks Lord Shaftesbury. 'He picked up some scores for me from the scriptorium.'

'Yes.'

'Good.'

'But he is not attending to his duties at present.'

'Why is that?'

'It seems he is afflicted. Some nonsense, says he cannot leave the house, leave his room even.'

'Sounds like an hysteria,' says Shaftesbury. 'My cousin Esme has a similar complaint.'

'Whatever it is, he needs to pick himself up.'

When they reach Hanover Square, Harry gets up to leave; as the door of the carriage opens he leans over and kisses his mentor, fighting back tears. Handel's stern features break into one of his luminous smiles. Once back at the King's he writes a note addressed to Rolli, leaving it with the doorman.

'You can always trust me, yer know that Guv,' his friend says, emitting a dunghill's whiff. His grime-laden fingers can barely wait for Harry to turn his back before opening the note.

He writes another note to Peter and finds a boy to take it. In it, he says how sorry he is, he pleads for forgiveness, he begs to see him, and tells him he loves him.

In the evening, after dinner, there is a knock at the rectory door. Harry's heart starts to race, but it is only a message for his father.

'Oh dear, the sexton, he says he must attend to his sister who is ill. I must go round to the church to lock it.'

'Papa, you most certainly will not; give me the key. I'll do it.'

As he crosses the courtyard, the large medieval key in his hand, he sees a figure by the gateposts. When Harry hugs him, he finds he's shaking.

'Come with me to St Bart's. I cannot embrace you here.'

'I'm not well.'

'You will be. I'll see to that.'

The Norman columns rise up in the darkness, their footsteps cry out then get swallowed up by the shadows, arches repeat like so many reflections.

'The sexton usually keeps the stove filled in the vestry, we'll go there.'

In the warmth of the dying embers, for even in September it is necessary to light a fire, Harry opens the cupboards, finds some choristers' gowns and throws them across the floor. He opens another cupboard and pulls out a heavy clerical cape. Once they are lying down he lays it across them. Then he takes Peter's face in his hands, touches his hair, caresses behind his ears and looks into his eyes. He is relieved to be with him again and that his decision is made. As they make love he can feel the heaviness of a large embroidered cross along his back.

1735

22. Mr Tyers' Views on the Opera

Harry is in a studio belonging to Mr William Hogarth, the artist. There is a harpsichord in it and he is giving young Emily Trebeck, who is chaperoned by her younger sister, her singing lesson. Next door, their mother, Hogarth himself, Mr Jonathan Tyers, and an untidy shock-headed fellow, called Captain Coram, are discussing matters of great charitable import. It is their intention to open an institution for foundlings. In Harry's eyes, they are commonly afflicted by a desire to meddle in others' affairs.

Emily's progress under his tutelage has been most gratifying. He is also flattered by the way she blushes with confusion when he praises her. The other day he saw her near the front row at Covent Garden. She and her sister were staring up at him, open mouthed, as they sat next to their father. Esther and Deborah were sufficiently Biblical to convince the Reverend Trebeck that he was watching a morally uplifting work. But they had enough earth and spice to appeal to the young ladies. Theirs were not the only eyes. Now that he has more solos he sees them, men and women, staring hungrily up at him, hanging on his every note. He learns that it is not just the voices of Handel's castrati that have the power to seduce. His does too.

'Walsh, dear boy, you are teaching this young lady to sing, I gather. Excellent. The sitting rooms of Polite Society are always in need of a good soprano.' Tyers and the rest of the committee have ceased their prating and are now taking their leave. Harry agrees to accompany Tyers down to Fleet Street where he is having a pamphlet printed about the work of this new committee. It is such the fashion nowadays, thinks Harry, to rush into print the moment one has an idea about anything.

'So tell me,' Tyers asks as they hit their stride, 'how are things at the theatre? This rivalry with the King's, it cannot be good for business.'

'Mr Rich is delighted that Handel's oratorios are permitted in Lent on the days when all other places of entertainment are forced to be dark.'

'They must be a sound commercial proposition, these oratorios. The costs are lower, too, I surmise; no sets, no costumes.'

'But audiences are fickle, the theatre is sometimes only half full. The queen, though, is steadfast.'

'You know, Walsh, my wife and I, we have been to the opera but once. One of my clients owed me money. He had lost his all in the South Seas Company, a most unwise speculation, and gave me tickets in lieu of payment. I would never have wasted my money otherwise.'

'What did you see, Sir?'

'A gripping tale about that figure of historic renown, the Roman leader, Julius Caesar, and his ill-fated encounter with Cleopatra, seductress of the Nile. As you must surely know, the auditorium at the King's is a very grand affair and a most pleasing prospect by candlelight. But the noise was indescribable and many people, it seemed, had come merely to eat, drink and greet their friends. There was much chat and laughter, and shouting from one box to the other. At one point a chicken bone landed in my wife's hair.'

'The audiences at Covent Garden, I find, are more sober.'

'I am sure you are right. I detected about the King's an air of immorality. There was a group of ill-featured women in the Royal Box and behind them stood two negroes decked in finery, like decorations. I did not like to see men so treated for we are all equal in the sight of God.'

'When Handel entered was there great cheering?'

'There was. The audience only kept silent when one of the principal soloists was singing. But Julius Caesar, dear me, he wasn't to our taste at all. When he opened his mouth he made a most unmanly sound. Squeak, squeak, squeak.' Harry recalls Senesino's agile voice. 'Can you imagine the barbarism of the act that had got him to such a state, and the immorality of the country that allowed it? The nobility, they love all things Italian. Soon, I thought, British choirboys will be forcibly mutilated for the pleasure of fashionable society. As these eunuchs were trained originally to sing in church, the thought also crossed my mind that we were witnessing, there in the opera house, another manifestation of the primitive instincts of Popery.'

'It sounds, Sir, like a most unhappy experience.' They are nearing Fleet Street and almost every house is either a tavern, full of noise and laughter, or a print shop whose machines clank and groan with great monotony. The builders are in evidence; for a whole stretch there are half-built dwellings, taller, and straighter, than their decrepit neighbours.

'Not at all, do not get the wrong impression, Walsh, for it was there, that evening, that I had my moment of inspiration, as I call it, my vision. While the music had lulled many of the audience into a state of repose - a good number were peaceably sleeping at the end of four hours - it had had quite the opposite effect on me. My mind was positively racing. We are here, I thought, because all of us wish to be transported from the dirty and dangerous, care-worn world which is our lot. I was sure that there must be ways of offering beauty and escape which all classes could enjoy.'

'In other words you saw a market for a pleasure garden?'

'Exactly so.'

'Your gardens, Sir, they are most pleasing. I go there often.'

'As do many,' he shouts triumphantly. 'I had one other thought that night, it was this. Should I ever encounter the great Handel face to face, then I would most surely ask him to compose his works in a language we all understand. I laugh because, of course, that is exactly what I did. Cheerio, Walsh, this is where my printer resides. Forget about the Italian opera, that is my advice to you, boy. It is works that are written in English that will triumph.'

It is a shame, Harry thinks, that the maestro does not take heed. He bids goodbye to his companion and turns north towards the theatre. First, he intends to meet Peter in Button's. He will try to lift his spirits with scurrilous impersonations of Arne. If Harry is successful, Peter will do equally scurrilous impersonations of his uncle, Anthony, who is forgetful and has a bad knee. He will chatter about his progress teaching Lucy to read and write and ask Harry if his singing students are doing well. But if he is not, Peter will look pale and distracted and leave Harry feeling helpless, for there is nothing he can do about the war being fought between Covent Garden and the King's.

23. Late at Night at the Three Crows

'Come into the Three Crows for a nightcap. Harlow is meeting me there.' Lord M has accompanied Harry to the Little Theatre to watch a show by their mutual friend, John Christopher, son of Johann Christoph.

'How are things, John?' Swiney is standing behind the bar looking unsettled.

'Not so good, My Lord.'

'I am sorry to hear that.'

'The taffies are after me, I'm in debt. My brother, Owen, is in Venice, says I should join him and open a tavern there.'

Lord M puts his face close to Harry's ear and explains that this brother used to be manager at the King's.

'He had to scarper because the bailiff's men were closing in on him.'

'You can't go away, John, we'd miss you,' Harry tells him.

'Have you not learnt your lesson from The Rake's Progress?' His Lordship points to the prints of Hogarth's celebrated moral tale that Harry has so expertly helped Swiney hang round the walls. One of them shows a Farinelli figure being showered with gifts, the rake carousing in his company. There are twelve prints in all, the last three showing John Rakewell descending into debt and madness.

'Hogarth knew a thing or two about debt,' Swiney observes. 'His father started a coffee house where only Latin was spoken; this unwise restriction was why young William spent his childhood in the Fleet.' They nod thoughtfully.

'Ah, there's Harlow coming in now. Brandy, John, if you please.'

'Four hours,' his friend yawns. 'Four hours of complete boredom listening to something written by an anonymous fool.' Farinelli has been performing for five months. Such is his fame that he steals audiences from Covent Garden and is the darling of every female in society. Lord Harlow is one of the few to be unmoved by his charms.

'Why was the king so keen on going to the opera? After all, he can't stand music,' says Lord M.

'He has to be seen about. He goes one week to Covent Garden, the next to the King's. His son has broadcast that he is dying so it is incumbent on him to prove that he isn't. Trouble is, he has piles so he can't sit down. Instead, we wander from box to box, greeting all manner of numbskulls whose wives simply wish to ogle the principal singer.'

'The usual, is it?' John Swiney murmurs to Harry for he knows that a glass of flip, made up of small beer, sugar and brandy, helps to soothe his throat.

'The king is like some old mill horse pursuing the same unchanging circle every day,' Lord Harlow complains. 'I tell you, you could run your clock by him. In the morning it's walking and chaises, in the afternoon, levees and audiences. At night, if not going out, he plays at commerce and backgammon, the queen at quadrille.'

'Long may he stay like that.' Lord M raises his glass. Harry fears that he and his friend will now talk of politics. 'The fact of the matter is, he lets Parliament run the country and leaves God out of the equation. When Walpole upped the royal levy it was a good investment.' Inside, Harry groans.

'Yes, you're right, M. It's what I try to tell my Jacobite friends.' John Swiney joins in.

'Let us raise our glasses to the king,' he says. 'God bless him for having neither dignity, learning, morals nor wit.'

As they toast the king's inadequacies, the door behind them opens and they are interrupted. John Swiney looks up then leans over and mutters.

'Look who's arrived, the young princeling himself.' They turn to see Montagnana, Rolli, and an elegantly attired, rosy-cheeked gentleman with a number of jewels on his embroidered frock coat.

'Doesn't he just have the open, smiling countenance of a man who owns a lot of property in the Tuscan hills,' says John before extending a greeting. 'Signor Broschi, or do you prefer to be addressed as Farinelli? You are most welcome, Sir.'

Rolli takes in Harry's presence then turns his back on him.

'I was just asking myself,' says John with ingratiating bonhomie, 'what it would be like to set up an Irish tavern in Venice. Il Tre Corvi.'

'Who would be interested in this Irish tavern overseas?' Rolli scoffs.

'La bella Fenice. The idea, it is eccelente,' booms Montagnana. 'The Irish whiskey, it is most pleasing. Try it, Broschi, I insist.'

Farinelli's features are smooth. It is said that his family are aristocracy, not humble like the families of most castrati. Broschi Senior died, so the story goes, when he was young, leaving the family desperate for money. Swiney pours out three glasses of his best whiskey.

'You will like this Signor, it's the legal stuff with all Walpole's taxes paid.'

Like Lord M and Lord Harlow, Harry watches in silence as Farinelli sips from his glass with great caution and holds it up to the light.

'Antonio is correct, it is pleasing, delizioso,' he announces in a high voice.

'Fair play to you, Sir, you have a fine set of manners on you, and here's another on the house.' It is little wonder that Swiney is in debt. 'It's a pity we're not having a knees-up tonight. I'd love to hear you sing.'

'You want a song, Swiney? Let me oblige.'

Montagnana fills his bellows, a rumbling sound starts somewhere round his navel, then lets out an ear-splitting broadside. Their lordships look startled and bottles rattle on the shelves. Farinelli is the only one who doesn't flinch; instead he smiles politely and inclines his head. His second Irish whiskey sits untouched on the bar. As the man-mountain reaches his denouement, a carriage pulls up along the curb outside. A lady, her hair all puffed and powdered, wearing a vizard, looks out.

'A most excellent rendition, Antonio. Thank you. If you will excuse me, gentlemen, I have an appointment.' Farinelli bows gracefully and is last seen being sucked into the darkness of the carriage that awaits him. Rolli throws a hostile glance in Harry's direction as if to say, 'See, that could have been you, had you chosen to join us.'

'What a combination that would have been, Farinelli singing and Handel composing,' says John. Lord Harlow sighs. They all do. Harry sighs because of the sight of the elegant singer setting out on his assignation. Should he allow himself to embark on similar adventures? He is nearing twenty years of age yet has never lain with a woman, never lain with anyone except his love. A sort of despair grips him when he thinks of Peter. The relations between them are, by need, a secret, he can rarely see him and, when he does, he is often sad. Harry is certain that he loves him but he is not so certain about resisting temptation. He needs to widen his experience. The notes that are left at the stage door; the looks from the front row; to ignore these invitations is, surely, a form of madness.

24. Cavendish Square

Harry stands in the wings during the last opera of the season, Alcina, listening to Strada's showpiece aria where she swings from sad resignation to wild bitterness. He wonders, at times, whether Alcina, the wicked sorceress, speaks for the composer, mourning his waning power. There has been no end to Handel's machinations to draw audiences away from the King's. French ballets have been added to the entertainments on offer at Covent Garden, also organ concertos in the intermissions. Swiney comments, sagely, that, since the country has been at peace for near on twenty years, people must create their own battles. From the hale of slander and accusation in the pamphlets every day, it is clear that they have chosen to pitch their tents in the opera house.

Harry's voice has progressed under Carestini's tutelage. He has been given the part of Orante in Alcina, singing in Italian for the first time. But then, like Senesino, Carestini starts to argue with the maestro. As always, the subject of their disagreement is the music. His aria, Verdi Prati, he says, is pointless. Predictably, Handel is enraged and forces Carestini to sing it. Night after night, the audience beg for an encore; it is their favourite part of the opera, the aria is a wonder. Then, Carestini is enraged, for this is proof that, not only is the maestro wrong, the audience is as well. He calls Harry into his dressing room, one day in June, and announces that, when Alcina is over, he will leave.

'Ah Harry,' he says, 'now I go back to Venezia. The cold, the smoke, the filth in the streets, it is all too much for me. Besides, I cannot bear any more, this constant comparison with Farinelli.'

What will Handel do, Harry wonders. It is almost a relief when Peter tells him that the following autumn his employer will give concerts but stage no operas. At last, he thinks, the maestro realises the impossibility of vanquishing his rivals. In time, his supposition will prove to be wrong. Handel's wont, he will learn, is to retreat and retrench but never to abandon the fray. For the present, however, Harry's main concern is that he faces a lonely summer, performing for Arne and Lampe at Drury Lane. Peter gives him little sympathy, pointing out that it is his fate to accompany Handel and Johann Christoph to Tunbridge Wells.

One night in late July, as he leaves the playhouse, Harry forms the impression that a young man is following him. Not having looked closely at his pursuer, he wonders if he is some ne'er-do-well who is after his bung. He lets him walk behind him for a while, looking from left to right to ensure that others are around. Once convinced that he really is being followed, he turns sharply.

'State your business,' he says.

'I have none. I admire you, Sir. I want to offer you refreshment in my home.'

'And where, pray, is that?'

'In the opposite direction, Cavendish Square; it is part of a new town-land north of the Oxford Road.'

'I have heard of it, an exercise in classicism, I believe. How the aristocracy wish that London was ancient Rome.'

'I work for the architect James Gibbs. I am a lover of the classical world.'

'Like every young fop who fancies he's all of the crack. You're a familiar cove to accost me thus.'

'If I have caused you offence, I beg your pardon.'

Once at Cavendish Square, Harry is ushered into a large, top-lit studio where a naked, marble discus thrower, with half his parts missing, presides over a number of curly haired, vacant eyed busts. In a corner, across expanses of empty floorboards, is an easel and drafting board. Extensive windows open onto an untidy garden, a vine waves its leaves up against the glass. It is light still outside, but his host brings forth candles.

'Would you like to change?' the new acquaintance asks.

'Into what exactly?'

'This.' He holds up a Roman toga. Harry starts to laugh.

'Most certainly, and you will show me how I wear it?'

The acquaintance takes off Harry's clothes until he is as naked the discus thrower, then dons the toga and bids him sit. He draws up the long folds of the garment until the position of his model is suggestive, then withdraws to his easel.

'Can I draw you?' he asks.

Paper and charcoal are produced. He starts to make rapid sketches, and he tells Harry to adjust his position until it is more and more lewd, but at no point does he touch him. Long after dark, once Harry has changed back into his clothes and they have taken refreshment, Harry's host, Timon by name, calls for his coach to be brought round. He thanks his guest and asks if they can meet again. Just before reaching the rectory, as Harry dismounts, the young footman presses something into his hand; it is a box containing a woman's ring.

'From my master,' he says gravely. He is a handsome fellow who looks Harry straight in the eye when he says this.

'Tell him I will keep it until I find the right person's finger to put it on,' Harry replies.

The next day, Timon collects him in his calèche.

'Come and look at the new squares and markets north of the Oxford Road. I will expound on the laws of classicism.' Mr Beaker, Harry thinks, would be proud of him.

A few days later Harry revisits Timon's studio. He is urged to dress as a gladiator. Timon himself is already togged up as a Roman Senator.

'Would you like to see my drawings?' Timon asks, pulling large sheaths of paper from a drawer. He sets them out on his easel.

'Look at the intricate etching on that breastplate. My mother and I, we bought it in Rome during our grand tour.'

'It's a very fine sketch, most accomplished,' says Harry. He makes no mention of the fact that the model is wearing the breastplate and nothing else.

'Look at the embroidery round the collar of this cloak. It took me hours to understand the pattern, it is a perfect example of symmetry. My mother and I, we found it in a shop selling antiquities that was hidden away in a little back alley in Florence.'

Harry wants to ask him if he found the model there too. The cloak hangs over his otherwise unclothed shoulder, the folds barely covering his naked cock.

'Ah, see how I have caught the light on this shield.' It is not the only thing that has caught the light. The smooth, muscular buttocks are lovingly rendered, a pair of perfect orbs.

'Come,' Harry says, 'stay behind your easel, you will draw my buttocks for they are exceedingly fine.' But Timon does not stay behind his easel for long. After Harry has draped himself across a couch he presses himself up against him. He is furtive and depraved, and Harry's lust is roused. When he tries to turn round, Timon stops him from doing so. Immediately after their business is done Harry thinks of Peter and is pleasantly surprised to find that he feels remorse.

As Harry discards his skimpy tunic and absurd sandals, and changes into his clothes, Timon pads across the bare floor with his robes swaying, to a small chest of drawers next to the discus thrower. He takes out a box which he gives to his guest. It contains a necklace of moonstones.

'Please take this. Every time I sin I give a piece of jewellery away that belonged to my mother.'

'An act of propitiation to the She Goddess?'

'You could express it thus. Closer to the truth is that I do it to insult her memory. She taught me to love everything classical but, that apart, she was a monster.'

As summer changes to autumn, then winter, a duality forms in Harry's mind. He can find himself walking in St James' Park with Peter, while Sid and Nell jump round their feet, and tell himself that he is not unfaithful since Peter is still his special love. In thinking this, he underestimates the strength of his libidinous nature. Like Timon's mother, it becomes a monster. With two lovers, he thinks, his body's needs will be assuaged; he will no longer suffer the frustrations brought about by Peter's absences or his duties at Brook Street. He is wrong because his appetite is not assuaged. It grows.

1736

25. The Rule of Passion

The spring follows a pleasing interlude of concerts. While this lasted, during the latter half of the previous year, Harry and Peter could make monthly visits to the Vauxhall Gardens, Peter could work patiently on Harry's writing, and they could hone their skills at subverting Mrs Trebeck at the soup kitchen. Such was the state of peace between them that Harry was able to set out with Timon, in his calèche, with his heart and mind fully at ease. His one regret was that he could not share his growing knowledge of the churches, mansions and markets of James Gibbs, with Peter.

After the New Year their lives changed. A new castrato joined the company and Handel's maniacal rate of activity resumed. If the opposition performed something light and airy, he would outdo them with some playful fribble. If it was classic and tragic, his next show had everyone blowing into their kerchiefs. Harry became sick of it.

When Peter looks harassed one night, he is not sympathetic. The performance has just ended and he is still in costume. His loins ache, as they often do after a performance.

'I'm taking Handel home; his energy is depleted.' Peter announces. 'He's up every night composing.'

'I told Papa you'd be staying at the rectory tonight.'

'I can't. I have to go home with him. He's so impossible at present. He was at the King's yesterday, sitting in the middle of the pit, laughing his head off as loudly as possible. Why does he do these things?'

'Because he's Handel,' Harry says bitterly. 'You go. Heaven knows when I'll see you again.' He breaks off because someone is approaching. That is their fate, he thinks, never to be able to talk openly. It is also their fate to be part of a threesome.

At that moment the third part of their little trio appears.

'Valsh, your singing tonight, it was good. Those classes with Carestini, they were helpful. Your voice is developing, how you say, "character".' He nods gravely and Harry does his best to look gratified which, in other circumstances, he would be. Peter starts brushing a splatter of mud at the base of Handel's coat and fiddling with the shoulders to make sure they are straight. Harry is about to ask the maestro if he would mind if Peter accompanied him, so they could stop off, midway, at the Three Crows. But the composer is preoccupied, he says.

'Peter, stop fussing. Lord Shaftesbury is lending us his coach to take us home, we must go, now, this minute.' How typical of him, Harry thinks, to be so oblivious of anyone's needs but his own. Peter divests his master of the leather music case then follows him through the crowds that linger in the foyer. Before going through the door he turns back to gives his love a mournful look.

As Harry makes his exit from the stage door, wondering whether to trek up to Cavendish Square, the doorman, a dour fellow who almost makes him miss the rogue at the King's, hands him a note. All it says is 'My carriage is outside.' An image of Farinelli comes to mind. To the front of the theatre there are many carriages. Harry looks round, as it would be unfortunate to try and gain entry to the wrong one. A footman steps up to him.

'Her ladyship awaits,' he says. He leads him to a mighty chariot with two drivers to the front and a liveried lackey to the back.

Harry steps inside. To his disappointment the lady who greets him is not in the first burst of youth although she was clearly once a beauty; her lips are still full and sensuous. She has a quantity of powder on her face, which is beginning to sag, and on her hair as well, and heavy breasts that seem to seek escape from the confines of her bodice.

'Mr Walsh, I wondered if you would like to accompany me

back to my residence? It is not far, Great Ormond Street. My husband, I'm afraid, is waylaid in the country; I hope that does not inconvenience you.'

Her ladyship, Harry discovers, is not one to observe preliminaries. The minute they dismount, and enter her grand hallway, she turns to the butler and says, 'Keep the candles burning in case my guest has to leave later. Come, Mr Walsh, I must show you the wall hangings upstairs.' The butler's face is a perfect mask. If ever I needed a servant, thinks Harry, I would most certainly seek him out.

In her boudoir the candles are lit, as is the fire. There is a water closet next door, she tells her guest, and that is where she promptly disappears to. The elaborately carved bed is exceedingly large, with quantities of silk hangings billowing round crisp cotton pillow cases. The fabric has made its way from India, no doubt, but it is some seamstress, working in an ill lit hole near St Giles, Harry wagers, who has fashioned it with delicate lace edges and embroidered flowers. The luxury of his surroundings, he finds, is much to his taste although he is relieved to find a piss pot under the bed and an honest jug of small beer next to the bottle of champagne.

So the moment has come. Harry is both fearful and excited. He decides to remove his britches. His linen, thank goodness, is fresh, the girl who works for Samuel knows how particular he is. He lies on the bed and eventually she comes, a moving mass of frills and lavender scent. She closes in on him and he fumbles, not knowing where to start with his hands. Large breasts land on top of his chest; the softness of her, the catch in her breath, arouses him.

'You gelding. Do you not know how to touch a woman's quim?'

'I am an innocent,' he laughs, for her bluntness, in his estimation, makes them equals. He has no interest in feigning an experience he does not possess and he is of a mind that she would enjoy it if he spoke to her roughly. 'You lubricious whore, if you want me to perform you must teach me what to do.'

'Must I now?' She roars with lewd laughter. 'In that case, give me your hand, my merry swain. I'll show you exactly what to do.'

Harry's sweet, dear countess with her soft swelling thighs and pendulous breasts, puts him through his paces. They pant and heave until dawn when he wakes, after a brief sleep, feeling raw and chafed. Bedclothes are spread across the floor, an empty champagne bottle rests on a discarded cushion. His companion snores softly beside him. He is exhausted but triumphant. He has had his first ever encounter with a member of the opposite sex.

He lies still on the comfortable bed and is overcome by a bout of philosophising. How different it is to have physical relations with a woman. To jock a man, it strikes him, is like singing in English, the familiarity is what attracts; to jock a woman is like singing in Italian, it is the mystery that attracts. He punches his pillow and smiles; both in and out of the bedchamber, he cares not what language he sings in.

A few weeks pass before he sees the countess again. He catches sight of her from his vantage point of the choir stalls of the German Chapel at St James' Palace. She is in the congregation at the Prince of Wales's wedding. As he processes down the aisle he catches her eye; a small elderly gentleman, the earl, he presumes, is by her side. Afterwards, as he and Jonny walk along Piccadilly, he recognises her coach; it is waiting to one side of the busy thoroughfare attracting much bad language from the drivers trying to pass it. Harry makes his excuses, mumbles something about picking up a score from the Hickford Rooms, and waits for Jonny to be gone. He goes back to the coach and her long-suffering footman opens the door.

'You have disposed of the earl,' he says.

'I do it often,' she replies. 'He likes to attend the auction rooms near here. Dreadful service wasn't it? Their Royal Highnesses looked grim.'

Harry clambers in.

'Were you there when the Princess Royal married the Prince of Orange? The king and queen could hardly bring themselves to look at him.'

'I don't expect he could bring himself to look at her. All those pock marks, so desperately unattractive.'

As she says this she deftly pulls his hand and guides it up her skirts; she is moist, expectant, eager. The coach barely reaches the Circle of High Park before they are copulating like a pair of cats.

26. At the Vauxhall Gardens

The autumn weather has held and, despite his regular visits to Great Ormond Street and Cavendish Square over the summer recess, Harry is overjoyed to see Peter again. On the night of their reunion they make their way, as usual, to the back of the pleasure gardens at Vauxhall where the woods are.

'Come, let's go amongst the trees here,' Harry says. 'I want to hear every detail of what you have been doing. Did you like my sketches of St Bartholomew's Fair? I was meant to go to Essex but changed my mind.'

For a while they caress but Peter does not respond.

'You seem different,' he says.

'I'm not, I can assure you. It's you that's different.' Harry's heart pounds.

'Maybe I'm just being fretful.'

'Is it Handel? Is he being tiresome?'

'No, it's the fact that I torture myself with the same old question every day. What will I do when your father tells you to marry someone?'

'I'm only twenty-one, and marriage is a long way off. Young girls frighten me, I just can't imagine being married,' says Harry.

'The trouble is, I can, only too well. Then you'll leave me, I know you will. Maybe, I'll have to kill myself.'

'Good grief. And singers are accused of overdramatizing.'

'Just stroke my hair. That calms me down.'

Harry does as he asks and gradually the encroaching darkness takes them, the worries of the day slip away, they nudge and kiss and passion overcomes them. Harry is relieved to find that a surge of sentiment washes over him; he feels protective and full of gentleness to the one who lies in his arms. He finds him hesitant and vulnerable, like a fawn. At the same time, he cannot stop himself from thinking, you cling to me like a vine, your tendrils search out my feelings, you seek a declaration of undying love that makes me uneasy. Beyond that is the larger reality of their future, or rather, the lack of it. Peter will always have Handel to look after but who will Harry have? He is right: one day his father will tell him he must marry. The path to that state seems unreachable. But a future where he is all on his own, that would be unthinkable.

'I'm different,' Peter murmurs.

'You are, that's what makes you so special.' Harry does not wish to embark on further discussion about marriage, less still about a love which is as wide and lacking in direction as the skies he saw stretching above his head on his visit to Essex. 'Come on, let's join the other revellers,' he says. 'What wonders does Mr Tyers have in store for us this evening?'

They walk down the alee, through the gothic arches, to where groups are strolling in the light of the lamps. They share a plate of thinly sliced ham and listen to the band. Then the music stops and the stone waterfall that sits to the side of the main square comes to life. Water gushes forth. On every tier, stand clowns, juggling with wooden balls. At the very top a dwarf holds a rope ladder. Walking along a tightrope, way above them, is a female acrobat.

People start going ooh and aah and Harry watches, fascinated. She somersaults and he is sure she will fall.

'She's amazing, that woman, so graceful.'

'It's my mother,' says Peter in a small voice. 'Can we go? I don't wish to meet her and I don't want Attila to see me.'

'Who's Attila?'

'The dwarf with the bandana holding the rope. Her lover, no doubt; she'll have relations with anyone.'

'Will you tell me about your life as a travelling entertainer one day?'

'No. Why would you want to know?'

'Well, it's so jolly different.' Harry puts his arm round him and smacks his lips on his cheek.

'Oi, a pair of molly boys,' says a voice behind them.

'You calling me a tweedle poop, you clod pate?' Harry answers. Their accuser is a bow-legged apprentice in a worn suit. 'Looking for a cuff across the chops?' The apprentice is pulled into his group.

'He didn't mean to gum you, Guv.'

'You'll have to teach Handel your vocabulary. He loves bad language,' says Peter as they wait for a boat.

When they part at the Whitehall Steps they make a plan to meet again. Harry does his best to dissuade his lover from attending yet another revival of Amelia. His part in it, he tells him, affords him no pride.

27. The Actress

'Harry, dearest, you look quite magnificent without your clothes on.'

He is standing sideways on to the mirror in Susanna's dressing room. His virility is wonderfully displayed. Susanna is removing face paint. Her breasts, which are hard to the touch and blue-veined, fall from her shift, and her swollen belly protrudes from under it. Harry stands behind her and she looks up.

'When I'm whelping it makes me pant for a man but Theophilus, he won't come near me when I am in this condition.

Not that I want him to, the second-rate thespian, he's a drunk and a thief.'

'Why did you marry him?' Harry's hand strokes her neck and rubs the grease from under her chin.

'Because of his father, silly. My parents thought that, as Colley Cibber owns the Drury Lane Theatre Company, I would be assured work. The upholstery business has been running up debts, and they wanted my future to be secured.'

'They wanted their own future to be secured. Move with me to the chaise, dear one, I find it hard to stand.'

Harry pulls her on top of him, holding back for as long as he can as she makes little mewing sounds that he finds totally enchanting. Susanna, the pure, the player of virtuous heroines and wronged women. For so many years he has been slightly in awe of her, for underneath her air of innocence he detects a band of steeliness. Now they share each other's secrets, occasionally enjoying a physical intimacy, but as friends and confidantes rather than lovers. When they are done he takes her beautiful face in his hands and tries to raise a smile.

'You jade, you are using me merely to spite your rotten husband.' She gives him a little slap.

'It is you who is using me. Just to test your love for Peter.' Harry has told her about the two of them, the first person he has confided in, for she has enough secrets of her own to make her discreet.

'I am lucky, I don't detest Peter as you do Theo.'

'I am in so much trouble, Harry, for I truly hate the man.'

'If only your father hadn't made you marry him.'

'You don't realise, we were brought up under the shadow of the Marshalsea.'

'Yes, that's one of the first things Tom told me.'

'When my brother decided to be a musician it was Marshalsea this and Marshalsea that. "Your grandfather died there, now you'll do the same." Poor Tom.'

'My Papa was so relieved that I could do something that he encouraged my music, even if it was second to studying books or joining the church.'

'You are lucky, Harry. I often think that Lady Luck is your friend. Not so with Tom. Even at Eton the boys would rib him, they would block up their ears if he played and scream "Arne's at his music again".'

Susanna clings to his arms and starts to weep.

'It's terrible to hate someone. Only yesterday I opened the ebony box over there, in which I keep my jewellery, and found it empty. I confronted Theo, of course, called him the usual things, a weakling, a drunkard, a gambler, a beetle headed frig pig, but what was the point?'

'What does he say when you call him those thing?' She pulls herself away and dabs her eyes.

'Oh Mrs Cibber, dear, haughty mistress, or, as I like to think of you, foul, baiting, bitch of a stage queen. Don't tell me you aren't sleeping with every depraved braggart and blackguard in Covent Garden.' Her impersonation is masterful. 'Theo's nature is so intensely jealous.'

'He's an actor, maybe he relishes playing the part of the hurt husband.'

'How far, I wonder, will he take this little drama of his?'

'I'm sorry, dearest. It seems so very hard for you. I wish I could help. Tom, surely, will protect you against him.'

'Oh, he's preoccupied. He is full of his love for the singer Cecilia Young. Lampe is in love with her sister. How they swoon and tweer, like a pair of nugs, I envy them.'

'I do too.'

'Does that mean you don't love Peter?'

'I do love him, but my nature is wanton. I relish variety, new experiences. I fear that the really good people I know in my life will find me wanting in their eyes.'

'Harry, who are these paragons, these saints?'

'My dearest Papa, for a start, then there's Peter, who is kind and considerate and a terrible prude. And there's Handel who isn't a prude but does good works in secret. If I was ever tempted to become a philanthropist I would be quite different, I'd make sure the world knew about it.'

'Harry, you are amiable and good natured, your talent is immense and your body, well we will not speak of it just at present. Why would you be found wanting?'

'Because, dearest Susanna, I have this proclivity, just as you do, despite your fame depicting wronged and virtuous women, to sin.'

28. A Visit to Holborn Hill

When the winter cold sets in, Doctor Walsh decides to re-open his soup kitchen and begs his son to invite Peter and Mrs Trebeck to help them. Peter comes the night before and in the morning the two of them take pride in concocting a tasty flummery. They add extra vegetables. Peter cuts up and stirs in the cooked ham he has bought with him, and they argue over how much salt and water to put in. In the end they declare themselves highly satisfied with the mix in the pot. As usual, Mrs Trebeck arrives with company, her friend, Mr Tyers. Because of an incident that occurs, Harry finds he is glad that he happens to be present.

Very soon after they arrive, while Tyers makes himself busy getting in everyone's way, a fight breaks out in the line. It is started by two older boys who pick up a young lad who is holding a black case, and shout at him.

'Gravy-eyed bungnipper. Yer deserve a wherrit across the chops.'

'Get the autem cackler,' his companion says, pointing at Tyers, mistaking him for a preacher.

'Boy, state your business,' booms Tyers, disentangling the lad from his assailants. Harry rescues the case from the ground which has sprung open to reveal a violin.

'Nah, he's no bungnipper, you bufflehead, he's a string,' says one of the boys who had mistaken him for a pickpocket.

The undersized cull takes his case and tries to explain himself as Tyers marches him to the front of the line.

'Sell your violin? You will do no such thing, boy, it is the last thing you sell, that's your means of making a living. Now sit down and eat, then we will talk. Yes, I know, you are concerned about your sick mother and your sister. You are among friends here, boy, and we will help you.'

Once the soup kitchen has completed its business and the women have started to clean the pots, the young boy, Philip Krich by name, agrees to lead the party of men to a tenement on Holborn Hill which is where he lives. His father, now dead, was one of Handel's players, they learn. On hearing this, Peter walks alongside him. Tyers and Harry hasten to keep up, no easy task when the jovial Tyers insists on talking all the way.

Harry is relieved when they stop and Tyers says, 'So, Philip, lad, this is where you live.' He enters the Krich establishment first, showing no reaction to the smell of damp, urine and stale food that pervades the staircase as they climb. Chunks of plaster are missing from the walls, revealing crude brickwork. A woman sits and moans in a doorway, a child clinging to her. Harry looks back at Peter behind him, his face grave. It feels to him as if they have entered the portals of hell. People do not 'live' here, he thinks, they simply cling to existence.

As they enter the Krichs' miserable shelter Harry hands the flagon of soup he has to a girl who is tending the sick mother. Peter unwraps a loaf of bread and Tyers orders Harry out to get fuel. When he returns, laden with a bucket of coal and two bundles of faggots, he re-climbs the stairs and sets the fire. He waits patiently for Peter who has been sent to find more food.

The girl begins to weep in a corner, a shawl tightly wrapped round her shoulders. The mother sits up in bed, thanking her benefactor. It is clear that she is an educated woman. How wrong that an early death in the family should drive them to destitution. Harry does not have a stomach for philanthropy, and the sad sight before him fills him with a sense of utter helplessness. Mr Tyers, on the other hand, is more resilient, admirably able to show kindness and concern as well as the practical bent of his nature. As Harry sits watching him, he thinks to himself how precarious life is, how thin the line between success and destitution.

29. A Rehearsal at the Covent Garden Theatre

Harry growls with his teeth clamped together, makes grunting sounds with his tongue furled between his lips, then he snarls, emitting vowel sounds from the base of his rib cage. He intends to run up and down several sets of scales when Reinhold, the bass, drowns him out with breathy grunts. The winter season is just about to open, with a re-run of Alcina, and all about them is bustle: as well as singers, warming their voices, there are instrumentalists getting in tune and scene-makers banging the flats into place. These depict hilly desserts and the magical palace of the sorceress, Alcina.

A bassoonist is blowing noisily next to the harpsichord where Handel is sitting, perusing the score with John Christopher. Harry is feeling sentimental. For sure, the great composer is no starving artist in his garret. When home, composing, Betsy will be preparing tasty dishes, of game perhaps, brought in by his friends from the country; Anthony will be banishing rude smells from the street by putting sage in a burner; Peter will be turning his imperfect prose into letters of immaculate English. How fixed his life is, how attached he is to his routines. And we, his musicians, thinks Harry, are his family. His one-time celebrity has been damaged but we, at least, are loyal; despite his demanding ways, he can depend on us.

A clerical type sits on his own at the back, an official from the Censor's Office. Groups of players and singers are talking to friends who have decided to come along and listen to the rehearsal. Peter has entered with Lucy, the girl who Anne Donovan was so exercised about, on his arm. She is now an elegant eighteen year old with dusky skin, curly dark hair, and soft, kind eyes. When Harry goes up to introduce himself she takes his hand, firmly, and says, 'Mr Walsh, what a pleasure to meet you. It is so exciting to be in a theatre. How I wish the General was well enough to attend.' She is neither forward, nor demur, but girlish and natural. Harry takes to her immediately and is pleased for Peter, that he has a near neighbour who has proved to be, not just a good student, but a firm friend.

'I am more than delighted to meet you,' he says, bending over to kiss her hand. Peter seems, for a change, to be happy and relaxed.

Once the sopranos, Strada and Negri, arrive, looking, as ever, immaculate and overdressed, accompanied by the castrato, Gizziello, Peter goes up to Handel to tell him that all the soloists are present. He then bids the artists to assemble on the stage behind the band. Handel silences a violinist with a loud 'Shsh', Jonny and Harry exchange a smile. Peter has the leather bag and is busy straightening then re-straightening pages of music. Just before the band starts to play the overture, he tut-tuts, like a sparrow pecking at the back of an ox, and brushes a spec off Handel's shoulder. The composer barely notices his presence.

After the rehearsal Harry manages to find a moment to draw Peter to one side of the pit.

'So did you ever tell Handel what happened at the soup kitchen?'

'I did.'

'And what did he say?'

'Zo, Peter, you haf become a Christian. Vat more can ve expect?'

'What did he mean by that? Does he suspect anything?'

'I don't know. Why do you always think the world revolves

round you? He has plenty of troubles to occupy him.'

'Did he remember old man Krich?'

'Yes, he said he was glad that the son still had the violin, that it was a fine instrument.'

'Is that all?'

'Don't be silly, he's already sent money to them. On top of that, he's arranged for the sister to work at Johann Christoph's scriptorium; the father was evidently a composer in a minor way and she's an adept music copyist. He asked John Christopher to give little Philip music lessons.'

'Gosh. Is he helping them because they're German?'

'You say such stupid things at times. If only people knew, he's such a kind and upright person, he hates to see suffering of any kind. If you must know, the plight of the Krichs has spurred him to set about creating a fund to help the destitute families of musicians.'

'I'm sorry, I know you're right. He's a good man, a real Christian.'

Not for the first time Harry feels irritation and pride in equal measure. He is proud to be working for the great man, irritated that Peter's loyalties are divided, and in despair that their love is forbidden. That surely, he thinks, explains why he is unfaithful.

1737

30. The Bedroom at Brook Street

'Have you heard? Handel has had a fit.'

Rolli has been waiting for Harry outside the theatre. He looks perturbed. There are still many weeks of the music season to go, for it has been extended, but Handel's place at their rehearsal that morning was taken by John Christopher.

'If he has, it's your fault. What's wrong with him?'

'I'm not sure. I went to his house to proffer an olive branch, to show my concern, but the whey faced boy, the one who carries his music bag, he shut the door in my face.'

'You can't blame him.'

'Harry, if only you knew how bored I am with the opera factions in London.'

'Which you helped to create.'

'It is our patrons, they are racing men. They like to pit one side against another.'

'Come now, Senesino wanted to destroy Handel.'

'Don't talk to me of Senesino. He will retire to Italy; he has made enough money to live in luxury for the rest of his life. My situation is different.'

'You speak as if your opera company will fold. So, you lasted for just three and a half years.' Harry is hurrying in a westward direction with Rolli doing his best to keep up. Their progress is slowed by women out with their baskets, collecting provisions, men pushing barrows, and small boys hopping in front of them, asking for coins. Harry tells Rolli to let him be, since he wishes to arrive at Brook Street on his own, but the man is a sticker.

'Our opera company cannot continue now that Prince Frederick has lost interest.'

'So that's it. I suppose you think he's a backslider for asking Handel to compose the music for his wedding. Who else could have done it? He towers above all other composers, and you knew that even before you were in the suds.'

'It is true. And now the Princess Royal is out of the way, the fun is gone from the prince's little game.'

'Is that what it was, a bit of fun?'

'You underestimate the intensity of dislike in that family. Not that the father cares what the prince does any more.' Rolli shakes his head. He is thinking of the king's current obsession with his latest mistress. 'If women took suddenly to intelligence and charm, the king would have a lonely existence.'

'Well they don't, so the king is safe. I will report back to you, but if you have destroyed a worthy man, let it rest on your conscience for ever.' Harry imagines Senesino's Madonna looking up at Rolli in horror and letting out a scream.

'How were we to know that there is room for only one Italian opera company in London?' he says, ducking to avoid a man with a yoke of live chickens.

'Many people could have told you that, years ago.' Harry does not add that they tried to tell Handel as much. At the Haymarket, Rolli bids him goodbye.

When Anthony opens the door at Brook Street he does his best to turn Harry away but Peter comes to the top of the stairs and calls down.

'Uncle, let him in.' Betsy's sobs can be heard below stairs.

Handel sits stiffly, surrounded by scarlet bed curtains and a matching coverlet. His body is still and slanting to the right. His face makes no reaction when Harry comes in; in fact he is hardly recognisable with his untidy, stubbly skull emerging from a soft cap, and a woollen shawl round his shoulders. His left arm sits lifelessly to the front of him. Peter resumes his place, kneeling by the bed, and takes the arm, rubbing it gently, murmuring, weeping. Harry kneels on the other side and takes Handel's free hand, then stretches across the bed to pat Peter's.

'He'll be all right, I promise,' he whispers, unconvinced. They sit like that for a while until Harry thinks he will scream from his aching knees. Then there is a kerfuffle below and he can hear Mrs Pendleton.

'Anthony, we are his friends, of course we must see him.' There are footsteps on the stairs and Mrs Pendleton, her kindly face looking frightened, comes in, followed by Anne Donovan. Her panniers and hoops are so wide that she hardly fits through the door.

'Heavens above, he does look poorly. Handel, can you hear us, my dear?' No reaction although every village surrounding London will have heard Mrs Donovan.

'He is melancholy,' she announces.

'He's exhausted,' says Peter. 'He has taken so much work upon himself, he's been up, composing, every night.'

'Peter, dear. It is a paralysis, I gather. Here, let me rub his arm. Go downstairs and get something to eat, Anthony tells me you have been up all hours. Anne, I suggest you go to the apothecary, bring back a tonic.' The room feels twice the size once Anne Donovan has gone.

'Tonic, pouf, what nonsense,' are her last words, 'it is a treatment for melancholy that he needs.'

As she rubs, Amelia Pendleton prattles, doing her best to look cheerful.

'Handel, my friend, do you remember when we first met? The architect, Mr James, was showing us round the new church in Hanover Square. Pendleton was alive then. What a tedious man he was, Mr James, I mean. Vitruvius this, Vitruvius that, what we didn't know about the laws of classicism by the end of our tour. Then, when we came out, there you were, standing looking up at the facade with Johann Christoph and his family; they had just come over from Germany.'

'I think I detected a blink of his eyes. I think he's trying to smile,' says Harry.

'Do you remember, Handel, Ambrose was with us and he

hung on your every word. He was so pleased with your choice of Mr Rosengarve as the organist. "He should be good, he studied in Venice under Scarlatti," you told him.'

'Arne attended the audition,' Harry tells her. 'He said Rosengarve was a wonder.'

'Johann Christoph's wife was like our old king.' Amelia Pendleton tinkles. 'She couldn't speak a word of English. You won't remember the old king, Harry, but I disliked him because he did not allow the little princesses to see their parents. He and his son hated each other, you know, which led to a family feud.'

'And now King George hates his son, just as his father hated him.'

Harry wants to add that it must be difficult keeping in with a family who don't talk to each other. But he is mindful of Handel's delicacy on matters of royalty and deliberately avoids any further comment.

'Do you remember, Handel, we came back to your house for tea? What a bachelor's apartment it was then, Anne and I had yet to take over the furnishings which you, wretched man, promptly covered up with boxes of music. Dear Peter, he had just joined the household. He was so shy and awkward.'

Handel's face softens; he is definitely trying to respond.

'I remember Peter smiling shyly at the young John Christopher, I think he welcomed the company of a boy near his own age. "There are horses round the back, would you like to see them?" I heard him say. And do you recollect what you said, Handel, in your usual gruff way. "No horsehair in ze house!" Betsy had just made a fruitcake that day and you took two slices. That's how it's always been,' she says, turning to Harry, 'Handel and me, we are a little too fond of the delights of the table. Isn't that so, Maestro?'

Her recollections are broken off by more noise downstairs, hurried footsteps and heavy breathing. Anne Donovan makes an unwelcome reappearance.

'How have you been able to get to the apothecary and back in so short a time?' her friend asks.

'Good Lord, Amelia, I got no further than Hanover Square. Handel, I have something to tell you, a piece of gossip, it will cheer you up. As I walked towards Mount Street, on my way to the apothecary, I had my eyes out for Rachel Trebeck. That's because she was the last person I wished to see.' These words are said in a whisper that could be heard at the end of the street. 'I am still wounded, you see, about her taking against Lucy. She believed, as the General's son claimed, that she was a "young baggage" as he called her.'

'Really, Anne, it is not a matter that is worth worrying your head about. Lucy looks after the General well. Ask Peter.'

'I am sensitive, Amelia, I can't help it. That son of the General's, Portland, he made himself busy finding out what went on in his father's household. So you can imagine, it was with a degree of stealth that I was walking along the gardens, for while I didn't wish to talk to Rachel, neither did I want to show I wasn't talking to her. But instead, who should I see but a most unexpected family group. It was the General, leaning on the arm of his young wife, with a toddler beside them, dressed in a wool bonnet.'

'Why, Anne, they walk round the square every day.'

'I do not live here, Amelia. I hadn't realised that so much time had passed since we first found out she was with child.'

Anne decides to sit down and makes herself comfortable on the red coverlet, pushing Handel over so he lists the other way.

'I was just wondering whether to address them when the General addressed me. "Mrs Donovan, how very nice to see you. We are having fine weather, are we not?"

' "General, you look remarkably well. Lucy," I said and nodded, not knowing what to say. "For a long time I have been wanting to talk to you," he replied.

'I was now feeling flustered because it is possible that, in the past, I hadn't been very polite.'

'Calling someone an "ageing lecher who should know better" really can't be construed as polite in any context,' Amelia Pendleton chips in.

'So then the General said, "I wanted to thank you. You made me do something I've never regretted. To marry this young lady here. Yes, I know she is more of a nursemaid than a wife." He looked at her, fondly, and she smiled back and squeezed his arm. "Look how much better I am; besides I need to look after this young fellow." We all turned our attention to the bonny-faced toddler who smiled up at us with big brown eyes, like his mother's.

' "Your son," I said, not really thinking.

' "Oh no, he's not my son," the General replied. "He's my grandchild. Yes, Portland took advantage of Lucy when she was very young and misused her dreadfully. But I am an honourable old soldier, Mrs Donovan. I intend to protect this boy, and his mother."

Lucy then spoke for the first time, her voice quite free of a London accent. We can thank Peter for that.

' "I realise that people construe my need for privacy as secretiveness," Lucy said, "but all that matters to me now is to look after this good man and my child. They are my family."

' "Lucy, I am so very happy for you," I replied. Great tears were rolling down my face because, oh dear, what selfish beings we are, because I felt that I had been exonerated.'

'Of course you were, my dear.' Amelia pulls out a kerchief from her bag and hands it across the invalid. Anne Donovan trumpets into it; clearly a great weight has sat in her heart these past two years.

'No, Amelia, it was me being self-centred. I should have been thinking of her happiness, of the General's, and of the wellbeing of that little boy. But the only person's happiness I could think of at that moment was of my own.' She dabs her eyes.

'Well, it has all ended happily enough.'

'And you, Handel,' says Anne, turning towards their host who was being partially propped up by the ample presence next to him. 'You were quite wrong, were you not? To impugn Lucy's motives for being on the Haymarket?'

The maestro's face twitches, as he is incapable of telling her that Peter corrected his misassumption a long time ago, but he is able to make a small lop-sided smile. With great effort his good hand reaches out and pats Anne's. Whether he will ever compose again, Harry is not sure, but at least, he thinks, he will get better.

31. St Paul's Church, Covent Garden

'What do you think of the script?' asks Arne as he sits across the table from Harry and Jonny in Button's.

'It's prime; the theme of the wicked landowner, the lampoon of Walpole's taxes, it has appeal,' Harry tells him.

'You mean it is marketable,' declares Jonny and they all laugh.

Arne lets Harry keep the script of the Dragon of Wantley. Carey's words have been set to music by Lampe, Arne will conduct, Jonny and Harry will sing. Susanna will join them if she is recovered from the death of her infant, otherwise Lampe will avail of Kitty Clive. John Rich, the producer, will get richer still.

They order chocolate from the addle pate of a waiter who has a drip on the end of his nose. Jonny and Arne have a funeral to perform at St Paul's across the way. Some of the people in Button's are clad in black, mourners for the member of the Russell clan, owners of the Covent Garden Estate, who has recently departed this world.

'What did you think of my friend, Tyers?' Harry asks Arne.

'He liked my masque, Comus, said it was full of delightful melodies and easy airs.'

'Yes, he is mighty fond of those.'

'He may even invest in a production of it so of course I think he's a fine fellow with discerning taste.'

'He will enjoy the Dragon of Wantley because it is full of nonsense and comicalities. He said the Beggar's Opera had him roaring until the tears ran down his cheeks.'

'Then I'm glad I wasn't sitting behind him,' says Jonny.

They are joined by two men carrying instrument cases, trumpeters who will also be playing at the funeral. One is young and Harry doesn't recognise him although his name, Valentine, suggests that he may be the son of the royal trumpeter, also of that name. The other, Caspar, is nearer to Handel's age, and like him he is from Saxony. Valentine's cheeks are red and apple-hard, from the blowing, his hands large and muscular, like those of a ploughboy, with splayed finger tips from the pressing. Caspar looks round at the top hats and hooped skirts, all in black with ribbons of crepe attached to them.

'Zis crowd, es ist gut.' That is the way with musicians, where even a church service is seen as a performance.

'I'll come with you and listen for a while,' Harry says, for he has an appointment with his fubsey, the countess, but not for an hour or so. Her note sits in his coat pocket.

'My husband, sadly, is detained in the country,' is all it says. His answer, for it is their little joke, simply said, 'I will try not to be inconvenienced.'

They cross the Piazza, avoiding the mounds of rotting vegetables and trying to ignore the usual summer stench. A group of pedlars huddles under the pillars of the church and one calls out to them.

'Yus looks like a set of bang up coves, buy me dobbin, woncha? Me dab of a husban's in prison.'

Harry has no interest in the ribbons she is pressing on them but he fishes out a coin; the girl examines it then hides it in her skirt.

'How is young Philip, the boy saved by Tyers?' Harry asks. 'I glimpsed him in the pit at Covent Garden.'

'John Christopher tells me he is a talented musician. I think the girl works for his father,' says Arne. The younger Smith is a close friend of his.

'Just think,' says Harry, 'the girl could have ended up like that pedlar woman.'

They go through a side gate off the Piazza, along a garden path that leads to the front of the church.

Caspar is right, the place is full. Harry whispers good luck to his friends then slips into a small space on the very back row. The choir opens with a composition by Byrd. English. Arne's choice. Harry's tiresome neighbour looks cross at his arrival next to her and refuses to give ground in her pew. She has him jammed against the wooden end.

'Dearest brethren, let us come together,' the priest says.

Harry thinks of all the brethren, and sisters, he has come together with recently. Too many. There would be more if he could summon the energy to respond to the notes that keep coming to the stage door.

All of a sudden he is gripped with a desire to turn to his disapproving neighbour and ask her to explain why it is he has such a temptation to sin. How it is that he is attracted to members of both sexes? How it is that he is unable to stop his libertine ways? Surely, he would like to ask her, this cannot be normal?

'Oh Lamb of God, that takest away the sins of the world, have mercy upon us.'

Amen to that.

The congregation stands. He recognises the piece that Arne is playing. Tallis. It is full of gentle promises and conjures up hedgerows in spring. This is a very English death.

The hour for him to make his assignation approaches. He tries, as inconspicuously as possible, to make an exit. His erstwhile neighbour, who made him so unwelcome, casts a furtive glance in his direction. Does he detect disappointment? He pulls his stomach in and hopes that she is impressed by the shapeliness of his thighs. He has an urge to lean over and suggest that they meet at the stage door the following night.

Two urchins stand at the entrance to the gardens and come towards him. He shrugs, and pushes them away, for he has given his last coin to the pedlar woman. When he arrives at Great Ormond Street, his countess is waiting for him. As he is led up the stairs, in order to sink beneath her shuddering, enfolding flesh, he realises that he hasn't heard from Peter for weeks, nor has he paid a visit to Brook Street.

Some time ago he had sent him a sketch as a penance. He showed himself sitting at the rectory table, with books all around him, struggling with his quill and paper as he traced over the letters Peter had set out for him. Behind him, his father, his hair standing on end, was stopping himself from falling backwards at the sight of his blotchy scrawl. Harry smiles, for he is proud of these sketches, and hopes that Peter understands that he is squeamish about Handel's frailty. He decides he must call round to Brook Street on the morrow.

'Harry, you scoundrel, I do believe you are not concentrating. Your mind is elsewhere.'

'Your Ladyship, forgive me.' He pushes her off him, sits up and climbs on top of her so his knees are astride her. Then he leans over and plants a quantity of tiny kisses on her face, her neck, her breasts.

'You are such a dear boy. The tailor will call with the suit I've had made for you, on the hour of four, so we must not linger.'

'I have no intention of lingering.'

He has his way with her and she shudders with delight.

32. Meeting Nanette

It is Anthony who opens the door.

'The master is away.'

'Away? Is he better then?'

'He is taking the waters at Aix-la-Chapelle; he is seeking a cure.' Harry knows that Anthony wishes him to go but he continues to stand on the step.

'How long will he be gone? What made them choose to go so far?'

'It was Mrs Pendleton's idea. She had heard that the waters there are most efficacious.'

The cause of Anthony's anxiety becomes apparent when a woman appears behind him and takes her place right next to him. She has high cheek bones, a black velvet ribbon tying back her blonde hair, a suggestion of slightly wizened cleavage on show, and a neat, petite form. Harry would say there is barely sixteen years between Peter and his mother.

'Anthony, you cannot turn Handel's friends away. Come down to the kitchen, I will make you tea, the parlour, as you will see, is all shuttered up.' This is said with a strong French accent.

'That's most awfully nice of you, thank you.'

'I hardly think Mr Walsh wishes to be received in the kitchen, there are proprieties to observe, Nanette. The master would not approve.'

'The master, he is in Germany. He does not know. You are such an old woman, Brother. Come Mr Walsh.' She beckons to him and Anthony looks unhappy.

'It's bad enough that she has invited Mrs Plunket in,' he sniffs.

Lucy sits at the kitchen table, a small boy playing with bricks at her feet.

'I am reading a letter,' she tells Harry. 'It's from Peter. It arrived here today. He is having a troublesome time in Aix-la-Chapelle.'

'So what else does my lovely son say?' Nanette looks expectant in a way that is characteristic of someone who cannot read, being read to.

Lucy consults the letter.

'Where was I? Ah, here we are. "If Mrs Pendleton was so worried about Handel, she should have taken him herself. The sulphur baths smell like bad eggs. The nuns think their guest's recovery is a miracle and are about to beatify him. Now he is a walking shrine to every organist nearby. They come to hear him play in the convent chapel, then kneel to kiss his hand. If that isn't bad enough, Charlemagne lies buried in the cathedral so I am dragged there, daily, to study every stone. I swear, he'd be easier to manage as an invalid".'

'He is funny, don't you think, Harry, très drôle. Peter, he is now a beautiful young man, no?'

'A very beautiful young man, in every way,' Lucy assures her.

'You know him, 'Arry?'

'Yes of course, he's Handel's right hand man.' She is studying him intently with her blue eyes and smiles to herself.

'He was always a bit of a moaner when it came to going abroad.' Anthony, tired of holding back, has decided to join the conversation.

'When a trip was planned, he would beg to be left behind, but the master wouldn't entertain the idea. Handel's a tireless sight seer, Peter dreaded that.'

'Peter, he is spoilt,' Nanette declares.

'What a fuss he made when they had to go off to Italy to find more singers,' says Anthony.

'I would have done anything to go to Italy,' says his mother.

'He complained about the lengthy banquets, the lavish villas, the armies of retainers. Said it was like the Middle Ages.'

'Comme c'est délicieux, all those velvet robes, suits of armour and smoking flambeaux.'

'He didn't mind visiting Handel's family,' says Anthony. 'The old mother died a few years back, and she doted on her son. I always said it was his upbringing what made him a fighter.'

'I'm so glad that he is better. He's such a good person.' Lucy is folding the letter away.

'And you helping to nurse him, we appreciated that,' says Anthony to Lucy.

'Then, just as you think you can relax, Brother, I come to your doorstep. You see, Mr Walsh, I am destitute, my business partner, Attila, he run away with my money. What can I do but come here?'

'Handel won't like it, Nanette, he values his routine.'

'Look, I mend all his cushions, his frayed curtains, the holes in his tablecloths. I am, you see, Mr Walsh, a very talented needlewoman.'

'My friend, Tom Arne, his father is an upholsterer. Maybe he would welcome a talented needlewoman.'

'In the meantime, you can stay with me,' says Lucy. 'I'm sure the General wouldn't mind. Come George, we must be going home.'

Harry accompanies Lucy back to Hanover Square. The little boy allows him to hold his hand. As they walk together Harry is struck by the fact that they must look like a family. The autumn has stripped most of the trees of their leaves but the air is delightfully clear in this part of the town. How lovely it would be to live here, thinks Harry, to walk out with a wife.

'My husband,' Lucy explains, 'is elderly and not very well. I am sorry but I cannot ask visitors in without warning him.'

'Anne Donovan tells me he is a most upright gentleman.'

'He's a wonderful person, the first true friend I have ever had. My start in life, Mr Walsh, was not a happy one. I ended up in the workhouse because a blacksmith and his wife, who had care of me, both died.'

'It sounds sad indeed.'

'What made it worse was that they had a letter from someone, explaining the circumstances of my birth, but I could not read it. I held onto that letter for years until fate put me under the protection of General Plunket. He it was who explained its contents to me. It made such a difference, knowing who my parents were.'

'Is it always good to know the truth?' Harry asks. She is such a natural person that he has an urge to tell her about Peter and his betrayal of him.

'That is a very good question. Is it better to know the truth yet be hurt by it? That, Mr Walsh, I have no answer to. I cannot say.'

'No,' he murmurs. 'Neither can I.' Peter tends not to ask him what he does while they are parted and Harry has no inclination to tell him. He decides that it would not be good, for either of them, if Peter knew the truth and was hurt by it.

33. The Bedroom in King Street

A line of Venetian masks looks down upon the two of them from the wall. A pair of sequinned pantaloons hangs from a hook, and scarlet and purple cushions sit behind their heads. They are in Nanette's bedroom, the one she rents in King Street next to the Crown and Cushion, the Arne upholstery establishment where she now works. Peter lies in Harry's arms. Today they are due at the Abbey, soon, for the queen's funeral. With her death, Handel has lost a long standing friend, but at least he is well. And the demise of Senesino's opera group has most certainly put a spring into his step.

When Peter had first met with Nanette, after returning from Aix-la-Chapelle, he had been so surly and awkward with her that she'd made her escape next door and left the two men together. This did not stop her promising that they could meet in her room whenever they liked. Nothing was ever said about relations between them but somehow she knew. Harry, happy that they had a place so close to the theatre where they could meet, had been full of stories about the prodigious success of the Dragon of Wantley. In great detail he had described the crowds that packed into the theatre each night, the record-breaking run, and the joy of Mr Rich. Within days of their return from Germany, he had managed to drag Handel and Peter to Covent Garden to watch the show. Afterwards, the great man had accompanied members of the cast and orchestra to the Three Crows and praised Lampe for his music.

It was on that occasion that Handel had drawn Harry aside and sought his assurance that his success in such a popular show would not take him away from singing in his oratorios. Harry had said that to continue singing for him would be an honour. He also gave Handel and Peter news of Susanna which was not good. Theo's need for funds, he explained, had reached such extremes that he had insisted his wife take up with their lodger, William Sloper, a country squire, for the purpose of extracting money from him. Now, it seemed, she had decided to stay with Sloper and to ditch the feckless Cibber. The husband, fleeing creditors, was now in France, but had threatened to take her to court.

'Every detail of her life will be trumpeted from the street corners of London,' Handel had predicted. 'Yes, the idle praters will be busy.'

With the time to leave for the Abbey drawing close, Harry leans up on his elbow and strokes Peter's hair the way he likes him to.

'Just think, this room is but a few minutes from the theatre. Now we can rendezvous whenever we like.'

'He doesn't intend to hold his shows at Covent Garden next season, he's taken a lease out at the King's.'

Harry is aghast.

'He's going back to Heidegger? I can't believe it.'

'He's trying to prove something.'

'What, that he's a bonehead?'

'Something mighty close. He's even paying to have an organ installed.'

'Such activity in a man approaching sixty. He's a maggot.'

'He overdoes things then goes queer in the head,' says Peter gloomily.

'It means that you, as always, will be occupied.'

'I promise, we'll meet as frequently as we can.'

As they get up to leave for the Abbey, Peter starts to arrange the cushions, straightening them, then re-straightening them. He picks up the items of clothing that Nanette has strewn across the floor and folds, then refolds, them. When outside, they raise their coat collars against the cold. Harry glances at the translucence of his lover's skin, the blue of his eyes, and wishes that he had comforted him more when they were alone.

King Street all of sudden looks dismal. No longer does it describe a cosy world of theatre and assignation, it is just a row of decaying establishments that serve the needs of the playhouses: there are seamstresses, blockmakers, carpenters, candle makers, printers, and all the paraphernalia of costumes, wigs and make-up.

The short terrace of houses, in which Nanette has her room, is slightly different from the rest, being newer and taller, with basements that back onto a sunken area that looks up to the gardens of St Paul's. Because of its position, the terrace gets sun, but otherwise the street is dark. There are closed doors and drawn curtains along it that the citizens hurrying by, in the daylight, hardly notice. At night the street will take on a different prospect, many of the ladies will have vizards, and they will linger on the corners waiting for pies and jays looking for a shilling's worth of diversion.

In the Piazza two society ladies, dressed in black as a mark of respect to the queen, are accompanied by an elderly article whose stockings fall in creases round his spindly legs. His coat is of an ostentatious blue and in his hat is a blue feather. He is a Jacobite, keen to show his lack of regard for the Hanoverian line. How tedious these people are, thinks Harry, as if any of us wanted that festering old crackpot, James Francis Stuart, to be our king. He feels depressed and disappointed.

'There are railings here, do they trouble you?' His concern is instinctual, he hardly thinks about it.

'I am so much better, hardly at all.'

'So your stay in Aix-la-Chapelle, it has done you some good at least.'

'Not really. You were all I thought about.'

'You merely say that.'

'If you don't believe me I'll show you my diary.'

Harry does not fancy the thought of having to plough through the closely packed pages of someone's diary.

'Do you trust me enough to do that?'

'You're the only one I would trust enough, you and Lucy.'

Of course, thinks Harry, because she is good. He wishes at that moment that he was, too.

34. The Smile of Fortune

It takes Harry a moment to work out that the attractive young lady who opens the door, her curly hair wreathed in a garland, her shift pulled in by a plaited belt to reveal a tiny waist, is none other than Timon's footman. He knows him, not so much from his visits to Cavendish Square, but because he sees him in the pit at Handel's entertainments, listening intently to the music. Today he is holding a silver platter of grapes. With his free hand he takes Harry's coat and steers him upstairs to change. When Harry enters the studio he is not the only one dressed like Cicero with a wreath of laurels propped on his pate. Timon issues forth from the white-clad figures that are spread round the place on cushions, like so many statues come alive. He looks more comfortable in his Senator's garb than Harry does.

Along the windows are trestles covered in linen clothes that hold a veritable feast of game and fowl and much else besides. Silver bowls, all rococo curlicues that shine in the candlelight, hold pyramids of fruit, assortments of nuts, skewers of meat, whole pickled vegetables and steaming sauces. Harry picks up a skewer, dips it into the sauce boat, and looks around. He recognises two young milords who subscribe to boxes in the playhouse and go there regularly. Their companions, even in their togas, look like the assistants who work in the bow-wow shop off the Piazza. Harry often visits it, to browse through the second hand clothes, hoping to find something stylish. The cane he now takes everywhere comes from there. He smiles to himself for here, in this room at least, the occupants seem to have fought off the shackles of snobbery that so readily trip up strivers such as himself.

Someone catches his eye and signals him to come and sit down. He is older than Harry, bearded, and is wearing Timon's famous breastplate over his robe. He bids Harry lie down, calling over one of Timon's servants, a blackamoor, who is going round with a large stone ewer in his hands, pouring wine into pewter goblets.

'Welcome to our feast,' says Harry's neighbour, 'our little lectisternium to Bacchus, God of wine.'

'You are a pagan, Sir?'

'I am. But my God is not Bacchus, it is Janus, God of doors and gates. You see, Mr Walsh, you do not mind if I call you that but you are famous, your show, the Dragon, excellent by the way, I have a particular fondness for them.'

'For doors, how so?'

'It is my profession. To open doors.' Harry thinks that his comment must be lewd in purpose, that it has some double meaning that he should surmise. It turns out that he is wrong. Simeon is a man of business, a trader, he says, to the West Indies. Normally his boats come into the port of Bristol, bringing sugar, then taking back brandy from France. On its return from the next trip, one of them, Voyager, he tells him, will come up the Thames; she needs some timbers replaced at the yards to the south of the river, near Southwark. He invites Harry to visit her. Harry declines for he has no interest in boats.

'You are rich now, are you not, with your success in the Dragon of Wantley?' Simeon comments.

'What is rich?' Harry asks. He makes a mental tally of the ten-guinea suits that his fubsey has had made for him. Occasionally, when it is wet, he takes a sedan, to save walking. In the dining room at the rectory is one of Hogarth's prints, an extravagance when he bought it.

'I have developed a habit of spending what I have,' he says.

'All of it?'

'Not quite.'

'Perhaps you should invest, Mr Walsh, make your stash grow. If you invest in a share of the cargo of the Voyager then I can pay you back twice the amount.' Is this a case of making money with money as described by Lord M? Harry wonders if he should discuss this proposition with his titled friend, who is ever the money man, for he knows little about such matters.

'I am not a speculator, Sir, surely those who are older and wiser than us have taught us the lesson they learnt from the South Sea bubble. I would be ever wary of tossing my money into some venture I do not understand.'

'You are wise, Mr Walsh. Stocks, shares, bonds, what do they mean? My trade is a much more straightforward one, that is why I urge you to come and see the Voyager, feel the solidity of the wood, leather and canvas, from which she is made, and meet the rogues who do my bidding.'

Their conversation is interrupted by a beautiful young boy, his cheeks rouged, who takes up a harp and starts to play. The footman climbs onto a dais and tosses his garland at the crowd of men who stand round it. Slowly he removes his clothing to reveal his magnificent nakedness. One by one the candles die down, the living statues start to bind together, their togas becoming loose and dislodged.

Harry can see Simeon's teeth shine in the darkness for he is smiling. The breastplate catches a shaft of moonlight that comes through the window, and for a moment the clear shape of a vine leaf flickers across it. The man leans over to whisper in his neighbour's ear, not a term of endearment but a promise.

'You are young and good looking and getting very well known, Mr Walsh. Now I will make you rich. You really should come and meet the captain of the Voyager when he arrives on our shores.'

Timon makes his way through the now writhing bodies and sits himself down beside Harry. Simeon rises to go.

'How I wish Mother was here,' he says, 'a real Roman orgy.'

'Surely,' his friend says, 'she would have called it a lectis-ternium.' His intention, when he returns home, is to ask his father what the word means.

35. A Visit to the Country

Desperate to avoid going home after the theatre closes one night in June, Harry decides to be rash and to go up to Great Ormond Street in search of his fubsey. With luck, her long-suffering footman will open the door and he can make discreet enquiries as to whether she is at home and on her own. The summer recess is upon them but Harry is performing still in the Dragon which has broken all records for the length of its run.

As he approaches her house he can see carriages and hackneys disported, willy-nilly, about the street. The shutters are open on the tall elegant windows of the first floor revealing the outline of people, their shadows dancing in the candle light. Sounds of conversation seem to rise and fall, there are crescendos of laughter followed by a lull when the even tones of a harp break through. Harry turns on his heel but, as he does so, a coach and four bars his way. The diminutive earl flings open a door and disembarks. Before Harry can escape he hears himself being addressed by name.

'Mr Walsh, I believe. So my wife managed to contact you?'

'Contact me, My Lord?'

'I'm delighted. We leave for the country in a few weeks. Did she discuss the entertainment?'

'Just briefly, that is, not in detail.' He tries not to look bewildered.

'My dearest Bumbo, she is, I'm afraid, insensible to matters of detail. Come, Mr Walsh, join our party.'

It is very late when he leaves, weaving his way back home as best he can. He has promised to join their country house party in Rutland, directly the Dragon's current run is over, in order to organise an amateur production of the Maid's Merry Tale. The earl, who is a keen amateur musician, will adapt the music, and a bevy of boisterous young ladies, they really were jolly, Harry recollects, will be acting in it. Leaving London in July; acting in some amusing entertainment; being under the same roof, no doubt the same set of bed clothes, as his fubsey, the earl's "Bumbo". At last he is to be a real gentry cove. What sport, Walsh, your fortunes are turning.

When the time comes, Harry climbs into the stagecoach, knowing that he has several days of travel ahead of him. There is no coach to the village of Edgestone but the earl's carriage will come and pick him up from Oakham. His head has been in a spin about what clothes to wear, for his new striped satin britches and brocade waistcoat seem hardly appropriate. He sent a note to his fubsey, asking her advice, and a few days later, a plain jacket of grey linen and two sets of pale cotton breeches, had arrived from the tailor.

When he looks out of the carriage at Edgestone he is amazed to find it as picturesque as a set from one of Arne's pastorals. Yokels, dressed in rough fustian garments, disport themselves to the front of thatched cottages of golden stone. One guides a pig with his stick. He can hear humming in a nearby garden and sees that the flowers are alive with insects; bees burrow through petals or hover, lazily, pondering which bloom to excavate next. Amidst the cottages is a tavern overlooking a village green. Barkham Court is close by but hidden by trees. When the carriage makes its approach, he sees that it is built in the modern, Italian style, with fine gardens, dating back to an earlier age, to one side. Beyond the gardens are fields.

The earl, who Harry takes to, accompanies him up to his room. While a manservant unpacks shirts and waistcoats from Harry's valise, many of them paid for out of the earl's money, he looks out of the window. All he can see is an uninspiring view of sheep in a field of grass with crooked trees dotted here and there and wooded hills in the distance. The earl looks out with him.

'What spectacular scenery,' he sighs. 'I never tire of it. Look at those noble oaks. My grandfather planted them. The other side of the family come from Scotland; my cousin is here, Douglas, you'll meet him at dinner. He too has some fine woodland on his estate but the feel of his place is different, more wild.'

Douglas turns out to be a whiskey-swilling, shock-headed cull whose toast at table is:

'To His Majesty in Rome, King James.'

'Douglas, spare us your Jacobite sympathies, I may be a Catholic, but I, for one, would not welcome the Pretender to the throne,' says the merry dame to Harry's left.

'And I wouldn't wish for the Archbishop of Canterbury to be replaced by some Monsignor from Salamanca,' adds the earl.

'Come to Scotland, the both of you, Nancy, Dorian, then you'll know how oppressed we are. Walpole and the rest of the Whigs, they care not a damn for us. If a Stuart arrived on our shores tomorrow, I, for one, would fight for him.'

'That's hardly likely,' says the earl, 'but I'm sure he will tell you if such an excursion is planned.'

'Is everyone here Catholic?' Harry asks quietly of his fubsey. He is intrigued, there is something slightly different about the company, a certain warmth and informality, a happy-go-lucky quality that is absent from the Whig circles he is accustomed to.

'Dorian, Mr Walsh wants to know if I am a Catholic,' the countess shouts across the table to her husband.

'She is not, Mr Walsh. My Bumbo is a pagan, much given to the worship of dark natural forces. When the moon is full I half expect to see her riding past my window on a broomstick.'

'There, Harry, you have nothing to worry about,' she says. He wants to assure her that he is not in the least worried, that he is a taster of exotic fruit, on a constant search for new diversions, just like the bees he saw earlier.

In the coming weeks the party sets all other matters aside. Their one concern is rehearsing the entertainment. Carey's moral tale is about the ineffectual attempts of a bawd, named Demos, to seduce Cecilia, a high minded young lady. She is eventually rescued by her brothers although, in Rutland, her rescuers are two elderly sisters and a wild Scottish uncle. Harry's licentious encroachments, as Demos, prompt Nancy, as Cecilia, to sing of the need for temperance and chastity while her actions suggest otherwise. The earl simplifies Lampe's music to suit his three fellow musicians; fireworks are obtained from Oakham; the servants, who have entered into the excitement, place candle holders round the garden. There is a good deal of hammering by the gardeners, as a stage is erected, and much laughter can be heard from the ladies and their maids as they deploy a quantity of old curtains as costumes.

Rehearsals, directed for the most part by the countess (looking fresh each morning despite busy nights in Harry's bedroom), take place straight after a late breakfast. If it is fine, hay wains are bought round to the front door in the early afternoon, baskets and cushions are loaded onto them, and the guests walk an hour, over meadows, to a secluded river valley. As the servants set out a humble repast, say a cold rabbit pie, guests take off their shoes and stockings. For the first time, Harry experiences the world through the soles of his feet. Grass, cool and soft, stones, round and clammy, water exquisitely cold and fresh, suffusing his legs with a feeling of vigour.

When the day of the masque is upon them, neighbours arrive for a lavish dinner of game from the estate. This takes place while the servants rush out to the garden to light candles and drape curtains across the stage. They arrange seating for both the guests and villagers, many of whom arrive early, to help with the preparations. House servants move the earl's drawing room organ to an open doorway from where he is going to play.

No sooner have the benches become occupied than the heavens open and start to pelt them. The party shrieks and runs inside. Fortunately, the fireworks are stowed still in the shelter of a summerhouse. The organ is moved back next to the fireplace, chairs are arranged in rows in the drawing room, and an awning is improvised, outside, for the villagers. The masque goes ahead to great applause. By the end of the performance the rain clears. Gardeners then put out the fireworks and a boy lights them, rushing off to avoid getting burnt. Punch is served to all who are present, including the villagers, some of whom fail to make it home and sleep, instead, in the bushes.

The following day, as Harry lies in his bed, he anticipates telling his father how jovial the evening was, how carefree the laughter of the past few weeks. He looks out of the window and appreciates that the view before him is no longer tedious but restful. After breakfast, as the guests' trunks are brought downstairs, Harry finds himself in a small anteroom that leads off the main drawing room. It is full of cabinets of fine china. The earl takes him through each beautiful object, one by one. Having money is not enough, Harry muses, one must desire things to buy with it. At home in the rectory their needs are simple, and stretch little beyond warmth and food, good books for his father and beds that are free of vermin. Maybe those who accumulate wealth have an appetite for ownership which is what drives them.

'Mr Walsh, look at the coral colouring of the fish on this vase, the turquoise water with the little wavelets in relief. It is a hundred years old, made for the third Emperor of the Qing dynasty. Hold it, feel how delicate the china is; only the Chinese know how to make it like this.' He allows Harry to take it in his hands.

'I must thank you, by the way, for looking after my Bumbo. I'm a bit of a Smithfield jade when it comes to the affairs of the bed chamber. Careful, don't drop that, I think I better take it off you. I am no athlete when it comes to being of service to the ladies. I gather you are. For that I thank you for I would do anything to make the countess happy.'

'To be married to such an expert, on china and so forth, that must make her very happy.' Harry is blushing and prattling the first nonsense that comes into his head.

'I can hear the coach coming round to the front of the house. Our guests are getting ready to set off. Yes. I'm so grateful, I just wanted you to know.'

Harry climbs into the coach with Douglas, who has a headache and looks more wild and hairy than usual. They are joined by jolly, ever-smiling Nancy and her maid. He is not sure if he has been warned, or genuinely thanked. The earl makes a fuss of them and hands in a basket of pastries and a flagon of small beer which he puts on the floor.

'Have a good trip, see you all in London,' he says cheerily. His coachmen calls out to the horses, the carriage jolts, and they start off down the long drive.

36. The Boat Yard, Southwark

The autumn of '38 affords a memorable visit to the gardens at Vauxhall for Tyers has unveiled a statue of Handel by a Frenchman, Roubiliac. Handel's airs have become increasingly popular as entertainment in the gardens and Tyers is mighty pleased with his statue which depicts the composer, as Apollo, playing a harp. He invites both Peter and Harry, when he sees them mingling in the crowds, to join him in the Prince of Wales Pavilion. It is pleasing to look down at the crowds from the balcony, catching sight of young couples looking up at them. Harry, in particular, enjoys such a visible position.

'Peter, my man, where is your master?' Tyers shouts above the hubbub around him.

'Closeted at home, working on his compositions.' In fact he is suffering from melancholy, Peter tells Harry, and is much burdened by debt. He will not resume staging his oratorios until January. He is also concerned, as they all are, about Susanna's plight. The wretched Theo, for the first time in his life, has proved true to his word and taken her to court. He has caused her to flee to the countryside, with William Sloper, after the details of their private life, as Handel predicted, were revealed in public.

To divert Peter's attention, Harry relates anecdotes about the musical interludes that Arne and he have developed for an ambitious young cove called Garrick. The man is obsessed, he tells him, with a sixteenth century playwright, William Shakespeare, and his intent is to make his works the most bang up in the playhouse. It must be a ruse, comments Peter, to bypass the Lord Chamberlain; so many new plays are banned now, under the new Licensing Act, that it is best to avoid controversy by aiming your arrows at those who have been dead a good few hundred years.

Besides his affairs at the playhouse, Harry is developing a new interest. He has business to do with Simeon. He decides not to reveal to Peter the details of his proposed speculation.

The following day, Harry makes his way to Brindley's gold merchants on Lombard Street. He is full of regrets at having had no opportunity to talk through Simeon's proposals with someone knowledgeable like Tyers or Lord M. He sits for while in Lloyd's coffee shop, wondering if what he is doing is wise. Timon's friend is most persuasive but Harry does not trust him. Lured by the promise of riches, he eventually proceeds to the gold merchants and borrows £500 worth of coin. This will supplement the entire sum of his savings which he will invest in the Voyager's next consignment of brandy and linen headed for the West Indies.

After his business at Brindley's, it is only a short walk to Simeon's office above the Royal Exchange. The piazza below the offices is crowded and he has to push his way through to reach the stairs. It annoys him that, no sooner does he arrive, than Simeon insists that he walks with him down to the river to accompany him to Southwark to see the boat.

The wharves between London Bridge and Limehouse Reach, he explains, are completely full which is why the Voyager is docked to the south of the river in a sufferance wharf that is unreachable by road. It will be necessary, he says, for his supplies to be delivered to him downriver for, if his boat has to wait for the availability of a berth in the docks, she will be unable to sail before the October storms set in.

With great reluctance, Harry clambers with him into a small craft that will take them across the river. He is fearful of the currents that swirl around them and of the enormous timber barges which are sure to bump into them. In the centre of the river, lighters, collecting coal from the colliers, bar their way and the oarsmen have to row around them. Once at their destination it takes fully an hour of searching through the assembly of creaking brigs and clippers, their masts and ropes darkening the sky above them, to find the Voyager. When they do, she is bobbing up and down in the turd-infested water, groaning, as if human.

The man whom Simeon calls captain is a queer cull and when he shakes Harry's hand he fears he will pull his arm off. For what purpose, he wonders, has he been brought here? To disprove any suspicion he might have that the boat exists only in Simeon's imagination?

'We need to set sail, Master,' the captain says, urgently, as he bends his ear towards him. 'There's too many gin shops and bawd houses here, I can't keep control of the men. Give 'em a chance and they'll be macing some gorger and stealing his bung.'

Then the sheriff's men will be after them and they'll end up in prison which is where they belong, Harry thinks. Savages, the lot of them. Dark brows and bearded faces look out from behind the rigging and eye his fine clothes. In the middle of the deck is a set of ship's irons where recalcitrants are flogged, he assumes. It is a revolting sight but his companion looks unperturbed.

'Gerry, you'll be setting sail very soon. Why, Mr Walsh here, is one of my investors. He was keen to see the boat.' Simeon's lie suggests that it was he who wished Harry to be seen on this boat, keen for the captain to see him all togged up in his expensive suit with his ivory headed cane.

'You can have your blasted money but get me off of here,' Harry says under his breath. The movement beneath his feet makes him feel unsteady; the smell of fish wafting across from a neighbouring vessel, that has lampreys and flounders wriggling across its deck, makes him feel sick; the stares of the men fill him with discomfort. He has the gold coins in a purse tucked into an inner pocket and hands it over. Simeon removes some of the coins then hands the rest to the captain.

'Here's the bung, now do as I've told you,' he rasps. The figures behind the rigging start to melt away. Tension on the brig seems to ease.

Simeon positively purrs as their hired craft takes them back under the London Bridge.

'Don't worry, Harry, that you haven't enjoyed your first taste of the seaborne life. I open doors, remember. The purpose of the Voyager is not to give us pleasure but to make us rich.'

'I don't trust you, take note, and if I never see my money again I'll thrash the breath out of you with this stick.'

'Dear boy, I won't let you down.'

38. A Meeting with Mr Rich

Mr Rich looks ordinary when in his office above the theatre foyer, yet he's a buck of the first head. His burlesques and pantomimes, so the news sheets claim, have so debauched the souls of society, and lowered the tastes of the town, that all people crave is crude spectacle and noise. He is proposing a revival of the Beggar's Opera, he tells Harry, and wishes him to play the part of Macheath. Miss Fenton and Miss Clive will be the female leads.

Harry does his best to act the weary worldling, fiddling with the lace of his cravat and blowing a fleck of dust off the ivory deity that leers at him from the top of his cane. He is playing for time in order to contemplate the fee he can get away with.

'Your mime, in the intermission last night, it was masterful,' he says. And he means it, for in his guise as Harlequin, Rich comes alive; his face contorts, his lips pucker, his body arches and cringes, his very eyeballs seem to change expression. The theatre manager chuckles and lifts a pipe off a small stand to the front of him.

Inwardly Harry groans, not just because he dislikes the smoking habit, but because he does not want the new suit he is wearing to smell like some joskin's pinafore at straw-burning time. Rich catches sight of Harry's fleeting scowl, carefully replaces the pipe, and leans back in his chair.

'Mr Walsh,' he says, 'when I do my mimes I am like your friend, Handel, writing his arias.'

'I'm sure the composer would be much flattered by the comparison.'

'I am a mirror, reflecting back to the audience the emotions in their hearts. Be they in a box, the pit or the gallery, it matters not, the emotions are the same.'

'So which dominate, or do we chop from one to another?'

He thinks a while. 'To be sad, that is the natural condition of man. To be lewd, that is human. To be gay, that is necessary. So there you have it: to be sad, lewd and gay, those are the states that predominate.'

'I must remember that when I play Macheath.'

'Exactly so. And now, Sir, to the matter of your fee.' He looks Harry straight in the eye. Harry stares back and names a sum which he thinks he will reject. To his surprise he simply says, 'You're a smart jemmy fellow but I have faith in your looks. I think they will keep the young ladies happy. After the Dragon, we are even making an actor of you.' Harry flashes his teeth and pushes back the locks of his loose poet's hair.

As he makes his way up Bow Street he does a little courante and tosses his cane into the air. He paid no more than a few coppers for it but to have it in his hand makes him feel like a swell. Gaiety, he thinks, is surely manufactured; happiness is what he seeks, and success. With Mr Rich's help he will have all the work he needs and very soon, he hopes, his fortune will be made. When the Voyager returns to Bristol, loaded with sugar from the Caribbean, life will be sweet.

1739

The Wings at Drury Lane

Garrick advances round the stage with an athletic grace, an animal ease. Arne and Harry watch him from the wings, reluctant in their admiration. His Lysander is so convincing that they almost believe in the fantastical confusions going on in the fairy forest. This William Shakespeare, who he is so keen on, is an ace story teller. They chuckle at the incompetent Puck, whose potions make everyone fall in love with whomever they first set eyes on, and hoot like the audience at poor Nick Bottom who is transformed into an ass. Colley Cibber, sadly, is all affected poses and proclamation; what a penance the man is. He may be the manager of this troupe but, in Garrick's company, he looks like a relic of a bygone age. His Oberon, King of the Fairies, could as well be Lord Foppington in The Relapse.

When Bottom leaves the stage, Harry jostles him and hisses.

'Look where you're going, you silly ass.'

Even though much encumbered by his equine head, Bottom can be heard chortling from inside it. Arne smirks. Harry is in the happiest of moods, buoyed by his recent meeting with John Rich. It will be some months before the Beggar's Opera will be staged, but at least his earnings are assured. He is also happy because he has secured the lease on a new apartment in Cavendish Square.

Only yesterday he had visited it, timing his journey from the theatre to the square. First he cut through side streets in order to avoid the pannies of St Giles. Then he pushed through the crowded market at Soho. In no time at all the cries of the mackerel sellers and tallow merchants were replaced by the trundle of roll carts carrying bricks still hot from the kilns. The houses gradually disappeared, being replaced by the sight of labourers' cabins strewn out along the Oxford Road. His fob watch told him that he'd arrived at James Gibbs & Co, Architects and Surveyors, in a mews behind Cavendish Square, in less than half an hour.

Timon, he learnt, was not available but, to his surprise, the footman who'd made such an excellent handmaiden on the night of the Roman orgy, was. He took a bunch of keys down from a row of hooks by the front door then swapped them, for another set, when Harry explained that he could not afford the rents for the ground or first floors. The footman told him he would show Harry a single room at the top of the latest terrace to be built round the square. He promised it was spacious and Harry wasn't disappointed.

The place had its own water closet. 'No dung carts to collect waste here,' the footman pointed out. Recessed windows, he said, they make fire less of a hazard; egg and dart mouldings round the architraves, chamfered shutters, Rococo sconces, a back staircase just for tradesmen and servants. The list went on; Harry's guide had a patter like a pedlar from Soho market. Looking out of a small window on the back staircase, he could see the brick works and clay pits of Marylebone and beyond them fields of corn. They were on the very edge of the town, he thought; but to escape the fog and smoke that so besets the City, that will be ample compensation.

The guide seemed uncommonly assured in his knowledge of the property so Harry asked him if he really was a footman. His eye lashes, he could not help noticing, were thick and dark, his body he remembered from their bacchanalian feast.

'I am as much a footman as my name is truly Tiberius,' he laughed, 'my identity is part of Timon's little fantasy.'

At those words he did something rather surprising. He took hold of Harry's jacket and slowly pulled it off, releasing his arms and pulling them around his waist. He drew Harry's lips down to his, the fingers of his other hand running down the centre of his back. Harry, with uncustomary restraint, pulled himself away.

'You take yourself for a bang up cove but your manner is forward. You may be part of Timon's fantasies, but you are not part of mine.' The words were harsh but he resented the cocksure manner, the assumption that Harry would find him attractive. Besides, he already had a plan fixed into his head; it was to bring Peter up here as soon as he moved in. He imagined taking him up the stairs, throwing open the double doors, and exhorting him to stay, not just for an afternoon, but for a night. His vision, he realised, was not infused with lust but something sweet and calm; it was domesticity. The floorboards will be left bare, he'd decided, only a large bed will be installed. Maybe one of Timon's artistic friends could paint a group of cherubs on the wall, frolicking in some enchanted garden.

Tiberius released his grasp, held up his arms as if in surrender, and smiled enigmatically.

'So, let me tell you about the rent and conditions,' he continued smoothly, naming a hefty sum and saying the property would be available soon. Harry had signed some attorney's scribble, handed over a purse of gold coins, and was about to go when Tiberius had taken hold of his arm and helped put his jacket back on. The keys lay abandoned, still, on the floorboards, Tiberius' own jacket, a fine one, hung on one of the sconces. Harry had thought for a moment that he was going to embrace him again but instead he said, 'I've watched you since you started to come to Timon's house.'

'Have you now? And what have you noticed?'

'Subtle changes. For a start you have become successful. It wasn't always so, of that I am sure.'

'You are right.'

'Elaborate then, tell me the story of your climb to fame.'

'There is none. Besides, I am not an introspective, literary type for whom everything has some significance.'

'That much I guessed.' Tiberius laughed, tucked the paper and purse into his pocket, looked round to check that nothing had been left, then picked up his own coat, and the keys, and guided him back down the main staircase.

'I envy you singing with Handel,' he said as they reached the last step. 'His music is sublime.'

'I see you often, in the pit,' Harry replied. 'Sadly not everyone agrees with you. Audiences are fickle. Alcina was a hit but sometimes we play to half empty houses.'

'People are gross and stupid in their tastes.'

'Next time I see you in the audience, Tiberius, I will sing only to you. Handel's greatness, our little secret.'

As they came out into the street Tiberius turned and said, 'If you plan to live here you must meet Marcel. He has a coffee shop on Holles Street, it's called the Le Faux Pas. Come, tope for a while, you're not in a hurry are you?'

He led Harry round the corner and, there in front of them, was a street of new shops with their goods artistically displayed behind the glass fronts.

'Where I come from, the shopmen use the windows for storage and the gathering of dust,' said Harry. 'A person could entertain themselves simply by looking at the windows here.'

A narrow alley led round the back of the shops to small, noisy manufactories. My every need will be catered for, Harry thought with satisfaction, he could get his bed made here and find a woman to do laundry. As they reached the Le Faux Pas Tiberius explained.

'Marcel, the proprietor, is no more French than his coffee shop, by the way. That why the inhabitants know it as the Fox's Paw.'

The sound of a lute tells the two musicians in the wings that it is time for them to enter the land of the fairies and for Harry to sing Under the Greenwood Tree while Arne plays the harpsichord. Half way through the song Harry, his spirits still high, pretends to miss his footing when leaning his arm back to rest on the harpsichord. He makes an exaggerated face, as if to say it is the harpsichord that has moved. The audience laugh. Arne picks up on his horsing; he lifts his hands as if completely carried away, and Harry fans him, suggesting a fit of the vapours. By the time they leave the stage there is whooping and calling.

'Walsh, you're a comedian,' says Nick Bottom as he passes him in the wings.

The plan, once they are finished, is to meet with Jonny who says he has news for them. As they leave the theatre, he is standing and waiting. This night, he explains, he has been performing in two separate entertainments, rushing from one theatre to another between acts, for he needs to increase his earnings. Such feats he describes as his acts of desperation.

'I'm sorry, fellows, I'm so tired, now, that I must go home so I will not keep you. I wanted to tell you that Henrietta and I, we have found a priest at last who will marry us.'

'Excellent,' says Arne, 'but Henrietta is a Catholic, is she not?' Arne is conscious of such matters. Harry is sick of his whines that his Catholicism excludes him from Church commissions, how pointless it is to agonise over the circumstances of one's birth.

'The priest was a rogue, as a matter of fact, who is trying to work his way to freedom from the Fleet. It was hardly a romantic ceremony and took all of five minutes,' laughs Beard. 'As far as he or I were concerned she could be a Mohammedan. I love her so dearly.'

'We are very happy for you.' Harry hugs his dear friend and kisses him on both his cheeks. Lady Henrietta Herbert he first met, the same evening as Jonny did, at one of Mrs Pendleton's parties. She is, to his mind, most highly strung and a figure of tragedy, haunted by her first marriage to a member of the avaricious, grasping Herbert family, Earls of Powys. Despite Harry's misgivings over this union he says, brightly, 'So, Jonny, now you, Arne, and Lampe are all taken. I have no wife and no prospect of one.' He does not add that, despite his growing success, his heart is prisoner to someone he can never marry. He thinks of Tiberius and his relationship with Timon. Would Peter ever leave Handel, come and live with him at Cavendish Square, seek out pupils, perhaps, to give lessons in writing to? Would he, Harry, ever try to encourage him to leave the composer? He knows in his heart that Peter would never desert his employer and that he could never live with himself if he pressed him to do so.

He wishes his friends goodnight and, once they are out of sight, crosses the road back to the theatre. Perhaps Miss Fenton, who has exchanged a number of lingering looks with him, will give him the benefit of her company. When he gets to the stage door he finds that the theatre has a new doorman. It is Attila. The cheeky fellow tries to dun him for money and, when Harry refuses, he says that Miss Fenton is not available. Harry wonders if this means that Attila has already been richly remunerated by another party. His speculations are ended when Lavinia, looking resplendent in a velvet boisson and aigrette hat, comes out with a state-cook type, a politician, in a close coat and cockers with a buckled wig. She smiles and nods at Harry, as if to say, "Keep away", then gives the simpering Attila a knowing smile. Harry chuckles as he walks away; he and Lavinia Fenton, it seems, are cut from the same fabric.

For a moment he contemplates going in search of Tiberius, but decides against it, for the young blade irritates him as much as he attracts. His keenness to improve himself reminds Harry, oppressively, of himself at an earlier age. Besides, he has, in his estimation, an exaggerated notion of his own charms. Instead, Harry skips northward, to Clerkenwell, to the bagnie, for the Turkish steam rooms help his throat and ensure that he sleeps deeply.

39. The Mall
It is less than a year since General Plunket died so Lucy is still in

black. She spends much of her time at the Foundling Hospital helping in the kitchens. It recently opened in temporary lodgings in Hatton Garden. The fellow sitting opposite them, with the gooseberry wig and rubicund face, is none other than its founder, Thomas Coram. The three of them are taking young George to the Mall, where they will feed the ducks and enjoy this June day in Lucy's open chariot, paid for out of the generous proceeds of the General's will. The little boy sits on Harry's knee and exclaims as they look down on another little lad, with his nursemaid in tow, who is inexpertly pushing a hoop along the road as they make their way to the park. Lucy looks sad. Is it grief that has led her to seek out his company, Harry wonders. She remains silent while her companion starts to prate.

'We were hit by the queen's death, that's the honest truth, for she was a great supporter of ours.' Harry taps his fingers. It is in the nature of philanthropists to be preoccupied with the good causes they espouse. Coram's voice has an American twang; maybe that's where he learnt to meddle rather than accepting things as they are.

'We have many subscribers now and we hope the Duke of Bedford will give us land for a permanent institution,' Coram continues.

'A most excellent achievement. You are lucky, Sir, to have Mrs Plunket helping in the kitchens. I am sure she applies herself mightily.'

'Lucky, in more ways than one, Mr Walsh, for when Mrs Trebeck brought her along, I, at last, found the girl I had been seeking for a long time.'

Good lord, Harry thinks, surely she is not going to tie herself to another old cuff.

'And I recognised you, instantly, even though I'd been so young at the time.' Lucy looks sadly but fondly at the Captain.

'I better explain, Mr Walsh. Lucy's mother was my house-keeper. She came back with me from the West Indies. She had been enslaved, Sir, but I freed her. If only I could have helped more of her kind.' Is there no limit, Harry muses, to the extent of his charity? 'Alas, she was seduced and ran away from my house, in shame. By the time I found her it was too late; she was dying, leaving me with a tiny baby.'

'Heavens, and that was Lucy, Mrs Plunket, I mean?' This information is a lot more interesting than the generous intentions of the Duke of Bedford.

'I put her into the care of a blacksmith and his wife. I was not in a position to care for her for I still served at sea then. When I returned from my last voyage I found that they had died. I knew that the child had survived but I lost touch with her and my heart was near broken.' He leans over and squeezes her hand. 'She looks so unbelievably like her mother,' he chuckles.

Harry looks at Lucy but she is far away, not really listening to the Captain. He is of a mind that she is holding back tears but that they have nothing to do with the memory of her unhappy childhood.

'Driver, stop here,' says the Captain, for it is forbidden to take carriages down the Mall. 'Got your bag of crumbs ready, young George?' The little boy wriggles off Harry's lap and squeals with delight.

In the chariot next to theirs an elderly man is being helped to don a coat by his coachman. The Captain's face freezes.

'You, Sir,' he gasps.

'Captain, you recognise me. I am old now, and sick, but don't think I have no regret for the things I did in my past.'

'Duke,' says Lucy, for the man speaking is obviously very grand, 'the last time I saw you, outside a tavern in the Haymarket, you bid me never to cross your path again, even though, for all you knew, I was homeless and in need of friends. And I did as you asked.'

'Yes, daughter,' he replies. 'It was wrong of me. I thought you were after my money. I realise now that you weren't and, in any case, you had every right to chase me.'

'George,' she says, turning to her little seven year old, 'this old man is your grandfather, your other one, not the noble one who cared for you when you were born.'

'Lucy, I am sorry that I denied you, sorry that I never got to know young George.'

Captain Coram is greatly distressed.

'Come Lucy, George, Mr Walsh, we will feed the ducks now. I have no time for this man with his lack of morals.'

As Lucy and Harry hurry to keep up with the Captain, and the little boy who has his arm, he suppresses a feeling of amazement. Apart from the Captain, he wonders if he is the only one who knows that she is the daughter of a freed Caribbean slave and a British duke. The vision flashes in his mind of three old dames, Mrs Donovan, Mrs Pendleton and Mrs Trebeck, their chatter silenced as he, playing a young shepherd, tells Lucy's story in a solo aria. What a wonderful theme for a drama.

'You won't discuss what you have just witnessed, will you?' she asks him. 'I am, as you know, a very private person.'

'I do know that,' Harry says with regret as he lets his vision fade. She threads her arm in his but he can feel the unhappiness within her and finds it impossible to restrain himself. 'Lucy, forgive me if I intrude, but I noticed in the carriage that you were holding back tears.'

She walks on in silence. Eventually she says, 'Sometimes I feel my heart will break. To love someone, that, surely, is to open oneself to pain.'

'I am sorry, Lucy, I cannot think who would break your heart; it is such a loving one.'

She goes mute but it is as good as saying, 'Well, broken it is.'

'Look, you two, look at how popular young George is.' The little boy is surrounded by a group of eager, quacking birds, and is chuckling with delight as Coram hands him bread to throw at them. The old man is not happy, though. He tears vehemently at the black crusts, angry at the memory of the pain the duke caused.

As they pass Brook Street on their return, the Captain asks, 'What is the news of Mr Handel? We have failed to raise his interest in the foundlings but he does much, I gather, to help destitute musicians.'

Let us all continue to be dismal, thinks Harry. First the plight of foundlings, then destitute musicians. If we go on in this fashion, Lucy's mood will never lift. Lucy's shoulders shudder, then she answers.

'He is burdened by problems, my Father. Like the cause of the Foundling Hospital, he suffered a reverse in fortunes when the queen died.'

'And the king,' Harry adds in a suitably gloomy voice, 'has proved to be no sort of friend, he is less and less interested in music and graces Handel's entertainments hardly at all.'

'Poor Handel,' says Lucy after a pause. 'Mr Heidegger now wants him to leave the King's again. I gather he intends to move to Mr Rich's old theatre at Lincoln's Inn Fields.' She retreats into silence. Eventually she stirs herself.

'Harry, he is too proud to accept offers of help from his friends. Please talk to him.'

This, then, is the purpose of Lucy's invitation, not to tell Harry about some unrequited love but to ask him, as Lord M did in the past, to wield some influence, which he does not have, on Handel. How can he tell her that he is, in any case, much taken up with other matters? He intends to visit the country soon, then to move to his new apartment. He is also busy working on new diversions for the intermissions at Garrick's shows which are hitting well with the public.

'Everyone tells me his operas are at a great personal cost. If he needs financial support from his friends, we will help him,' Lucy explains.

'Handel is his own man,' Harry murmurs gently. 'Ask Peter,

when he and his master return from the spa. If anyone has influence on him, it is he.'

40. The New Apartment

The earl's Chinese vase sits in a niche. He has also given Harry a China rug with peacocks flaunting their feathers against a blue-green background, his beloved "turquoise". The fine chair, brought up the stairs by the fubsey's footman, has ball and claw feet and Chinese style tracery on the backrest. Harry must explain to his visitors, she says, that it is made is by one Richard Wood, a master joiner and woodworker from York whose furniture surpasses all others'. A half-finished wall painting of a Roman market, started by Timon, adorns one wall. So far it depicts the figure of a woman in a striped, Turkish turban, selling fruit while seated on stone steps at the base of a tall fluted column; large paving stones recede to infinity, showing Timon's mastery of perspective. On the floor in front of the wall is a set of Timon's oil paints and varnishes.

Tiberius offers to sit for him, wearing nothing but the breast-plate, but Harry explains that he intends to teach his pupils in the apartment, which is why he has had his father's old harpsi-chord moved from the rectory.

'I hardly want Miss Emily or Miss Matilda to have to stare at a man's dangler when mastering their vibrato,' he tells Tiberius. This does not stop the young man from visiting often. Or from removing his clothes, saying he will model a Roman statue, for he likes an audience, for his cock to be admired, magnificent beast that it is.

At this moment Miss Trebeck is present, with her younger sister and the one person whom Harry would not trust to chaperone any daughter of his; their brother, Timothy.

'So you live here alone, do you?' He is pacing up and down inspecting everything. 'I like the lack of furniture, the large windows. I get sick of the medieval stuff in my rooms at Oxford.

This is all so modern. The streets, they're straight, I see they have lights. Emily, let's skip your class. We could go down to the new market, find a place for chocolate.' He has already pulled Harry aside and asked if the town-land has bawdy houses. Harry is delighted at his excitement and envy; he really feels like a prime article in his new accommodation. He is pleased, though, when Emily rebukes him and insists on her lesson before he shows them round Marylebone.

Her voice is clear and unadorned, his creation, and her progress thrills him. He has six other young ladies, now, whose mothers wish him to work the same magic on their unpromising offspring. His specialty is to take simple airs and to make them sound portentous through the addition of ornament and vibrato; but then, when they sing songs of real quality, he strips them of trimmings and gets his singers to reach for the emotions beneath.

'Lascia ch'io pianga,' he shouts at Emily today, when she sings the aria from one of Handel's early operas. 'What does it mean? Let me hear you weep, you are sad, young lady, sad.' Timothy looks unmoved and irritated by her efforts but her sister is reduced to sobs and Harry is satisfied.

The day before, Handel had puffed his way up the staircase, sat in state in the fubsey's chair, and admired Timon's half-finished painting. When Tiberius had come knocking, with the sealed copy of his lease, he'd looked in wonder at his guest.

'Mr Handel,' he stammered. 'Your Alexander's Feast, I saw it earlier this year.' Harry thought he would bow down before the great presence and kiss his feet.

'I will be putting it on again,' Handel said munificently. 'We have decided to move to Lincoln's Inn.' We? Heidegger has decided. A new Academy Opera has been formed, by Lord Middlesex, but Handel has decided not to be part of it. Having tasted independence from aristocratic sponsors, he would rather, it seems, be free and impecunious than enslaved to others' tastes.

Peter had looked at Tiberius furtively while tidying the

rumpled bed clothes that were strewn over a mattress on the floor. He would admonish Harry, he knew, for not finding himself a carpenter to make a bed, and ask him all manner of difficult questions about Tiberius. The young jay acted, annoyingly, as if the apartment was his and as if Harry was his close friend.

The day after the visit from the Trebecks, Harry takes a sedan all the way to the City, for he has received a note from Simeon that was left at the coffee shop in Holles Street, the Fox's Paw. Marcel has increased trade by acting as a postal address for the local inhabitants. People come for their letters, then invariably stay, for it is a good place to tope and jaw. When Harry gets to the Exchange the loathsome man, his partner in business, looks mighty pleased with himself. He opens a drawer in his desk, pulls out a bag, and strews the contents across the top.

'You gave me five hundred guineas, Harry, now I return them. There are a thousand there, count them. I told you I would double your money. This trip, it has been a good one. The Voyager met none of those Spanish pirates, how they like to board our vessels and demand their taxes. They are a damnable crew of blackguards, those bull fighters.'

Harry is too well mannered to count the coins in his presence but has every intention of doing so later. To be in possession of such a sum makes him feel like a Colossus.

'We set out again in a few weeks' time, have to, to catch the trade winds. If you wish to invest again, come round here any time.'

Harry assures him he will. He intends to make him wait a week, in order not to appear too keen. Besides, he has owings to settle at Brindley's which he plans to repair to immediately; to carry so much coin makes him nervous. Once he has done his business at the goldsmiths, letting the assistants count the coins, carefully, and leaving most of his gains in the vaults, for Mr Brindley has taken up as a bank as well, he decides to visit the rectory.

Walking through the old stone pillars at Charterhouse Square, he feels as if he left years ago instead of just two weeks before. Samuel is in the dining room and tells him that Doctor Walsh is at the church. The dining room looks old, the beams feel oppressive, how little light comes through the lattice windows, and the place could do with a good dusting, he can't help noticing. He finds his father at St Bart's, in prayer, kneeling at one of the inward facing pews near the altar.

They embrace and Harry persuades him to come back with him to Cavendish Square. For what seems like an age they walk along the Oxford Road. How much Harry would like to tell him about his projections with Simeon. Instead, they chatter and laugh about his aunt in Essex and the new shire horses she is so proud of. They partake of lamb cutlets, washed down by glasses of ale, at one of the smarter ordinaries in Holles Street, then Harry shakes up the caretaker at the base of his lodgings who lights a candle and guides them up. That night Harry sleeps with his father who is quiet and contemplative. He is impressed, Harry thinks, with his new lodgings but he misses him, he says. One day, Harry promises, he will move into a larger apartment so he can have his dear father with him.

The following night he has Peter for company. He is waiting for him outside the theatre. Handel is preoccupied with his compositions, he tells him. Once they are "home" - how Harry loves the word - he takes him into his arms. This is the moment he has dreamed of for so long, the moment when they can spend the night together alone, free to do what they please, in lodgings that belong to him and no-one else. In the morning Peter places an untidy notebook, bulging with loose pages and old letters, on Harry's chair. It is his diary, he tells him.

41. Burning Texts
The sedans tend to cluster to the north of Covent Garden's Piazza,

near the theatre, but today there is just one waiting. The minute Harry climbs into it he realises that it is barely fit for purpose; the seat is worn and uneven, the curtain is torn and the bearers are two rough-looking buffleheads with toes, that are blue with cold, poking out of broken down boots. They are former soldiers, he presumes, unable even to afford the red livery that is usual for chairmen. He resents the fact that his uncomfortable journey this will cost him six whole pennies, but the streets are wet and he has no wish to muddy his new leather boots. He bids them take him to Lombard Street. After that he intends going to Simeon's office above the Exchange. Two months earlier he invested in a second voyage and must now pay the residue of what he owes Simeon.

He clutches Peter's diary, determined to flick through it so as not to offend him. He thinks fondly of the nights they have spent together. They afford him moments of sanity, of quiet, comradeship, laughter and love; sometimes Peter is his older brother, wise and protective, sometimes the younger one, needful and vulnerable. Now that the new season has just started at Lincoln's Inn he fears for the continuation of their pleasant assignations.

He unfolds the tightly written pages, heavy with a sense of duty. Since he is a slow reader he has made little progress so far. The first entry that he read, back at the apartment, was for October 1737. It had Handel unexpectedly encountering Lord M while sitting in the steam room in Aix-la-Chapelle. So great was the look of embarrassment on his friend's face that Handel thought it best to feign madness and let him escape. Harry had laughed out loud. No doubt many more such amusing anecdotes were contained within these pages. Nanette was right, her son can be très drôle when he wants to be. Harry is so full of sentiment, as he touches the worn pages, that tears form at the back of his eyes. Suddenly, the sedan lurches dangerously.

'Look where your prancer's fucking going,' one of the ruffians shouts to a horseman. Harry fears, for a moment, that he's about to be tipped into a pot hole and sticks his head out of the curtain.

'Sorry about that, Guv, he wasn't gumming you, just some grinagog riding a bone shaker.' The chairman smiles to reveal inflamed gums and rotting maws. Steam issues from his mouth in the cold November air.

Despite the rocking motion of the chair Harry flips the pages back and starts to read an entry for the year 1733. That, he thinks, was shortly after they met. It starts:

'June 16. A song just goes through my head: Harry, Harry, Harry. I love you, love you, love you. The coats and britches seem to hop into their right place on the rail, the shoes effortlessly find the order they should be in, the affairs of the dressing room, in other words, are under control. We met today in St James Square, NOT by the stage door because of the doorman.'

It makes him uneasy to see his name written down; what if someone should get hold of the diary and read it? The next few entries describe a yawn-filled stay at Tunbridge Wells, an incident where railings close in on him, then Handel's fascination with Lord Shaftesbury's collection of fossils. At the time they were in His Lordship's country home near Salisbury and Peter describes his desperation when Handel plays at the cathedral and promises to return to the music festival they have there. Then he is back in London. He describes in great detail a reunion with Sid and Nell, their eager yelps when he takes them to the park, after which he is meeting up with Harry again at Vauxhall.

'September 15. Tonight Harry and I followed the wall round the pleasure gardens to the back and hopped over it. We slipped in among the trees, held hands and embraced. I can't stop myself from touching his fingers, putting my lips to his hair, looking into his eyes. I am simply intoxicated!!!'

Harry can feel the spit drying in his mouth. This diary, it reveals much; it is intimate, it could fall into anyone's hands. Where will he put it when he gets to the gold merchants and when he meets up with Simeon later? His coat is of too elegant a cut to afford capacious pockets.

'April 12. 1735. We were back in the gardens today and I couldn't stop myself from asking the same old question although I know it annoys him. "What will I do when your father tells you to marry someone?" He says that girls frighten him, that he can't imagine being married. The trouble is, I can, only too well. Then he would leave me and I would...What? Kill myself? I better try to behave. Tonight as I lie in my bed the curtains float outwards, wafted by the night air, bringing thoughts from across London of my love. Where are you now, Harry, how it pains me to be apart.'

He flicks the pages forward and there is more of the same, his name plastered everywhere, endearments written that could undo him, ruin the name he has made for himself, and worse. His father's pained face flicks before his eyes; Peter, dead in Handel's study, a pot of poison to one side, an incriminating note to the other; Handel's raised arm coming down, the violins shrieking in unison as every member of the audience looks at him in horror. His relations with Peter, they have always been private, why has he committed such detail to writing? There is only one solution, decides Harry, this diary, it must be destroyed. His bearers swerve again, no doubt to avoid one of the many piles of horse dung that ornament the streets. An oath from the back confirms his suspicion.

'Fuck me, m' best kicksies, covered they are.'

Harry is filled with rising panic for they must be approaching Lombard Street. He sticks his head out again and sees that they have cut down Bucklebury and are passing St Mary Woolnoth. In the graveyard next to the church a group of fuddle caps is sitting, in a circle, passing round a flagon of gin. Next to them a doxy has lit a fire which she's feeding from a pile of rubbish taken from a collapsed house to one side of the church. Perfect.

'Stop,' Harry cries, causing the chairmen to all but pitch him into the gutter. He pays the wretches their fare, walks over to the fire. For a brief moment he pauses, then tosses the diary onto it. He watches as years of personal anguish, happiness, laughter and tears, shrivel and disappear. The stupefied creatures around him, surprised by his sudden appearance in amongst them, stare like sheep. The doxy sneers.

'Burning sacred texts?'

'Yes I am.'

'Yus an Aminadab?'

'I am no Quaker, Madam.' He straightens the velvet collar of his coat, cleans the dust off his calfskin gloves, pulls back his long curls from under the brim of his hat, and marches north. A group of curs, their rib cages visible, grovel and slink away as he passes them. By the time he reaches Lombard Street he is calm. Walsh can be quite the actor.

1740

42. The Duke's Daughter

Harry is meeting Lord Harlow and Lord M at a chop house in Candle Alley off Cornhill. As he makes his way there he is whistling and swinging his stick. He believes that Lord Harlow is seeking him out in order to ask him to sing at one of his private entertainments. Only the other day his lordship spotted him at Carlton Gardens where Handel and his performers were rehearsing in front of their Royal Highnesses, the Prince and Princess of Wales. He surely deduced from that what a bang-up cove Harry has become. Apart from an awkward moment when Handel stopped playing, on account of a lady-in-waiting leaning over and whispering something to her neighbour, the occasion was a great success. The prince was most welcoming. Since his mother died, relations with his father have reached a compete impasse, but he is now free to bestow his largesse on Handel without it looking as if he does so merely to please the queen.

'Harry, dear boy.' Lord M is immediately visible as he enters. 'You are looking most theatrical. Have you been to a rehearsal?'

'I am a performer, My Lord; it is my habit to look overdressed.' He is not ashamed of the flash of green silk under his jacket, or of the stripes on his britches, even though everyone else is in black. It is clear to Lord M that his young friend has become a fashion-conscious molly, a bit of a French dog.

'Harlow, there you are, come and sit down.' They make room for themselves amongst the crowded tables; Simpsons, like Batson's, is the haunt of City men.

'What are we having? The steak and kidney and a bottle of Burgundy?' Harry is happy for their lordships to choose.

Lord M has been away on some diplomatic mission at Potsdam. The court in Prussia, he assures the pair of them, is not to his taste at all but the king's sister has the misfortune to be the mother of the Prussian monarch, Frederick William. Her brother, George, is concerned for her welfare now that the talk in Europe is of war.

'Let us raise our glasses to peace, long may it continue.' Lord M drains his glass and refills it. 'Walpole once took the view that he and the king have much in common,' he says gloomily. 'That was because both believe that every man has their price. But the differences between them are beginning to surface.'

'You are referring, I suppose, to the king's liking for playing the soldier, and to the fact that he'd like to embroil himself in every dispute in Europe.'

'Exactly so, Harlow.'

'Don't dwell on it, M, while Walpole is our first minister he won't let him.'

'I just hope you're right. It amazes me that a man of his age could entertain romantic notions of heroism on the battlefield.'

Harry lets the two worldlings prattle on the politics of the day. But when Lord M mentions his travels across Europe, he asks him, 'Have you ever been to Aix-la-Chapelle, My Lord? Handel swears by the waters there.'

'I have. I was there when he was as a matter of fact.' Harry raises a questioning eyebrow. He is surprised that he is admitting to the fact. 'He behaved most oddly.'

'I thought he'd been behaving rather normally recently, calming down. He's almost stopped staging his Italian operas, I gather, cutting his expenses and so forth, a wise decision. What are you trying to say, M?'

'I'm not talking about now, Harlow; it was nearly three years ago.'

'In what way was he odd?'

'He mistook me for some character in one of his operas. Kept calling me Justinian. He was making as much sense as a Dutch almanac.'

'Where were you at the time?' Harry asks, looking puzzled.

'That's not like him.'

'In a steam room.'

'You in a steam bath? Taking cures? Had the pox, did you?' Lord Harlow throws his head back and laughs.

'No, I didn't have the pox, although, goodness knows, that's why most people go to Aix-la-Chapelle. I was spending a few days away with a lady companion if you must know. Nothing serious, un divertissement. It was most unfortunate, I was strolling down the road one morning when, who should I see but my wife. Mary was in the company of a group of diplomats' wives, they'd been staying near the Makt. Her intention was to take the waters then turn up and surprise me at Potsdam.'

'But she surprised you earlier than planned.' Harry is trying not to smirk.

'I dived into the nearest doorway which turned out to be some sort of convent in which there were baths. A creature with a white headdress bungled me into a steam room dressed in nothing but a flannel dressing gown. Gabble, gabble, gabble, all in German of course. It was only when the steam cleared that I became convinced that the lobster-like apparition before me was none other than the great composer. That's when he started talking a lot of nonsense and I decided it best to flee. If Mary had found me I planned to tell her that I was visiting Charlemagne's tomb.'

A small boy is peeping in at the window. When he sees Lord M he squeezes in among the chairs and hands him a note in a pretty pink envelope. The contents are read, a coin is fished out of his lordship's pocket, and a nod is exchanged. The boy makes his exit. This is not the first of such messages, that's for sure.

Harry half expects Lord M to give some sort of an explanation but, instead, Lord Harlow makes a request that pleases him greatly.

'My wife is holding a soirée in a few days' time to introduce our daughter's fiancé to the family. I wondered if you would sing for us.'

'I would be delighted.' Lord Harlow, he knows, pays generous fees; he will surely mix with the very top echelons of society in his drawing room. Maybe the Prince and Princess of Wales will be there. His current aviary of students, for the most part, are the daughters of merchants and professional men; they do not include in their number the daughter of a duke.

'Young Isabel engaged? A good match I hope,' says Lord M.

'Three thousand acres in Norfolk and another three thousand in Tipperary.'

'Excellent.'

Harry starts planning in his head the songs he should sing at Lady Harlow's soirée and wonders whether Caspar will be free to accompany him. After only a single glass of wine his head is slightly dizzy. To his relief, when it is time to go, Lord M offers him a ride in his coach. It is parked, he says, on the main thoroughfare which makes it necessary for them to negotiate an open channel of human waste that runs down Candle Alley.

'The streets in the City of London, they're a disgrace. It does not look good to foreigners,' says Harry. This observation is for the sole purpose of adding, nonchalantly, 'Why, in Cavendish Square they are laying the roads with cobble stones. I much enjoy living there.' Sadly, Lord M is not listening. Once seated, he observes,

Those awful steam baths, they do nothing to improve one's "performance" and that's for sure.' He lights a pipe and Harry fears for his suit; it will be like a kipper after five minutes in his lordship's rattler.

'Are you on your way home, Sir? The coach seems to be moving south.'

'Most certainly not, I'm on my way to a little establishment I keep in St Clement Danes. Young limbs, that's what I need, to keep my old bones warm.'

'It's just what I need too,' his companion replies, the wine having loosened his tongue.

'Why, come and join me. You'll like the company I keep.'

The luxury of satin sheets, the opulence of brocade drapes round the bed, the soft light of finest whale oil, plump pink limbs. Lord M laughs at Harry's enthusiasm and stamina although, in truth, it barely matches his host's, for he has a horn on him the size of a stallion's. The young ladies giggle and tease. They recognise him, they say, from the playhouse.

'You'll have to come again, you young stag,' says Lord M.

'I most certainly will if I'm asked,' Harry replies. I am a libertine, like you, he thinks. His last, contented thought, before the company allows him a moment of sleep, is that, if he is going to sing at Lord Harlow's, he must ask Tiberius for the name of his tailor.

43. Lady Harlow's Drawing Room

Caspar says he will arrive just before they are due to perform for he has a trumpet solo to do first, round the corner, at the Hickford Rooms on James Street. It annoys Harry that he is nervous, as he climbs the ornate staircase, and that he recognises no-one. The grandees in silk evening suits, handing their top hats and gloves to a flunkey, seem oblivious to those around them, relying on quick flicks of their eyes, like a lizard's, in order to take in their surroundings. The women are worse, merely staring ahead with a disdainful look on their faces, terrified that they may have to converse with someone who does not match them in rank. They look mountainous in their wide skirts and plumped up hair, and confined by the quantity of furbelows and fal-lals about their person.

Harry looks round to see if his fubsey is present but then realises that, since she is part of the Tory camp, this is not her set. As his name is announced at the entrance of the drawing room Lord Harlow comes to his rescue. He separates himself from a group of what look like Parliamentary men, and walks through the crowd to greet him.

'You must meet my mother, the Dowager Lady Harlow,' he says. 'I have to protect Isabel from her for she is very free with her advice.' The dowager is indeed formidable and stares at him, rudely, through her lorgnette. The mousy little creature who stands next to her, with knots round her head, is dressed rather soberly in grey silk with her eyes lowered to the ground; she must be the Harlow daughter. Somewhere in the room, no doubt, will be the much landed marquis who is due to tie his acreage in with hers.

'Mr Walsh, you sing at the Lincoln Inn's Theatre, I gather. Not one of my haunts, I can't stand that awful man, can I, my dear?'

'No you can't, Grandmama.'

'He's very arrogant you know, and rude, that's so typical of his race. Thinks he can rule the musical tastes of this country. '

'I have never found that, Your Ladyship.'

Clearly, anything Harry has to say is not of interest to her. A decrepit old battle axe in pink chiffon has just tapped her arm with a fan and the dowager turns her back on him so that she can sneer at the guests' outfits with her companion. That leaves him with the mouse. He wonders what item of small talk he can amuse her with.

'She never loved Handel.'

'Sorry?' The eyelids have snapped upwards and she is looking at him full in the face. The eyes are a surprising violet blue. His breath is fair taken away.

'She never loved Handel; she's in the opposing camp, running him down whenever she can. I, on the other hand, have always loved him.' The mouse's habit of stressing certain words makes her views sound very firm. The grey silk doesn't do her justice. Her chest is the most beautiful milk white. Harry has to force himself not to look at it.

'Yes, I love him with a passion. I first saw you perform when I was sixteen. I like everything you sing, what you do with your characters, your voice.'

'And which of his works is your favourite?'

'Why, Semele of course.' She stresses the last word. You little minx, Harry thinks. One so pure and innocent yet with a taste for Handel's erotica. There is nothing oratorio-like in this tale of a young girl's lust for the God Jupiter and her spurning of her fiancé.

'And is the marquis your Jupiter?'

'What do you think?' She looks directly at him again but this time the curious stressing of certain words is absent, in fact he can barely hear her, instead he is reading the movement of her lips. Jupiter was always his part. The sounds around them seem to fade; in their short exchange so much has been said. He realises that, to continue talking to her will be considered impolite, so he bows to take his leave. As he does so he glimpses Caspar standing at the door looking for him. When Isabel puts out her hand he lifts it to his lips, holding onto the fingers for a moment longer than he should. Their eyes meet, hers violet, surrounded by a milky whiteness.

'There's the marquis,' says her grandmother scowling at Harry, having forgotten who he is and why he is standing there. 'You must go over to him, Child, and at least give the appearance of being happy to see him.'

Harry is almost shaking as he greets Caspar.

'A slight change of plan,' he whispers. 'The first song will be Where'er you walk.'

'Nice. Jupiter's aria. Are you pining?' Caspar laughs.

Isabel is in the front row of the semicircle of gold and scarlet chairs that form a wide arc round the harpsichord. His opening song is addressed to her but they do not exchange looks. Harry's voice soars, capturing the beauty of the melody. Everyone becomes quiet so that his singing is the only sound; he exaggerates the rise and fall of his voice and lets the pauses between the phrases become long and tender. During the applause he throws a momentary glance in her direction. Her cheeks are flushed, her eyes sparkle. The marquis is next to her but has his body half turned away. Harry is shocked by the lust and longing she stirs in him.

After the performance, Lord Harlow's wife approaches, smiling, her skirt impossibly wide, with a youthful duchess in tow who insists that he must sing at her next assembly. Praise is being bestowed on him by all and sundry but Harry and his accompanist must leave because they have a rehearsal to attend early the next day. Harry bids Caspar good night at the Long Acre, watching as he cuts up to his lodgings on the top floor of a tenement on the Seven Dials.

'Be careful, my friend, don't get yourself into all sorts of trouble,' are Caspar's parting words.

As Harry walks on, he reflects on the fact that his life has become a muddle. He revels in variety yet Peter is still central to his life. Handel is the only composer whose work he really respects yet he makes money singing in satires and ballad operas. Now he is burning with passion for a young girl who is above him in station and due to be married to another man.

44. The Parlour at King Street

Attila, feeling penitential after running away with Nanette's money, has bought the lease of her house so she can make her living renting out the rooms. He has become rich in his position as the doorman at Drury Lane for, like Mr Tyers, he is an impresario. From husbands, he takes bribes to spy on wives who perform at the theatre. From wives, he takes bribes to arrange access for those whom they wish to entertain in their dressing rooms. Late at night, when the theatre closes, Peter claims, he is a stripper at one of the taverns by the docks that caters for fribbles and bully traps.

'Can you imagine,' says Peter, raising his eyebrows, 'he's bad enough with his clothes on.'

Peter has begged Harry to meet him at his mother's house so, with haste, he makes his way to King Street after an early morning rehearsal at the Covent Garden theatre. Harry's head aches and he can sense a fever coming on. He feels possessed by what happened at Lady Harlow's the previous night, not in a way that gives pleasure but which torments and confuses.

When he arrives Nanette is in her kitchen, kneeling on the floor. He is surprised to find that the person whose gown she is hemming is Susanna Cibber.

'Dearest One,' he cries, 'you are up from Devon. We all miss you.'

'I am, Harry, I cannot remain in hiding for ever. Dear William, he looks after me well, and we have our darling little Molly, but I hate the fact that my living as an actress is at an end.'

She stands magnificent in cerise coloured brocade, a long train attached to her back, hoops widening her skirts, and frills issuing forth from the low cut of her bodice. She is like a stickleback as large-headed pins stick out of her at all angles. Peter sits holding a tin of them within Nanette's reach, some bent with age but still looking perilously sharp. Harry is unable to kiss her, without getting caught, so he bows instead.

'Queen Susanna, let me proffer obeisance, guard you with my life.'

'Harry, darling, do stop playing the ass.'

'I was at your second court case, a wondrous performance.'

'You don't think I overdid it, saying Theo forced me into William's bed at gun point?'

'Not at all, when you said that he did it for money, because you had no possessions left which he had not stolen or pawned, the crowd was in tears. Why, even the judge looked dewy eyed.'

'So did he get damages, this rap scallion man you marry?' asks Nanette through her pins.

'Theo was awarded £500, more than the paltry £10 paid first time round,' she says. 'But he'd been looking for much more,

£5,000, because of the threat, as he put it, to his "peace of mind, his happiness and his hopes of prosperity".'

'That must have made you laugh.'

'It would have if he hadn't turned me into a public farce and portrayed me as a drab.'

'My poor, dear Susanna.'

'I am a Londoner, Harry, my home is the stage, acting is in my blood, to be hiding in the country is like a death.' As she describes to them the kindness of the country folk who work on Sloper's Devon estate, and the mean-spiritedness of the local gentry, Harry glances across the table at Peter. As is usual in company, he is quiet, but he steals shy looks at his lover; the light catches his blond hair and makes it shine. How Harry used to marvel at the radiance of that hair, at the license he had to stroke it, to run strands of it through his fingers. Now, all he feels is dread that Peter might ask him for the return of his diary or wish to spend the night with him.

Nanette gets up from the floor.

'Now you must step out of this dress but not so that the bodice comes away from the skirt.'

'Look away, you naughty boys, I don't want you peeking at me in my shift.' Susanna giggles and for a minute is her old self again.

'We will retreat upstairs and so protect your modesty,' says Harry, making his way to the door. Peter rises gracefully and follows him up to the back parlour which is on the same level as the street. Harry knows he wants to embrace him, to be stroked and petted, and so find solace from the trials of his life. But today he has no wish to do this. He wants to close his eyes and see the flash of violet, her milky skin, to hear her clipped emphatic voice, so sure in its opinions.

'Harry, are you unwell? You seem far away.'

'Forgive me, I hardly slept.'

'I wanted to see you to explain why I rarely come to the

theatre. It makes me melancholy, the Lincoln's Inn. It's such a tub of a place. I know he wants to save money but it's so out of the way. The fashionable crowd have dropped him.'

'It won't always be thus, I'm sure of it.' Harry does not know what else to say for, like Peter, he feels that Handel has been humiliated, yet again, by Heidegger and his set. Peter then asks the question that Harry feared he would.

'My diary, you've had it a while; have you read it?'

'Oh yes. I am honoured to be trusted with it.' Guilt flutters in his chest.

'You can keep it for the present time. I'm going away, to the Netherlands.'

'Going away?'

'The Princess Royal has asked Handel to stay with her at Haarlem.'

There was a time when, to hear about the composer consorting with royalty, and to know that he was one of his singers, that he was an intimate of Brook Street, would have been the apex of Harry's ambitions. It encased his relations with Peter in glamour. Just now, it is merely a relief that Peter will be gone for a while.

'Please don't be angry, my love. When you read the diary, you'll know my feelings.' Peter's need for him, it is suffocating.

'How can I help but be angry. You know how sorry I am when we are parted.' Gracious, Harry thinks, I sound like David Garrick in one of his plays.

Peter kneels and puts his arms round Harry's knees. He brushes his face against them.

'You're not yourself today.'

'No, I don't think I am.'

'You do still want me, don't you?'

'Of course.'

'You seem distant.'

'I could say the same for you. This trip to the Netherlands, how long will you be gone?' Harry has no taste for play-acting. All he wants is to be gone. 'I am sorry but I don't feel well. Say goodbye to the others, I have a mind to go home.' Peter's soft features look hurt.

'I'll come with you.'

'No, not today, I need to be alone.'

As he walks towards Cavendish Square, Harry forgets Peter's mournful look almost immediately. Instead, wild fantasies fill his head. What if Isabel broke her engagement and chose him in place of the marquis? The feeling between them, it was mutual, there was this sense of being of the same mind, as if their hearts had spoken, one to the other. Lord and Lady Harlow as his parents-in-law, would they accept him? Surely not. If, in her persistent and headstrong way, she insisted that they did, he would become an habitué of soirées like the one last night, he would learn to talk freely with Parliamentary men and all those trussed up chickens with their severe expressions and voluptuous eyes.

Harry starts to plan his new life. He would never live off her, no, he would invest in trades as he does now, maybe even give Lord Harlow a spot of advice every so often. He'd make sure not to let Isabel down, he would dress in satin britches and buckled shoes from the finest French cobblers, get himself a long-bobbed wig and a hat with a Denmark cock. Rising above one's station, his father would not approve. On the other hand, he it is who wants him to find a wife. If he ever married it could only be to one person, the lovely Isabel. All of a sudden he craves the idea of marriage, of having someone to share his life with. For sure, it is the most unnatural of things to live alone.

At home he finds that a letter has been pushed under the door of his apartment. His hands shake.

'Mr Harry Walsh,' it says, 'My Jupiter. Wait for me, won't you? I have plans, so many plans, I will tell you about them soon.' The note is written in an elegant hand, and he is certain he can smell a waft of her scent off it. Straight away he finds a boy in the street and sends him to Piccadilly with a coin and a note, hastily written, that says, 'Jupiter vaits, you wixen.'

Two days later another note comes.

'Jupiter,' she writes, 'We leave for the country on the morrow. I pine for you, my beloved.' Oh to be called her beloved. 'How I long for you, how I hate the marquis, he is cold, he is a Mr Tattle with time only for cards. You will vait for your little wixen?' she pleads. Immediately, he replies; it is urgent, for his note must arrive before she leaves, poor darling, for a dismal month on the Harlow country estate. On account of his difficulty with writing, all the note says is:

'I will, my dearest.'

Harry watches as his small messenger darts between the coaches down to Piccadilly. He begins to feel like a proverbial worm writhing on a hook. Unable to bear the isolation of his room, he turns into the Fox's Paw which is crowded with the usual set of swells, showing off their duds. In the corner a young City clerk, Edmund by name, sits on his own. Harry sees him there often. He is Marcel's landlord, so Tiberius tells him. When Marcel approaches he has a strong desire to indulge himself by voicing Isabel's name.

''Aree, what is eet I get you?' Marcel's accent travels from Paris to Shoreditch in the space of seconds.

'A chocolate. I am in need of sustenance, I am bitten, Marcel, so in love. Isabel, it's a prime name, don't you think?'

'Ooh, ah, 'Aree, you are a notey boy.'

'This is one occasion, Marcel, when I believe I am not.' Not only is he in love with a woman, he wants to marry her. He is about to give a long description of the colour of her eyes, the soft curls round her face, the sharp inflection of her voice, when Marcel leans over.

'Edmund,' he says, 'you like eem, he is handsome, no?'

'Oh yes, decidedly so.'

Everything about Edmund, a runner for the underwriters who frequent Mr Lloyd's coffee house, is grey. Poor Marcel, he is totally deluded.

45. Trouble

Weeks pass, during which time Harry receives just one letter from Isabel saying that she is going mad, for she is scarce left alone, but that she pines for his company and dreams each day of the time they can be together. Harry bids an unsatisfactory and awkward goodbye to Handel and Peter in August, accompanying them down to the port at Harwich to see them embark for the Netherlands. He then cancels a visit to Rutland, in case Isabel should suddenly decide to come back to London, much to the annoyance of his fubsey. When he goes round to Great Ormond Street, to explain, he blurts out his hopes to her and she puts her head back and barks with laughter.

'The Harlows,' she snorts. 'Whigs! Harry, dearest, people like that, they have hearts of ice. They mix with the hoi polloi when they need them in order to increase their wealth, which they do by such means as transporting slaves and coal. You can be damn sure that, in their drawing rooms, they mix only with their own. This Whig Parliament, what does it do? It passes no laws except those that help their friends - merchants, traders and bankers. Why, it has even trumped up a war against Spain, not to serve some moral purpose, but because the Parliament men resent our shippers in the West Indies having to pay dues to a foreign power.'

'Dearest, I am so sorry to have upset you.'

She stops her tirade, which shocks Harry for its vehemence, and takes pity on him because he looks worried and forlorn.

'You think I am presumptuous because she is so above me in rank,' he sighs.

'Not that, you poor boy. I'll tell you something about myself, you might as well hear it from me rather than someone else. My father was a foreman in a glassworks. The earl happened to be the owner, he made his money from the fact that much of his farmland was on the edge of Birmingham and the town had a need to expand. We've travelled far, me and him. He liked me because I had spirit, and I liked him because he's a gentleman.'

Harry embraces her for taking him into her confidence. He nestles his head in her bosom, letting shiny brown curls spread across her cleavage. He secretly takes hope from what she says. He most certainly admires Isabel for her spirit; does she see in him the makings of a gentleman? Harry does not confide to his dearest fubsey that the past few weeks have felt unbearably lonely in his spacious and lofty apartment. The only person who, it seems, is not away or planning to leave the metropolis, is Timon.

When Timon has the time, he comes up the stairs and adds to his mural. It now has a group of clean-shaven, strong-jawed citizens in white togas, buying fruit, all looking like Tiberius. A group of ladies take their leisure under silken awnings, held by Negro slaves. The stone pavement stretches to an infinity of hills and scrubland. Sometimes Harry feels as if he is on that pavement, walking into a distant haze, not sure where he is going.

In mid-August, Harry hears from Isabel again. In her letter she promises she will find a way of meeting, on her return, in September. She pleads with Harry to come and abduct her which is the last thing he wishes to do. Again, she refers to herself, strangely, as his little 'wixen'.

In vain does he wait to hear from her once September is upon them. Each day his hopes become, progressively, more like some fantastical delusion. He is busy enough at the playhouses, thanks to Garrick and Rich, but the sense of isolation in his apartment increases. His singing classes resume, but often he chooses to give them in Hogarth's studio in St Martin's Lane.

It is October when Isabel writes, at last, to say she is back in town. His 'wixen', she swears, loathes the marquis more than anyone in the world, so much so that she plans telling her parents, outright, that to marry him will kill her. Taking heart from her words, on a whim, Harry takes himself to Piccadilly one Friday afternoon. He sits by the window of Gloucester's Chocolate House, which is conveniently opposite the Harlow mansion. For over an hour he reads The Spectator from cover to cover, The Craftsman and then The Grub Street Journal. He drinks five cups of tea, a beverage he likes only in moderation, and looks out at the blank gaze of the windows glinting in the autumn sunshine opposite.

Coaches and carts arrive at the courtyard to the front of the house, but all they contain is quantities of stuff that is taken in boxes indoors by menials dressed in long aprons. Neither Lord Harlow, nor any member of his family, emerges. Eventually, Harry gives up his vigil, for the following day he has some fatuous wedding to sing at, in St George's, and must get prepared.

As it is a Friday, and the theatres are dark, in the evening he goes to the rectory so that he can share a modest fare of fish with his father. At dinner, Doctor Walsh tries to make conversation, for he takes delight in Harry's new habit of familiarising himself with the news. Admiral Vernon, he tells his son, the bully cock who beat the Spaniards at Porto Bello, has received the Freedom of the City this day; he saw the Lord Mayor's coach make its way to the procession as he walked to his church.

'The Battle of Porto Bello may have been a victory,' he says, between mouthfuls of haddock, 'but it marked the end of our many years of peace. I am concerned that Admiral Vernon plans to attack the Spanish again.'

'Old Grog Vernon's the type what can't keep his bone box shut, I'm sure he won't provoke another bout of conflict.'

'You see, Harry, I am not persuaded of the rightness of our nation's cause.'

'Not paying the bull fighters their excise, you mean?'

'As you know, I find every aspect of slavery disquieting. Should we really be supporting the slavers, that's what I'm asking - it's not so much the unpaid duties to the Spanish.'

'It's a repugnant activity, to be sure, but the slaves harvest sugar and we all have a taste for that.' Harry has not told his father that he has investments in the sugar trade and that these now amount to 1600 guineas.

'You sound like a cynic, my son. We all lived perfectly well without sugar. I, for one, intend to have nothing in this house that comes from the labour of slaves.'

The following day Harry walks to St George's in Hanover Square rather than taking a chair. He is standing in for Jonny who has troubles to contend with over his wife, poor Lady Henrietta. The Herberts, so Jonny assures him, are landed rogues. They are determined to take little Bridget from Henrietta, the daughter she had from her union with young Herbert, on the grounds that Jonny may not allow her to practice her Catholic faith. As Harry sits in the choir stalls, waiting to do the opening solo, he wonders, as he does twenty times a day, where his Isabel is. The organ reaches a crescendo then quietens. As it plays the opening bars of Scarlatti's Caro e dolce, Harry plants himself between the choir stalls looking down the aisle; the music is in his hand although he knows the words well.

The west door opens. Coming towards him, lightly veiled and dressed in ivory, is Isabel on the arm of her father. The marquis is standing with his best man at the step between the aisle and the chancel, Harry feels foolish not to have recognised him; he notices his features looking set and grim. Harry hardly knows what he's singing, his face flushes with anger. He despises his own self-deception, but he also feels that the veiled figure, coming steadily towards him, deceived him too. Her letters and notes, they were misleading. As she relays her vows he can see her looking at him but he cannot read her expression. The marquis looks miserable, Lord Harlow looks bored. When the nuptials are complete, and the couple process pass the choir into the vestry, to sign the book, Harry creeps round to where the organist is sitting.

'I'm going,' he whispers.

'You can't, you have an Ave Maria to sing when they come out,' the organist hisses.

'I know but I'm not going to. Just play this piece again, no-one will notice.' The organist looks scandalised and goes painfully sharp.

If I had more style, Harry thinks, I would run down the central aisle and shout obscenities, that would give the congregation something to remember. But instead, he leaves discreetly down a side aisle, his head down. On the street he starts to run, he wants to howl. Not knowing what to do, he makes his way to Cavendish Square and pounds on Timon's door. Tiberius opens it.

'Timon, I must see Timon.'

'He's not in.'

'Where is he?'

'I am not in a position to say.' Tiberius' manner is cold for he resents Harry for ignoring him, not succumbing to his harlot charms.

'Damn you for your stupid secrets, tell me where he has gone.'

'To Simeon's office, that is all I can tell you. He needs to find Simeon.'

'Oh, so he's there. I suppose he invests in the Voyager as well.'

'You seem to know much about it.'

'I'm an investor too.'

'I am sorry, Harry, I didn't realise you were going to be affected. I suppose you have read Lloyd's List today. '

'Affected, how do you mean?'

'The Voyager, it's gone down, no survivors, everything is lost.'

'The cargo, lost, the brandy?'

'It wasn't carrying brandy.'

'Damn you for contradicting me. What was it carrying?'

'Slaves.'

46. The Dining Room at the Rectory

Even though Harry is gloomy, he notices the pleasing shadows the candles are throwing across the panelled walls. At the far end of the room, holding pride of place, is the gift he gave his father, several years back, which he'd bought as soon as he had funds to spare. It is a print, by Hogarth, depicting worshippers leaving the Huguenot church which Peter's uncle happens to go to; as they do, their overstuffed offspring look on at the street boys playing in the mire. The print will hold its value, he'd explained proudly, when he gave it to his parent, for Hogarth is ever the businessman. He had pressed Parliament into passing a Copyright Act in order to protect his works from pirates and copyists. Hogarth is certainly more sensible than I am, thinks Harry.

The lease on Cavendish Square has been returned, the deposit forgone, and his few belongings moved out. He has agreed with the gold merchants to put all his future earnings aside. It will be years before he can repay the sums he owes, which include a hefty rate of interest. Curious, how savings tend to remain static while debts balloon so. To return to living with his father is a hindrance to his liberty although, he has to admit, he was wanting company in his airy garret. The heavy chimes of St Paul's, that used to keep him awake at night, the early calls of the night soil men, and the shouts of the hawkers all day, that once vexed him, are pleasingly reassuring to him now.

To feel poor again weighs heavily. He thinks, briefly, of the jewellery sitting in his bedside drawer which Timon used to give him when they first met. Maybe he should pawn it, although Timon may want it back. His friend has lost money but, being more worldly than Harry, he was insured against his losses. If only he had discussed his activities with Lord M, he would, no doubt, have been advised on how the practice of insurance works.

He stabs his meat as he brings to mind the new suit, that will now have to go to the popshop, and the wonderfully ornate bed that he will never be able to collect from the carpenter. Lucy, he reflects, with just a touch of envy, has become rich, for her father, the duke, has made her the chief beneficiary in his will. If Harry asked her to lend him money, she would readily assent, but his pride prevents him from doing so. All of a sudden he understands, so much better, the pain that Handel must have experienced these last two years when so many of his entertainments failed to make money. Some say he is near bankrupt although Harry would never press Peter to tell him if this was so. The thought strikes him that, while one is happy to trumpet one's wealth, debt is an intensely private matter; acknowledgement or discussion of it is unwelcome.

Harry looks across the table at his father and wonders if he has any inkling of why his son has returned to the rectory. He had some old cuff in church this day, a visiting preacher, raising money for the Society for the Propagation of the Bible in Foreign Parts. He'd described to the congregation, in repulsive detail, the conditions in which the slaves were shipped from the West Africa coast to the Carib Seas. They were forced to lie beneath the decks, naked and chained, wallowing in their own filth, itching unbearably from smallpox. On hearing this, Harry's bitterness towards Simeon increased, no longer because he used other people's money to finance his adventures, but because he involved them in a trade that Harry had learnt this day was utterly barbaric. His rumination leads him to the next source of bitterness, Isabel's latest note that sits in his pocket.

'Jupiter, what were you doing running away from your little wixen? Did it not delight you that you and I shared a secret while everyone around us was so solemn? Now that this tiresome marriage ceremony is over with we can meet in my coach, whenever we like, for the dear marquis hardly cares how I spend my time.' Rantum scantum. Was it so wrong of her, that all she thought was that he would enjoy grafting her husband as much as she would? Harry thinks of the character of Semele; Handel has her standing in front of the mirror singing "Myself I do adore". Is there no manner of personality that he does not understand?

'So what was Cliveden like? You must tell me all about it,' says Doctor Walsh. Harry realises that he is being poor company and that he must do his best not to mope. He also realises that he is filled with a longing to see Peter, to feel his loving hands, to welcome him back. He must be due now, any time, from the Netherlands.

'Cliveden was surprisingly homely,' Harry says. 'The Prince of Wales, he is charming. Next to the canes in the hall-stand was a cricket bat. He captains for Surrey. Princess Augusta, she is severe and very German.'

'Was the little boy there?'

'George? Yes, with his nursemaid. What a solemn fellow. Although he is a baby still his face looked grave throughout Arne's masque. But when I sang a tub-thumping air, called Rule Britannia, he waved his hands as if conducting.'

'You always said you would become a successful singer. Now that you are performing in the private drawing room of the Prince of Wales, I believe you are.' Doctor Walsh looks up as Samuel enters with the sole, puts one soup dish on top of the other, and passes them to his old retainer.

'Yes, at least I have fulfilled one half of the promise I made to you as a young man.'

'And will you be presenting Arne's masque on the London stage?'

'Alfred? Possibly, he is in talks with Mr Rich.'

'Thank you, Samuel, you can clear the rest tomorrow.' Old

Samuel places on the sideboard Doctor Walsh's favourite, a hasty pudding, then retreats, his limping footfall receding down the stone corridor. When the reverend is sure that they are alone he stretches out long white fingers, his scribe's hand, across the table. Harry realises that he is about to receive a lecture but he takes the old man's hand in his and looks at him with love.

'Son,' his father begins awkwardly, 'you were out again until the early hours this morning.'

'Papa, I am twenty four, I am used to doing as I please.'

'I know, I know, forgive the fretting of someone who is past their prime. But I am concerned. I know you did as you pleased when you lived by yourself but, now you are back, I cannot help but keep a watch on you. This is hard for me to say, and may be based on a gross misconception, but if you frequent bawdy houses, get the pox, what then of your marriage prospects?'

'Papa, the company I consort with is respectable.' He thinks of his fubsey, a libertine; of Timon, a pervert; of Susanna, a fallen woman; of Lord M's companions, courtesans. Yet all of them to his mind are honest. The prigger, the rook, is Simeon, who took other people's money but never shared in the risks, who could tolerate the thought of transporting fellow human beings, and allowing them to be shackled, beaten and starved.

'It embarrasses me that I have no idea where you are. That nice young man, Handel's assistant, he came round last night.'

'Peter is back from abroad?'

'Yes, Peter, that's his name. He waited so long I had to explain in the end that I had need of my bed. After that, I believe, he waited outside.'

'Peter was looking for me?'

'Yes, I asked him to leave you a message, but he said there was none.'

While Peter was waiting for him Harry had been rolling round satin sheets with the two rosebuds who Lord M kept in St Clement Danes. It was a risk, to go to them without their protector, but he needed to forget the ache in his heart. How happy he would have been had he known Peter was back.

As he climbs into bed, of one thing he is certain. Peter will be hurt and angry. His wasted visit to their house the previous night, he cannot help thinking, foretells disaster.

1741

47. Anthony Remembers

Tears and recriminations Harry had expected; having to rock Peter on the bed at Nanette's, promising him that he would never stray again, accepting to meet only when he could spare the time and being grateful for it. All that he was prepared for. What he did not expect was a wall of silence. At the theatre, Harry found, Peter had an ability to appear, then evaporate; if they passed each other in a corridor or in the foyer, he said nothing. Harry became consumed with a need to break Peter's silence. Regret, guilt and gloom, he thought, put that in your pipe, Mr Rich, turn that into one of your little mimes.

One day he hears the calamitous news that Sid has been trampled to death by a horse. Peter, he knows, will be distraught and badly in need of comfort. Determined to track him down, Harry knocks on the door at King Street, in the hope of finding him there, for he knows he visits his mother when Handel does not need him. Nanette gives a shout of surprise and Harry bows deeply.

'Ah, what a nymph you are today, a vision from some Elysian glade.' She is holding a broom and is dressed in her old work clothes.

'Come in, come in, I have a visitor.' For a moment Harry's hopes are raised. But it is only Anthony, who sits, looking out of place among the Turkey rugs, in one of the armchairs in her back parlour. Beside him the fire is lit. On the mantle above it is a row of blue china dancers in Breton headdresses holding out their aprons. Arne would most certainly have admired them for their rusticity. The old man half rises.

'Master Harry, how pleasant to see you. My time is free so I thought I would pay my sister a visit.'

And bore her to death, thinks Harry, knowing that he is being uncharitable.

'So Handel has no need of you,' he says jovially.

'It seems like it. Peter really runs the household now.'

'You look well, Sir.' He looks decrepit. Harry tries to work out his age and decides that, even though he is just over fifty, he is well on his way to becoming a relic. He scratches around for a topic of conversation, while Anthony pokes the fire.

'So, did your master enjoy the Netherlands? A fine place, I gather, cleaner than London.'

'You wouldn't see the dunghills that you do here in London, that's very true. Least, you didn't when I was there. The truth is, though, I haven't been since before Peter joined the household.'

'Tell me, Sir, when was that, a long time ago?'

'A long time ago,' says Nanette. 'Tell him about your first meeting with him, Brother. I will be back in five minutes, I have a dress I must deliver.' She winks at Harry and he scowls back at her. Nanette will be in his debt for this.

'I have to say, that when I first came across him, it wasn't what you'd call auspicious. I had this note, see, from Nanette, who I hadn't seen for ten years. I really didn't want to meet up with her if I'm honest. When I eventually tracked her down, I wasn't too surprised to find her dangling upside down from a tightrope with a dwarf below her.'

'Attila,' says Harry. 'Jonny Beard and I think it very droll to tip our hats and go, "Ahoy there Captain", as we leave the theatre, because he looks like a pirate.'

'No, he was never a pirate, least I don't think so. She was ever so light, with her little acrobat's feet, Nanette. She still had an accent about her. Once our parents moved to Spitalfields I'd lived in London. But my sister ran off back to Paris. She had with her a Bavarian juggler who used to perform outside the theatre at Lincoln's Inn Fields. The two of them joined a troupe of travelling entertainers.'

Had the man stayed long enough to become Peter's father? A

Bavarian juggler. Suitably exotic. Anthony's drone is devoid of colour or cadence.

'I won't tell a lie, I rather hoped that I'd seen the last of her, living as I did in a respectable household. It was unfortunate, as far as I was concerned, that she'd found her way back to London. She was camping out in a field next to the New Spring Gardens at Vauxhall. It was a most disreputable place, needless to say. That was before Mr Tyers took over the gardens and made them so famous.'

'Mr Tyers is a mint of energy.'

'He is that. So the first thing I asked her, Master Harry, was how is it that you managed to find me? You know, how had Nanette tracked me down. "Everyone knows your employer's at the King's every day with his trolls and mollies from the opera," she answers, "that's why I left a message there."

'The wretch of a doorman had handed Nanette's note to me, he was looking for a tip.

'"Nice bit work she is," he'd wheezed. "Well done mate, figure like a fairy."

'"She's my sister," I told him.

'"Oh yeh, course she is."

'So, next thing, I'm saying to Nanette, "No and no again, I simply can't take responsibility for your son, Handel hardly needs some itinerant from a travelling circus."

'"You make him sound like one of his bleeding eunuchs," she said. Nanette could be coarse at times. Attila, I could tell, was laughing 'cos his earrings jangled.'

'What was he like when you met him?' Harry asks. He is enjoying finding out about Peter's background. At the same time the teacher in him wants to say to Anthony, "Lift your head, loosen your jaw, project".

'Dishevelled and speechless, that's what he was like. His feet were bare and he smelt of horses. Under his breath he was counting. You're laughing, Master Harry. It seems unkind to describe him like this but he really was a sight.'

'So you relented, allowed him to work for you?'

'Not exactly. Next day, after dinner, when I was polishing shoes in the kitchen at Brook Street, he came round. Music was wafting down the stairs from the parlour. Sometimes the master would have Johann Christoph round, such a gent he is, as is his son, and the organist fellow, Mr Rosengarve. They were playing together that night. It was a liberation for the master to live in his own home and enjoy such simple pleasures. Before, he'd always been the guest of one nobleman or another. He wasn't a great man for the bended knee.'

'Particularly in regard to musicians and clerics, I've noticed.'

'Peter was nervous, he was shaking and looked wet, he'd been caught in a shower. He liked the sound of the music, though, it seemed to calm him. Then the master called down. "You have company, Anthony? Bring your visitor up, we need an audience."

'This I was reluctant to do. Peter was only ten at the time, his face looked pale and girl-like. In other words, he was a bit of an oddity. He mounted the stairs, unsure of himself, and stood stock still in the doorway.'

Harry, knowing Brook Street, can picture the scene.

'Eventually, the master spoke. "So, Anthony, this is your nephew, is he seeking work? Do you need an assistant, someone to look after the dressing room, to collect manuscripts from the publisher? You decide, as you know, I am too preoccupied with the opera." I tried to say something but the music, at that point, resumed and everyone, including Peter, was ignoring me. His face in repose was slightly less abject, the trembling, thank goodness, had stopped. For some extraordinary reason, I just couldn't think why, the master seemed to like him.'

Harry recalls the first time he saw Peter at the Abbey. He was still diffident then, still shy, but graceful, like his juggler father or his acrobat mother. Maybe Peter aroused protective feelings in his employer just as he did in Harry. This silly game he is playing, of pretending Harry doesn't exist, he wishes it would cease.

48. The Theatre at the Lincoln's Inn Fields

'What's that boy doing?' Harry asks Jonny as they walk down the Strand.

'It looks like he's tearing down posters. They're our posters, damn it.'

They race after the little cull.

'Explain your business you grubshite.' There on the ground are the remnants of Handel's printed programme for the season.

'Spare me, Guv, the bum traps are closing in, me sisters n' bruvvers are gut foundered 'cos there's so little food, we all are.'

'Who asked you to do this?' Jonny's jovial features have become dark and red.

'Some auld gentry Gill, she offer me money to do this so I tiksit.'

'It's that fussock, Lady Brown, I'll be bound.'

'How much did she pay you?' Jonny asks. They immediately put their hands in their pockets and double the sum so that the boy will leave the posters alone. He's shaking with fear and hurries away.

'Poor little flat.'

'I was passing the King's yesterday,' Jonny sighs. 'Had to pick up a score from that revolting doorman. He said that Strada's husband was suing Handel for unpaid fees. "Ware hawk the shoulder clappers," he cackled.'

'At least singing at Lincoln Inn means we don't have to consort daily with that hog-grubber.'

'Yes, I suppose that's one advantage of being banished to such a flea hole.'

'Seen Peter recently?'

'That's what the doorman asked. "Where's the bleached mort, then?" If I think about it,' says Jonny, 'Peter's become rather elusive. He doesn't seem to follow Handel round as he used to.'

Harry wishes so much to divulge to his friend the rift that has developed between them. But how could Jonny understand; he is loyal, uxorious, monogamous. Not a wanton, thinks Harry, as he forms a fist and bangs the railings. Jonny puts his arm round his friend's shoulder.

'I know. I'm cross as well. That ghastly old hag, Lady Brown. Did you know, she's taken to holding assemblies on Handel's first nights, just to entice people away. Oh for the queen, she was loyal.'

'While the king isn't. Too busy capering round Hanover.'

'It seems London's love affair with the opera is over.'

To add to the gloom, Jonny reverts to a subject he is much taken up with, the opprobrium and gossip that has been generated by his marriage.

'I wish Anglicans didn't treat Henrietta's Catholicism as an affront to decency,' he says.

'Her father, I gather, has renounced his Catholicism for the sake of an earldom,' Harry comments.

'What an unprincipled jackass he is. He hates me for being an entertainer. Now the old gorger has cut Henrietta out of his will.'

While Harry listens to Jonny's retelling of this tale of family fealty his thoughts are far away. Does Handel treat him with the same warmth as he used to? He is convinced that he and Peter exchange looks between them when he is in their vicinity. He is also convinced that Handel has become more possessive towards his secretary. Does this possessiveness amount to jealousy, jealousy for anyone who Peter feels affection for? For his life as a composer to continue running steady and firm, like the working of a clock, he has need of Peter. Without him, Handel cannot be Handel. Why even decrepit old Anthony ceases to be of consequence.

As they pass Lockets they see an arm waving through the lattice. It is Johann Christoph, in the company of Caspar. They go inside, wait until the two men are ready to progress to the

Lincoln's Inn Theatre, then walk four abreast along the Strand.

'Don't you mousle me,' mutters a heavily laden hawker as Harry knocks his yoke of swinging pewter mugs.

'Johann Christoph, Casper, tell me something,' asks Jonny. 'You two should know better than anyone. Do you think Handel will pack his bags one day, return to Germany? He's being treated so shamefully by London society.'

Harry can feel fear fluttering in his gut. Maybe that is why Peter will not talk to him; he is leaving London. The thought had never crossed his mind before.

'You mean, will he return to Herrenhausen?' asks Johann Christoph.

'I suppose I do.'

A rider pushes his horse between Harry and his companions at that moment. He does not hear Johann Christoph's next words but then Casper says, 'Das ist richtig. No social mixing like you have here wiz your cricket pitches and coffee houses. Business and commerce first, not class. Yah?' Jonny laughs.

'Herrenhausen, it is a different world, I don't think it possible for people here to understand,' says Johann Christoph. 'Among the nobility alone there are ten classes: princes are in the first class and a field marshal in the second.'

'Yes, then there are working privy councillors, generals of the cavalry, generals of the infantry, the high chamberlain, high marshals of the court, high masters of the horse, the secretaries and pages.'

'You miss out the Hofjunkers, Caspar.'

'Yah, land owners.'

'And where are musicians?' Harry asks.

'At the very bottom.' Johann Christoph chuckles. 'So, now I answer your question, John. No, Handel, he will not be going back to Hanover.'

Harry's relief is immense. He stops at a brazier and insists on buying paper twists of roasted chestnuts for everyone. Despite his dislike of letter-writing, he decides to write to Peter, to beg him on bended knee to forgive him.

49. The Dublin Rebuff

Doctor Walsh has gone to Essex and Harry is in retreat from St Bartholomew's Fair. Jonny sits opposite him at Button's, Arne beside him. The trumpeter, Valentine, with his big flappy ears, waves at them from further down the aisle. He is toping with Mr Rich's clown. The wretch of a waiter, his eyes seeping and nose running, takes their order.

'I hate those Herberts,' Jonny says. 'They are threatening to take Henrietta to court in order to get custody of Bridget. I cannot countenance the fact that she is the butt of gossip in every drawing room.'

'I don't envy you, how my sister suffered. Cibber's antics occupied the idle duds for months, he turned the law courts into a bear garden, the news sheets crowed like cocks.'

'Poor Susanna,' Harry says. He knows that Arne is a devoted brother. Despite his yearnings of the previous year, he is lucky, he realises, never to have got married. It is an undertaking that is full of risk. He thinks of Isabel and the contempt in which she holds her marquis. No doubt some other lamebrain has taken his place as the object of her fancy.

'Susanna is wilting. She intends to move abroad to get work,' says Arne.

'Where to?' Harry asks. 'To the Continent?'

'No, Dublin, the theatres there are always busy and they don't care that her household is not a virtuous one.'

'Is that why Handel is planning to go as well?' Jonny asks.

'Who knows?' Arne answers. 'He is up all night for the present time, so Peter tells me, composing another of his oratorios, in readiness for his visit. He thinks it will be his greatest yet.'

Harry tries to stop himself from choking. Once he becomes calmer, he asks casually, 'How firm is this plan, that he goes to

Dublin?'

'Well, you surely know as much as I. The Lord Lieutenant has invited him and he seems mighty keen. The soprano, Avolio, is to go with him, he's been communicating with Dubourg, head of music at the Castle there. I've told him I can't go because of the court case with Henrietta. What have you decided to do?'

'I'm still thinking about it,' Harry lies. To go to Dublin would be so perfect; it would free him of the bitterness and regret that envelops his life here in London; every street, it seems, has reason to prompt within him unpleasant recollections. Away from London, he and Peter would surely reconcile. Going to Dublin might enable him to increase his earnings and pay off his debts.

When it is time to go Harry trudges across the Piazza and enters St Paul's Church. He walks down the echoing aisle, aware of the fact that the verger is padding around somewhere near the altar. He takes off his hat but puts his head down in case the verger sees him. His heart burns like a coal in his breast. His whole body feels weighed down, heavy in the knowledge that he will not go to Dublin, that he has been passed over. We artists, he thinks, as he falls to his knees and wonders if the good Lord is looking down on him, our experience of rejection is so intense. Handel's slight stabs him like a knife. He is overcome by a sense of utter worthlessness. When the news spreads that Handel intends to go to Dublin, that august outpost of the Empire, and maybe even hold the debut of his latest oratorio there, how will Harry explain to his friends, his rivals, to his father, that he has not been invited?

50. The Fight with Peter

Peter is making his way down Kingsgate Street towards the Lincoln's Inn Fields when Harry comes across him.

'Peter,' he says. 'For goodness sake, stop, I know you are angry but please, give me a chance to explain myself.'

'What is it you want?' he asks coldly. The man can most certainly sustain a sulk.

'What do I want? To be friends of course. I miss you.'

'It's too late to say that.'

'I think you treat me ill.' Harry can feel anger rise up within him. Why should it be Peter who holds a grudge when it is himself, who, over the years, was always kept waiting until Peter was able to spare a few moments? Was it any wonder that Harry sought diversions elsewhere?

'I wrote to you but you never answered. Why is it that you continue to cut me?' Harry's voice is slightly higher than he would wish it.

'If I "cut" you, as accused, it is because you have no further need of my company.'

'That's not true.'

'I think it is.'

'And is that why you have even managed to turn Handel against me?'

'In what way have I done that?' He narrows his eyes.

'That's right, play the innocent,' Harry snarls. 'You know full well what you've done. You've stopped him from inviting me to Dublin.' Harry's voice sounds so menacing that a dell with a basket of fish on her head steps neatly away from them to the other side of the thoroughfare.

'Oh, it's always your way,' says Peter bitterly, 'to miss the point or to get the wrong end of the stick.'

'Is it now? We all know how dammed possessive your beloved employer is about you. Oh, I can't have Harry in Dublin, he'll take my beloved Peter away.' His voice has travelled up an octave causing two labourers, shoring up a tumbledown doorway, to look up and jeer.

Peter makes a theatrical laughing sound, his voice beginning to sound no less hysterical than Harry's.

'But, of course, I'm forgetting, you're a singer. It's always got to be about the singer. He has to be centre stage, doesn't he? Oh dear me, there's a draught, created for the sole purpose of hurting my poor little throat. Oh ah, that note's too high, it must be the composer trying to kill me. Oh mercy, Handel isn't inviting me to Dublin, that's because someone is better than me, someone he prefers. I'm dying, help everyone, gasp. My voice, it's such a delicate instrument.' Peter clutches at his throat and falls about.

'Stop your silly sarcasm. Have you any idea of how much it hurt me, not being invited?'

'And have you any idea of the real reason why he didn't invite you?' Two Jewish barkers pass with a cart full of rags. They stop, briefly, to see if the men are to come to blows. 'Money, you idiot. He's run out of money. Can you imagine what that feels like to him?' Peter grips Harry's arm painfully and thrusts his face forward. 'To be owing people money?' The barkers move on, disappointed.

'Don't give me a lecture,' Harry growls through his teeth. He wants to sneer that he knows full well about problems with money.

'London's turned against him. It's let him down.'

'Fuck me if you aren't going to start giving a lecture on flax and soil.'

'What the hell are you talking about?' Peter hisses.

'The fact that you just can't face the truth, that's what I'm talking about. And your diary, by the way,' now he wishes to hurt him, anger seeps out of him like liquid decay from a dung heap. 'You had no right to write about us, to put my name in print. I've burnt it.' Harry is rubbing his arm where Peter gripped it. His adversary looks at him, wide-eyed.

'Why, you're still just the same little shit you were when you were young. You're spiteful, full of yourself, and so, so stupid.' Peter is almost spitting.

Harry turns to run down Kingsgate but Peter catches his arm

then takes a swing at his opponent. His fine cheek bones have blotches of red on them. Harry puts up an arm to defend himself.

'You bilk, paillard, how dare you burn that diary,' Peter grunts as he bends down and punches Harry inexpertly in the stomach. This makes Harry's head shoot forward and he hits Peter's nose. It starts to bleed. Harry staggers backwards and lands in a puddle. The damp coldness on his backside pulls him back to his senses. Peter is crouching on the side of the pavement, holding his nose and weeping.

'You're right, I am a bastard,' Harry rasps. A ragged group of drinkers is standing outside the Blue Boar Tavern across the road and he notices them for the first time.

'Well if it ain't a couple of twaddle poops having a tiff. Fancy a wap up the windward passage?' one shouts. His companions laugh loudly, awed by their friend's wit.

Harry is immediately fearful, after this taunt, of having his brains beat out of him. But then he notices that they are all in chains. He remembers that Kingsgate is on the route from Newgate to the platforms at Tyburn. This day must be a hanging day and the dabs standing there, prisoners. The Blue Boar is where they are allowed off the wagon one last time for a final drink. Well, they've had an extra spectacle today to savour during their last moments, he thinks.

As he starts to stagger home he looks briefly round to check that the crowd across the road is not moving towards Peter as one foul body, clanking their chains. He sees that a man with three dogs has stopped and is leaning over him. It is Hogarth and his beloved pugs. He has probably been walking them in the fields at the top of the road. Harry tries to run but the damp on his trousers is clammy and his legs seem devoid of strength. He tries to steady his breathing, as he does if he feels nervous before a performance. His heart starts to ache for he realises, for sure now, that he has just lost a friend for ever. It is hard not to feel at this moment that the life he has known has come to an end.

1742

51. The Weariness of London

Nanette brings the letter from Susanna round to Hogarth's studio.

'Harry,' she says, 'you look sad. I miss them too. Come and see me, I have heard from Peter.'

How can he tell her that he looks sad because he feels so oppressed by the newspaper reports from Dublin? They are filled with accounts of Handel's successful concerts, the crowds at church when he plays the organ, his attendance at the Duke of Devonshire's receptions, and the courtship between him and every charity with a begging bowl. The latest report in the London Journal has him staying at a place called Clontarf Castle. It is owned by one Colonel Vernon, a relative of the Admiral who managed to dump Britain in the brine with his rout by the Spanish at Cartagena.

Susanna's letter chides Harry for the note he sent her which, he unwillingly agrees, was full of complaint and resentment. How small of him not to rejoice in the fact that she is working again and that Handel has disregarded convention by asking her to sing for him. It is typical that he has no interest in her private life, only in her vocal ability, the skill she has in wrenching emotion from every note.

'Dearest One,' she writes, 'it is too impossibly tedious when people are jealous of someone else's success. I know that Acis and Esther are your special shows but our dearest Harry is not with us so of course the maestro must find other singers.'

How it hurts him to read these words.

'Handel's old friend, Mathew Dubourg, who is Head of Music at the Castle,' the letter continues, 'has been scouring the drawing rooms of Polite Society and managed to flush out a surprising number who can wield an instrument. As to singers,

the maestro has been stealing whoever he can from the cathedrals' choir stalls. Dublin, believe it or not, has, not one, but two
cathedrals - so profligate. He is quite spoilt for choice. So no more
getting into one huge funk(!!!).'

Susanna's words are designed entirely with the purpose of
getting him into one. Her next sentence only makes matters
worse.

'I have exciting news. Handel's plan is that we perform a
completely new oratorio. No one, I assure you, talks of anything
else. Guess who is going to be singing one of the leads?! Some
unseen hand is guiding us, I know it, for we all get on so well.
Our preparations for "Messiah", for that's what he calls it, are
truly blessed. Peter and Johann Christoph will sell tickets from
their lodgings in Abbey Street. Miss Avolio and I have become the
best of friends. The maestro has been warned by Dubourg to be
nice which he finds very hard; when the amateur musicians make
mistakes you can see him trying to control himself. He shouted at
Mr Lamb (such a timid little man who I know is madly in love
with me) when he was just a fraction late for his entry. "Where
are you Mr Lamb, not straying I hope." The boys all shake when
he booms out "Chorus", and as to those watching as we rehearse,
they live in fear of making a sound.

'Harry, you should hear the good charitable ladies whose life
is devoted to the relief of debtors at Kilmainham Jail, they delight
at whatever we do. Even the papers can find nothing ill to say,
now that would never happen in London. As a result, your little
Susanna is happy even though the Lord Lieutenant's awful
Duchess is unbelievably high and mighty and will not countenance the presence of a fallen woman (!!!) at Dublin Castle.

'As to Handel, he is loved by everyone and believes that, in
Dublin, they have yet to banish wit and conversation from good
company. He spends hours with a music publisher, Mr Lee, on
Cork Hill, and praises the works of an ancient bard by the name
of Carolan (I think that's what he's called). Whenever he can, he

gets Maggie, the maid at his lodgings, to stand on a chair and sing a ballad called "Aileen Aroon". Peter spends many hours with Maggie [indecipherable] to the poor in the Liberties. Handel is much exercised by the possibility that he might stay with her forever and never come back to London. The same could apply to me.'

Susanna's hand is childish and her underlining random. Harry cannot bear to read further. He is surprised that Handel even allows this Maggie to talk to his beloved Peter let alone do whatever they were doing at the Liberties.

He puts the letter away and attends to his student, Matilda, the plump offspring of a cheesemonger on Cheapside. His ability to get his young ladies to express themselves in a voice that is entirely their own - all of them, it seems, want to sound like Susanna or Kitty Clive - is a matter of pride to him. Matilda's voice is decidedly her own but, sadly, off-key for much of the time. He often catches sight of the kindly old fussock, who accompanies her, wincing as she hits a wrong note.

This afternoon her chaperone sits sewing in front of an oil painting by Hogarth. It depicts a set of worthies - goodness, how the world throngs with them - who have made it their business to improve conditions at the Fleet. The needlewoman looks as if she has stepped out of the canvas and is waiting patiently for the gentlemen to cease their prating and order refreshment. Matilda blushes and stammers, when Harry compliments her, then hits the same wrong note time and again. He is so relieved, when the class is over, that to bump into Tyers, yet another worthy meddler, is a pleasure. He agrees to walk with him for a while in the hope that this will take his mind off the wearisome sense of exclusion that sits so heavily on his heart.

Harry does not tell him that he is on his way to the King's Theatre, that he is singing this season for the Italian opera, for that would be to invite a lecture. Tyers will remind him of the virtues of singing in English and tell him that Lord Middlesex, who has resuscitated the opera, is a projector with no business sense. As they stride up the Haymarket, Harry sees that there are fresh posters on every pillar and shop front. They are seeking young men to join the British Army and exhort the candidates to report to the Earl of Stair in Wapping.

'Just look at these posters, Walsh,' Tyers pronounces. 'Mr Walpole was mistaken to oppose the maintenance of a standing army at home. Our troops are badly run down, not a happy situation now that we face the prospect of being overrun by Frenchmen.'

'Frenchmen? I thought King George was fighting the Prussians. Isn't the idea to save the Empress of Austria?'

'Piffle to that young man. Saving the seat of some Austrian Archduchess, Queen, Imperial Highness or what have you - Maria Theresa has so many titles it's hard to keep up with them - is by the by, Walsh. His real aim is to curb the power of France.'

'I never realised. I am no politician.'

'It's part of a Jacobite plot, you don't have to be a politician to understand that. They want to get King James' son, the Old Pretender, onto our throne.'

'Are we in danger then?'

'Yes and no. Fortunately, despite his pious attitude at home, Walpole was financing armies abroad. I know because I have a business trading animal skins; I was supplying the boot leather for 12,000 Hessian troops, a most useful contract, it helped pay for several new pavilions at my gardens. There were a further 5,000 souls being kept on standby by the Grand Duke of Brunswick-Wolfenbuttle, the king's relation. Sadly we failed to get that contract, we didn't pay a sufficient inducement to a certain milord.' He rubs his fingers together like a Jewish money lender.

'Walpole sounds like a sensible man, I'm sorry he's hung up his spurs.'

'He had to, Walsh, he was out of step with the nation and you can't rule under those circumstances. The new nationalism, that's what I call it, we've had enough of being pushed around on the high seas and we've had enough of the Catholic kings of France taking every opportunity to unseat our good Hanoverians. It's time to fight back.'

'Some say the king meddles merely to save his lands in Hanover.'

'Utter nonsense, Walsh, all patriots know that he fights solely for the cause of Britain and that our prime enemy is France.'

'It's a great comfort to know that about the king. If you'll excuse me, Sir, I have a message I wish to give to John Swiney.' Harry decides to turn into the Three Crows simply to save himself from being seen by Tyers to enter the King's.

The first person he catches sight of is Paolo Rolli.

'Have you seen the reviews for our new opera? They are quite dreadful. Look at this.' He opens a page of the London Journal. 'Is not Britain in a fine state,' he reads, 'when, notwithstanding our taxes, we can fling away a sum on a parcel of squeaking, capering, fiddling Italians and Foreign Buffoons? Your accent is improving, Harry, they think you are a foreigner. How they hate us, these savages, these quill drivers.'

'It's the talk of war, the new nationalism,' Harry tries to tell him but he ignores him.

'Now look at this.' He produces a copy of the London Journal that has the day's date on it, April 15th. 'Words are wanting to express the exquisite delight afforded blah blah blah... the sublime, the grand and the tender adapted to the most elevated, majestic and moving words, conspiring to transport and transform the ravished heart.'

'That's better,' Harry says.

'You are missing the point, bufflehead, this review is not about us.'

'What is it about then?'

'The first performance of Handel's new work in Dublin.'

'His oratorio?'

'Yes, exactly. It's called the Messiah.'

52. At Mrs Pendleton's

Harry is walking to the Grosvenor Square in the company of Arne and John Christopher. They are on their way to Amelia Pendleton's to discuss proposals for a musical performance in her drawing room to raise money for the fund for destitute musicians. Philanthropy, Harry comments to his companions, is so much the fashion that a musician could work full time without earning a penny. Arne has been gloating over the reviews from Dublin, not surprisingly since so many of them praise his sister.

Amelia's impressive new apartment faces out towards the as-yet-uncompleted western side of the square. Far beyond it, the platforms at Tyburn are still just visible, as is a steaming heap of filth sitting in a nearby field. These sights are partially camouflaged by newly planted cherry trees to the front of the houses, the blossoms of which are a most pleasing prospect. One day, Harry ruminates, this is the kind of place I would like to live in. The wide streets are so much better than the closed courts and alleys round the City. Then, with a stab, he remembers the straightened circumstances that have forced him to return to the rectory and wonders when, if ever, he will be able to fulfil his dreams.

'Thomas, Harry, John Christopher, do come in.' Amelia Pendleton stands at the front door in person and purrs her greeting, moving up an entire octave, then back again, as she says their names. She fusses, while her liveried butler takes their coats and hats. Once she was traditional in her ways, the servants were part of the family, as in Handel's house, but, since her move, they have taken on the aspect of anonymous persons who emerge from mysterious hiding places then disappear again. The visitors are pressed to accept tea before a maid is despatched down a hidden set of stairs. She shows them up the sweep of her staircase to the first floor, for this is where the Quality like to have their drawing rooms. The furnishings, Harry notes, are bang up to the mark. Mr Pendleton, an attorney, has clearly left his widow in the lap of comfort.

'I saw you last night. I was in a first floor box,' she whispers to Harry. 'The plot was rather complicated but your singing, as ever, was a delight.'

He acknowledges her compliment with a self-deprecating twitch of the lips and murmurs something about poor reviews. The heartache that is his daily companion begins to ease. He decides to walk to the window, admire the cherry trees, savour the pleasure of being part of this gathering, sip tea from the finest porcelain, persuade himself that his singing the night before really was a delight. He even allows himself a glance at the serving girl's neat ankle. How sweet it would be to feel at peace, to be able to banish for a time the painful thought that he is so alone. His reverie comes to an end with Amelia Pendleton's next words.

'I have a surprise for you all. Anne Donovan has just appeared; she has been on the stagecoach overnight from Chester. Only two days ago she was in Dublin. Her brother is a don at Trinity.'

'Hello, one and all, yes I am back. How I survived the journey, goodness only knows, for some of the roads were barely passable.' Anne enters and sits herself down. Her panniers occupy the entire settee, her nose looks larger and redder than ever, and the ears of her dachshund, one of Nell's offspring, are barely visible as the little creature settles among the layers of her skirt. Nell herself, old and stiff, lies asleep on a satin cushion nearby.

'Anne, we are all so excited to hear your account of the Messiah. Why, the papers are full of it.'

'My sister says it was wonderful,' says Arne.

'It must have been quite an occasion,' Harry murmurs.

'Yes, we want to hear every detail,' says John Christopher.

'Well, if you insist. But where to start? What a nightmare for Handel, so much drama, Dean Swift at St Patrick's, such a tricky man to deal with.'

'Meaning what exactly, Anne?'

'Meaning, Amelia, that he is quite off his head. He objected to the Vicars-Choral being used by Handel as his soloists and the Young Gentlemen of the Choir being his chorus.'

'Handel has a history of upsetting the clergy,' Harry interjects.

'It wasn't that, Harry, it was that the Dean knows as much about music as a Muscovite.'

'But he relented in the end did he not?' says Amelia.

'Handel flattered him into doing so. He praised the quality of the voices at the cathedral, allowing the Dean to boast that, in disposing of musical employments, he acted unlike a Minister of State in giving them only to those who deserved them. "An indifferent parson may do well enough if he be honest," he said, "but singers, like their brothers, the poets, must be good or they be good at nothing".' Those listening laugh at Dean Swift's words, maybe he wasn't as muddled in the head as people thought.

'Let's hear about this oratorio,' says Amelia.

'I think it was early March, or maybe it was the middle of March, that there was an announcement in Faulkner's Journal.'

'An announcement in Faulkner's Journal?'

'Amelia, I cannot concentrate if you insist on repeating everything I say. It said that a new oratorio was to be played at the Charitable Society's Music Rooms, a charming room, I have to tell you, in which the music sounds delightfully. The proceeds were to support the poor men and women languishing in prison.'

'That's our friend, such a good man.' They all nod.

'Did my sister sing well?' asks Arne.

'Mrs Cibber sang, as always, with great feeling.' It is painful for Anne, not being able to digress, given her brother's presence, on the subject of Susanna's adultery. 'The song Handel wrote for her, He was despised and rejected, so suitable.'

'The music, it was wonderful was it not?' asks John Christopher.

'It was a mix of everything he had ever written, only better. Phelim, my manservant, said that, sure, it was a host of angels standing over him when he wrote it.' If Harry needs a critique of Handel's music he will not be looking for it from Anne Donovan although Phelim's observation is an interesting one. This does not stop her words filling him with a desire to clench his head between his hands and rock back and forth while he groans.

'Tell us then, Anne, about the first performance,' says Amelia. The room becomes silent, the lady soloist strokes the silken ears of her near-invisible dog and Nell farts quietly in the corner.

'Well, as you can imagine, the clamour for tickets was prodigious. All members of the Law Courts, of Trinity College, of the church hierarchy, of the Administration at the Castle, as well as the local gentry, were determined to be there. Sadly, the Lord Lieutenant and Lady Devonshire had already returned to London.

'It would be hard to exaggerate the excitement throughout the centre of the city when the morning of Tuesday, April thirteenth dawned. So much had been spoken about this new work, it was as if we all knew that something rather special was going to happen. People barely had time to breakfast that day, before making their way to Fishamble Street, for we had to be in our seats in good time for the twelve o'clock start to the performance.

'It was quite impossible to get a carriage to the door of the concert hall so we parked way down the quays. It seemed to us, that, even there, the activity along the river had ceased. By the time my brother and I had gained entry, the room was virtually full. The ladies had been asked to attend without their hoops, and the gentlemen without their swords, the better to accommodate a greater number of people.

'Our dear friend looked cool and composed, as always,

perched at his harpsichord, riffling through his music, the pristine white of his collar contrasting with the brown velvet and gold trim of his jacket. The violinist, Mathew Dubourg, was leading the orchestra. The musicians looked nervous, for it was not in the normal run of things that they perform in public. The younger members of the choir, there were about twenty-six of the gentlemen in all, jostled each other and had difficulty finding their places. The lady soloists looked serene. Altogether some seven hundred of us had been squeezed into a space designed for six hundred.

'The maestro at last raised his hand, the hall went completely silent, and the music began. As a tenor voice sang over and over, Comfort ye my people, and the chorus sang of the prophecy of Christ's coming, it was as if everyone had stopped breathing. When, in the second part, the choir turned to the sacrifices our Lord had made for mankind, both the men and women, sat around me and my brother, started to weep.

'It is hard for me to describe to you, dear friends, how completely engaged the audience was, how it felt to us as if only one place existed at that moment on this earth. We occupied a space, no longer physical in nature, but defined by sound.' Anne looks pensive. 'At the end of the second part, the choir burst out with a glorious Hallelujah, the beginning of a celebration of the Christian soul's victory over death. After being so downcast by rejection and persecution, our souls were now uplifted. As one Hallelujah followed another, people could not stop themselves from smiling, some even stood. Mr Lamb then did a most affecting duet with the tenor, Mr Church. The words were from the Book of Revelation, so my tiresome brother pointed out to me; like Handel, he knows his Bible.

'All of us listening, I believe, could have sat there forever. Such was our absorption that, when the solemn Amen finally came to an end, we finished as we had started, with a silence. Then the maestro rose. The room erupted.

'"Sister," my brother cried over the hubbub, "wait and see, this work will be indestructible".'

Anne becomes silent. No-one present speaks. Then Arne says, 'Do you know? I intend to join my sister in Dublin. It sounds a wonderful place. Susanna says it offers many opportunities. Come with me, Harry.'

'No, I can't,' he says.

'Why can't you? Come, I say.'

'I can't because I am obligated elsewhere. I intend to fight for our king. I am joining the army.'

53. At the Fox's Paw

Garrick bumps into Harry in Covent Garden and declares that he too intends to travel to Dublin.

'I'm going to show the Irish my Hamlet, darling, and ravish every damsel in town.'

If anything could drive Handel back to London, Harry thinks, it would be the presence, not just of Arne, but of Garrick, in Dublin. In the July, he accompanies Tom and his wife, Cecilia, with their many trunks, up to the Oxford Road, where they intend to catch the stagecoach up to Chester; from there they will take the packet across the Irish Sea. Tom is full of suppressed excitement at the prospect of seeing Susanna again, and sadness that his friend will not join them. Garrick, he learns, is ahead of them and is awaiting their arrival.

Harry is not surprised to read in the London Journal, a few weeks later, that Handel and his entourage have plans to return home. During the prodigal's prolonged absence, sentiment in London has turned in his favour, driven perhaps by guilt at subjecting him to so many libellous attacks these past few years. To think of them being back, after what will have been ten months away, fills Harry with a mix of feelings that he does not fully understand. On one thing he is clear, though; by the time Handel and Peter return, he will be gone.

Once his season at the Middlesex Opera has finished, it is with relief that he leaves behind the quarrelling of the Italian singers. Performing at the King's has enabled him to pay back what he owes to Brindley's with the interest being met by a loan from Timon. He has signed the requisite forms with the authorities in the service of the Earl of Stair but cannot help regretting having chosen such a drastic means of escape. Had he not made such a public announcement at Amelia Pendleton's, he could have forgotten his terrifying and ill-conceived plan to join the army. What pains him most is having to find some logical explanation to proffer to his poor distressed father. Doctor Walsh is, not surprisingly, astounded when Harry disguises his simple desire to flee with an uncustomary bout of patriotism.

The day before he is due to leave, having nothing better to do, and feeling both sadness and dread, Harry walks as far as the Fox's Paw, seeking company. Marcel makes a fuss of him, declaring that he must not pay for what he orders. He sends a boy round to the architects' offices, to fetch Tiberius, who promptly arrives and sits at his table. Since the debacle of the Voyager all tensions between them have been forgotten. He takes his friend's hands in his and Harry starts to weep. He blurts out the history of his relations with Peter, about his infidelity and the terrible and precipitous way in which Peter cut him. It was Handel's jealousy, he implies, that came between them, the three of them were caught in a triangle. He is surprised to hear himself also say that his love for Peter had, in any case, no future.

Tiberius, pleased at being a confidante, is polite enough not to say he is being inconsistent. Instead, he strokes Harry's hands. Such is the pall of effeminacy that Marcel has managed to effect in his coffee house that no-one around them notices. Marcel even drapes his arms round Harry's shoulders and says, 'No 'Aree, yer murst not weep because zen I der too.'

As if to demonstrate that he is not the only one with secrets, Tiberius tells Harry of his own background. His parents were poor weavers from Leicester and he was one of ten, he explains. He came to London with nothing. Timon spotted him when he worked as a labourer on one of James Gibbs' sites. He was always the first to offer to run an errand or to point out difficulties if the design didn't work.

'I was hungry,' he says, 'for fortune and success.'

'Like us all,' Harry observes. 'Now you have it, Tiberius, mind you cherish it.'

Then, because he knows how genuine Tiberius' love for Handel's music is, Harry starts to talk about the man who, since he was sixteen, has been his lodestar. He is the one person, he explains, who didn't see him as an addle pate, unable to read, he didn't deride him as the masters at school had. Again, his words, as he speaks them, strike Harry as revelatory, for he is not much given, in the normal run of things, to introspection. Secretly enjoying the way in which Tiberius hangs on his words, he describes the subtlety, the genius of Handel's music, how Alcina must be, to any discerning ear, one of his greatest works, so profound and adaptable is its shape and character.

'When I first sung in Italian, it was like walking on air. It has the power to transport, music.'

'You are right,' says Tiberius. 'The world is so full of meanness, music is as necessary as food or wine. When you talked of Brook Street, it seemed to me, to stand for enlightenment.'

'Yes,' says Harry, his sadness washing over him again, 'and now I have been excluded.'

Unlike everyone else who he's talked to, Tiberius thinks his idea to join the army is capital. His friend points out, with a giggle, that he will be surrounded by men in beautiful uniforms.

Possibly for that reason, he arrives at the rectory, in Timon's calèche, with a driver, the next day, and insists on taking him down to the boat at Wapping. When Harry wishes a tear-filled goodbye to his father and Samuel, he bids a silent thank you to

Tiberius for being with him. As they proceed to the docks, where the army ships wait, he believes that he has never felt as nervous, not even on his first day at the King's.

Once they arrive they have to push their way through the crowds of well-wishers, and protect themselves from the exhortations of the hawkers. Tiberius looks hungrily at a group of officers with shiny boots and tightly fitting breeches. He watches Harry ascend the gang-plank of the Royal. As Harry turns to say goodbye, he cannot help thinking how out of place his friend looks. The weaver's son from Leicester in his foppish attire. This last glimpse of Tiberius is a fitting goodbye to the theatrical world that has been all that he has ever known. In the coming weeks he will try to remember him but the sight of his figure, standing there amongst the huddles of weeping women and young boys, envious of their older brothers, becomes less and less clear in his mind.

Harry's new home is an overcrowded bunk room below the deck of the Royal, reeking of unwashed bodies. He does not realise it at the time but he will inhabit it for the next six months. To begin with, he retreats into silence, keeping particularly quiet about his profession as a singer. After a time his natural sociability makes him warm to the uncouth company around him. He becomes adept at cards, does his best to speak of women only with lewdness, and marvels at how the battalion of London-based Scotsmen, who have become his friends, can manage speech consisting only of obscenities and blasphemy. He even grows to tolerate the stench of tobacco smoke. After weeks of itching, a fellow soldier, Angus, inexpertly shaves off his long, lustrous curls.

'Tha's better, laddie, you doon look like some feckin drab noo.'

'More like a criminal,' says his victim.

Such is the state of disarray in the organisation of the king's troops that Harry begins to think that this is all he will do. They spend the winter on the boat, bobbing up and down on the water at Ostend. The officers become bored and very often are hardly seen by the men as they stay in their cabins and get drunk. During the day, the men disembark with their young lieutenant to learn how to march and bear arms. Harry is grateful for his sturdy build, and skills as an actor, for there is nothing, otherwise, that makes him fit for soldiering. In the evening the men line up at the dockside whore houses, or enjoy a doxy standing up against the bollards along the quay. Harry creeps into town when this happens for his usual fear of disease makes him desist from such diversions. His secret wish is that his platoon will stay on the boat for a year and that, then, the Royal will return to London.

1743

54. The Battle of Dettingen

While it is still winter, the battalions docked at Ostend are ordered to gather their things, to leave Flanders, and form a brigade with other forces that have joined them from Austria, Hanover and the Netherlands. Some 40,000 men make their way through the Ardennes then down the Rhine where King George, and further regiments from Hanover and Austria, are waiting for them. For Harry, the days of marching through countryside are, at first, an exciting relief from tedium; to be part of such a large body of men, exhilarating. But what follows are weeks, turning into months, of aching legs, sore shoulders, and an all-consuming hunger. When they reach the north side of the River Main, word spreads that the king, now in charge, is heading them towards Würzburg, a name that means nothing to Harry and the men around him. All he knows is that, at times, they are shot at by unseen bands, said to be French, and that food is getting ever scarcer.

Finding their way barred by a stream coming off the main river, one day, having marched firstly in one direction, then been told to march back, the troops take their rest on marshy ground. The river is to the south of them and wooded hills to the north. They do not know that the reason they have been turned back is because a brigade of French troops has cut them off to the east. Nor do they know that, across the river, are lines of French artillery. Further battalions of Frenchmen have already assembled to the front of them.

For Harry, the moment stays in his mind because he sees the king for the first time, sitting astride a white charger with hundreds of cavalry around him. Beside him is the young son, Cumberland. Swords clatter against stirrups, hooves make a persistent thud on the ground, bridles jangle. All is movement and noise. The king, thinks Harry, looks utterly replete as he surveys the men lying in the flat marshes around him. What must it be like to look down from a horse and see 50,000 men? The uniforms would have told His Majesty if they were Austrians, Hanoverians, Englishmen, Scots or Dutch, but otherwise, what differences were there between them? We are all equally bored, equally hungry, thinks Harry, whose stomach now dominates his thoughts. We all share the same antagonism towards each other, for the fellow with a different uniform is just another foreigner.

The froggy features of both royal highnesses seem almost to glow with self-importance. The feathers in their helmets bob and wave in the breeze, what a lark it all is. For a moment, Harry is transported back to the Chapel Royal, to the sight of the king's droopy cheeks and blank stare in the candlelight. Now, he seems happy, for a battle is inevitable.

The following day, when the cannons start booming, the men become aware for the first time of just how trapped they are. The French, it seems, have them surrounded and they have nowhere to go. Harry's platoon sees the Duke of Arenburg, the Austrian commander, pass them. He is trying to organise an enemy advance ahead of them where 20,000 of the Duc de Gramont's forces have hemmed them between the hills and the river. For hours, it seems, the men press forward then are herded back; on the left flank, guns are being fired and men are falling to the ground, some screaming as they do so.

The sound of the wounded, crying, is then replaced by a great commotion. The king's cavalry to the front, with horses snorting with excitement or fear, is being pressed backwards into the ranks of their own infantry, men are being crushed, the riders' faces look fearful and uncertain. Behind the horses, Harry sees blue coats for the first time, hacking this way and that as they come face to face with enemy foot soldiers. All around, it seems, people and horses are now shrieking or groaning, metal is clashing, but the sound of guns at least dies down. The French coming in amongst them has loused up the enemy's artillery; they can no longer fire at the king's army from across the river. Harry draws his weapon and prepares for an ignominious death, for to survive this mayhem seems impossible.

Within seconds he finds himself exactly where he has no wish to be: on the ground where he can easily be trampled. He is aware of a swelling ballooning at the back of his head. When he presses his hand to his skull it feels numb and large, almost as if it is someone else's. It is so heavy that, try as he might, he cannot move. The ground round his head is getting damp as is a patch under what he realises is his knee, a mass of gore, which he can see stick out from the shreds that remain of his britches. A blue clad figure is standing above him, his sword raised, his face contorted either with hatred or fear. Curious, the metal doesn't glint because this summer's day in Bavaria is dull. Harry had been cold and stiff when he awoke this morning. The sword comes down towards him. What a lot of dupes they've been.

'No,' he cries, then everything goes black.

55. A Farmyard in Bavaria

When Harry wakes he's not sure where he is. Straw, pleasingly warm to the touch, is tickling his bare, lacerated feet. His knee, and a gash in his thigh, throb painfully. His friend, Angus, is pressed up against him. When Harry tries to push him back he realises that he is unnaturally cold. He looks at him properly then, even though it is hard to move his aching, swollen head, and sees that Angus is dead. He looks round him. They are in a large barn, bodies lie everywhere, it is night time; some groan, some simply lie with their eyes wide open. With difficulty, he raises himself. He struggles with Angus's boots and puts them on because his feet are bare. They feel uncomfortable and ever so slightly warm still. In time, he reasons, they may save him. Unsteadily, he gets to his feet; once he stops swaying, and the wound in his head stops sending out spasms of pain, he puts his hands under Angus's armpits and drags him round the edge of the barn. The body hits supine forms as he goes. A tall man, a Netherlander, judging by his uniform, rises up in front of him and takes Angus's feet.

'He's gone.'

'Must have had the fever.'

They edge the door open and moonlight catches the solitary form of a well. There are one or two corpses lying to the right of the door already. A French guard approaches them. With a mix of spoken language and gestures he indicates that, in the morning, he'll get a group of prisoners to bury the bodies over in the far corner of the field.

'I had no wish to sleep next to a corpse,' says Harry as if it is necessary for him to explain himself.

'No, of course not,' says the Netherlander.

After a while it comes back to him, where they are and how they got there. They've already been in the barn for a few days, he is sure of that. He estimates that there are several hundred of them as he looks round. He remembers being picked up off the marshy battlefield, its turf turned into an expanse of mud, and feeling the steady rumble of a cart underneath his body. On the road, French soldiers had been pushing and chivvying those who could walk, keeping them close together like so many sheep. What had happened to their own army? It must have fled from the battle, leaving the dead and wounded. Which side, everyone wanted to know, had won? Or did they want to know? He is not sure, everything seems so uncertain.

Harry had been aware of passing a dreary little village while still on the cart, then arriving at the farmyard. The barn they were sleeping in ran the full length of one side. Along the other were outhouses and a simple cottage from which, when they'd first come, they could see the frightened faces of a peasant farmer and his children looking out at them. They would be Bavarians, allies of the French. A wooden gate was banged shut at the opening to the farmyard which any one could have climbed over. But all the men, around Harry, wanted, was to lie down, to be left in peace, better still, to die, for they were prisoners, that much was clear. Their fate, no doubt, would be to be shot.

But then, curiously, they were not. The farmer's family did not have to watch, as one by one, the prisoners were put up against the byre and executed.

Each night, subsequently, Harry relived the battle in his sleep. In his dream, a shot would ring out, flaring close to his face, then he'd look down and see his uniform hanging off him. The dream always ended in the same way, the French soldier standing over him while he tried, without success, to move. He'd hear a low noise deep inside of him, then shout "No" and wake up. On the first night the ache of his empty belly was worse than the pain of his wounds. He'd sunk into a torpor.

The following day, to everyone's surprise, an aide to the Duc de Noailles, the French Marshal, had arrived on a horse, the equal in size to the English king's. He'd come into the farmyard, inspected the barn, ordered the farmer to unlock his tools, and sent out a posse of men to dig up an early crop of potatoes from the neighbouring field. Soon fuel was organised, fires were lit and cauldrons appeared. From then on, the pattern was set. The prisoners would work together to clean and boil the potatoes then the farmer, who had a cunning, foxy face - he was being well paid, everyone surmised - would provide buttermilk and salt. Harry felt that satisfying his hunger with that first meal was better than the thrill of being on stage.

On the same day, the guards had indicated that bales of hay, stacked up one end of the barn, should be spread across the floor. One of the Hanoverian captains, Von Bothmer, had then tried to get permission from the guards to dig latrines in the field but they had refused him. He'd shouted out to the men that they should use the far corner of the farmyard as a place in which to relieve themselves, and got a group of his men to spread hay across it. The English soldiers had jeered, even though what he said was perfectly sensible; one had taken out his cock and sprayed the barn door. Being late June, the warm humidity made any smell linger just as it would on a London street.

On the day of Angus's death, once the crop of corpses is cleared from their midst and the men have taken turns to wash their faces and drink from the well, a cart arrives on which strings of preserved pig meat, a local speciality, are piled. Those who have coins are quick to buy them. Then another cart arrives, and the French guards tell the men to unload barrels of beer and lay them up in a storeroom. From then on, at every mealtime, several barrels will be taken out, making the men mildly intoxicated and helping to dull the pain of their wounds.

After the first taste of beer, as the prisoners lie about the barn, their stomachs no longer wracked with emptiness, the Hanoverians set up a deep and mournful chant. After a while Harry recognises it. It is Queen Caroline's funeral anthem, the Ways of Zion, but it is being sung in German. He moves closer to the singers and joins in. His voice is hoarse and cracked. The Hanoverians smile, then one or two of the Scots and Englishmen start to hum along with them. Harry clambers to his feet, ignoring the throbbing of his leg and the spasms in his head; as best he can, he sings Gentle Airs and Melodious Strains, from Athalia, at least half the notes are poorly tuned. A Scotsman follows him, singing a ballad called Bonny May. A Hanoverian then sings a simple hymn, Die Ganze Weit.

The farmer and his family stand at their window and the French guards cluster around the wooden gate. It is the first time that any present have been able to banish the screams, the explosions, the flying dirt and the blood of battle. They are not gay at that moment but neither are they sad. Shortly afterwards, the farmer's wife comes out with rags and a bucket of vinegar and brine. Red-faced and squinting, she seeks out Harry, pulls back the cloth from his festering wound, dabs it until it stings, then binds it.

'Ihre Stimme,' she says, 'ist es gut.'

'Your voice, it is good,' the Netherlander translates for him. The farmer's wife moves quietly with her bucket among the other wounded men but Harry, exhausted by his singing, sinks into a fever. Each time he awakes, after that, he will be conscious of the presence of his new friend, the Netherlander, who is never far away from him.

Weeks pass, and Harry regains some strength. Gorringe, his companion who has nursed him so well, sits next to him on the straw in one corner of the barn. Being the professional he is, he has rifled through Harry's pocket while he was feverish and found some coins. With them he has negotiated the purchase of schnapps from the farmer.

'We're lucky we had to fight the French,' he says, 'not the Prussians. That infantry of theirs, it's the best trained in Europe.'

'How do you know this, who told you?' Harry asks. Together with red-faced Jock, of the Royal Scottish Fusiliers, they are a threesome, taking turns to sip from the bottle. It enormously relieves the pain in Harry's leg.

'Yes, you Butter Box Dutch bastard, how the fuck do you know aboot the Prussians?' says Jock, taking a generous swig from the bottle.

'Look at my height, my bearded friend. I am tall, am I not?' says Gorringe. 'The old king of Prussia, Frederick, dear old Fritz, he formed a brigade of men on a single criterion; we all had to be tall. When my mother heard about it she sent me to the court at Potsdam, said I would make a heap load of money. As it turned out, I was barely tall enough, there were some right queer culls in that brigade but, anyway, I got in.'

'The gorger was a fucking brute I'll be bound.'

'Jock, I give him credit for one thing,' continues Gorringe. 'Unlike his son, he didn't start wars. We soldiers were just a bit of fun, a hobby if you like. He took a childlike delight in watching us march.'

'His son, King fucking Frederick of Prussia.' The mere mention of the name has Jock fumbling for the bottle. 'You're right, Froglander, he's the bastard who started this business. Not that I care a piss for the Arch fucking Duchess of Austria, I just wanted to kick the shit out of them French cunts.'

'How can you say that?' Harry groans. Jock has had his shoulder blade cracked by a bayonet yet, as long as he can dull the pain with schnapps, he doesn't seem to care. Injury has had the opposite effect on Harry, it makes him sensitive to everything. 'I'm sorry to hear he was cruel, your old employer,' he murmurs to Gorringe. The thought of the king of Prussia being some sort of twisted pervert seems to him to be a great sadness, tears are filling his eyes.

'Jock's right, his son, Frederick, is the bastard who started this business, walking into countries that didn't belong to him,' says Gorringe. 'But he's a madman, of that I'm sure. When he was young, he tried to run away from the father, to his uncle, King George of England, that was before my time. But he was caught which was bad for the prince. The father, for his punishment, made his son watch as his best friend was slowly murdered. Charming, those Prussians. For certain, that's why he became a madman.' The son, mad, the friend, murdered, how tragic, more tears.

Von Bothmer has been listening and inches towards them, his eyes fixed on the bottle. Harry passes him the schnapps, all of a sudden feeling sentimental even though the fellow's a whip-jack know-all.

'Scotsman,' he says in what is intended as a chummy observation. 'I am sorry ven I see ze French cavalry, it break your regimental lines, ze loop in Main river, it mean you haf nowhere to escape to.'

'Och aye,' says Jock, 'them loons followed us in but they didna gang oot again. We gave 'em a basting alright. And I'll tell you for why, they're a lot of fucking bobtails and gilly gaupers.'

Von Bothmer looks stumped. Jock repositions his kilted legs and, being supine, Harry catches sight of two hairy bollocks. Those alone, he thinks, would have been enough to frighten off the French cavalry.

Before Von Bothmer can continue with his discussion on military tactics, Gorringe stands, stretches his long limbs, then bids Harry to follow him to the corner of the farmyard.

'Time you did a crap, Harry, we've run out of bumfodder. You'll have to use straw, I don't want you to grubshite your britches while you sleep, like you did last night.'

'Thanks Gorringe, you're a friend, you really are.' More tears. 'Jock, don't finish the schnapps while we're gone.'

'How canny while I'm being tapped by this smous?'

'Scotsman, I am not Jew, smous is vord for Jew.'

'Hoots man, you are if you dinna provide the next fucking bottle.'

'Yah, zat is funny. You, very funny man. I haf bottle, you don't need worry. Ve drink, zen ve sing. Yah, vhen you come back, Harry, ve sing. It is gut, gut for friendship.'

They never do. By the time Harry and Gorringe come back, the French guards are among them. They are chivvying the men to pack their things. All night they march although, if it had not been for Gorringe's arm, Harry would have fallen over and been left. At dawn they emerge alongside the banks of the Main where boats are waiting to take them to their scattered homes. Harry thinks, longingly, of the barn, the warm straw, the comradeship. What did the future have in store? He does not feel ready to go home - the very term means nothing to him.

56. Return to the Rectory

Samuel is in tears, Doctor Walsh is in tears; Harry is too. They sit round the dining room table, light pooling under two brightly lit candelabra on the sideboard. Harry looks in wonder at the comfort of his surroundings, at the gentle glow of polish on the table, at Hogarth's print lurking in the shadows, at the pewter dish in which a side of beef is oozing juices.

'It was while we were on the boat, coming back up the Rhine, that we learnt that our side had won and that the king had nearly been killed when his horse was shot from under him.'

'And did you know about the agreement?' Doctor Walsh asks.

'That prisoners and wounded on both sides would be kept alive, looked after? No, we knew nothing.'

'My poor son, how frightening. God be praised that your captors stuck to this agreement. I thought, when we read about the battle, that you must be dead. I have been in mourning ever since.'

'Oh Master, when I's open the door 'n saw you standin' there, was like I'd seen a ghost.'

'Now, Samuel, don't set me off again.' The poor man cannot stop his sobs and it makes Harry cry too.

'Come to the church with me after, son, let us offer up our prayers.'

'Of course I will, Papa, it is like a prayer come true that you are waiting for me. What fortune to have this lovely home to come back to.' A noise explodes in his head. Damn the noises that trouble him so, and the bad dreams, always the same one. A pain shoots down from the back of his neck. He groans.

A hand reaches across the table as Doctor Walsh steadies him. 'There there, son.'

'My friend, Gorringe, he wanted to rejoin the fighting men. I miss him. On the journey home, the men would drink every night and make me stand on the deck and sing Rule Britannia.'

'I expect they all roared with approval. Everyone here is in love with the idea of war although the victory at the battle you fought in at Dettingen was received quietly, I have to say. Eat, Harry, eat.'

'Oh, Master, I jist can' forgit opening that door there and my surprise.'

'Samuel, tonight you eat with us, we are a family.'

'No, Master, I'm better now. There, I've dried me ol' eyes. I'll get some bread from the pantry for yis.'

As he leaves the room he lets out another howl.

'Dear me, dear me, can't seem to get a grip, I thought I'd seen a ghost.'

'What do you think you'll do, son?'

'I'm not sure. I don't even know if my voice works. Contact Arne, Jonny, Lampe, my old friends, I suppose.'

'You may have to rest a while.'

'No I can't, I must get back on my feet.'

'What about Handel?'

'I doubt if he has need of me. Did the Town embrace him when he returned from Dublin?'

'They did at first. Jonny tells me his programme consists only of oratorios now. The opera run by Lord Middlesex limps on. Go round to Brook Street, Harry.'

'No, I have no wish to.'

'He's called round a few times.'

'Round here?'

'To see if I had news of you. And when I didn't, he looked worried. Once you're ready, son, go and see him. Even if you don't sing for him again, you owe him a visit. He said he felt responsible for you going away. I can't think why.'

1744

57. Dinner With Mr and Mrs Tyers

Harry loiters around the streets then loses track of where he's going; he's so queer that, as often as not, he forgets what his business is and returns home. The noises in his head persist and tears spring to his eyes for no reason.

'Oh, Papa, I promised you once that I'd be a success and look at me.' He cannot say more, that he is the author of his undoing.

'The horror is upon you,' is all Doctor Walsh says as he shakes his head. 'Lord M, when he came round, so kind of him, explained that images of war persist in a man's head even though he be safe.'

At least this day Harry has made it as far as the New Spring Gardens. Tyers has simply refused to accept that he is not fit for company and sent his coach over the London Bridge to fetch him.

'You, Sir, are a conquering hero. You answered the king's call and you went into battle for our great nation.' His extravagant claims on Harry's behalf are an embarrassment. The gardens are closed for the winter, but the sooty fogs that envelop the City are absent and the gardens are busy with country folk in smocks, hoeing the beds, scraping the gravel paths and piling any broken tables on a large cart that will go to the carpenters.

'Hogarth, my good man, look who we have here.' Tyers calls over to the figure inspecting the bucolic scenes on the walls of the pavilions. He is in the company of his fellow artist, Francis Hayman. A young assistant, who Harry does not recognise, stands behind them.

Hogarth greets Harry warmly, and shakes his hand, which makes Harry splutter for he cannot find words of reply.

'We've missed your presence at the studio. You can use it whenever you want. There are many young ladies, I wager, who wish to learn to sing under your expert tutelage.'

'So tell me, William, Francis, what is your verdict? Which paintings need repair?' asks Tyers.

'Hopscotch and Leap Frog, most certainly. Maids a Milking is damaged in one corner but Cricket round the Village Green just needs a touch up here and there.'

'Excellent, and who is your assistant? Introduce us.'

'A student of ours, he goes by the name of Thomas Gainsborough.'

'Mr Gainsborough, Sir, you are most welcome.'

'I would like to paint that scene there, if I could,' says the young man in a tone that suggests he hails from Suffolk. He points in the direction of an elderly gardener leading a decorated carriage that is being pulled by a nanny goat. The young occupants are urging the animal to trot faster but she has been waylaid by a few late blooms in one of the flower beds.

'My grandchildren, how they love it, I had it copied from a similar contraption belonging to the Prince of Wales. It will make a charming painting. I commission you, Gainsborough, here and now, although I wish you good luck with those two boys.' Both have dismounted and are pelting each other with gravel.

'Ah, look who we have over here, replacing the lamps that have blown. You will recognise him, Harry.' A freckled face looks up and creases into a smile. The red hair is thinner, the sinewy hands hold a glass shade which he puts back on a cart. The arms enfold him, the tears start again.

'You have left the Three Crows, then?'

'It's called The Pride of Dettingen now. I owed a lot of money, Harry. I took the honourable course, I did a runner.'

'You were a sinner, John, but we have saved you.' Tyers roars with laughter. 'You could have ended up like our friend, John Rakewell, isn't that so, Hogarth? But instead of going to the Bedlam, you came here.' Tyers is almost overcome by his little joke, and it gives Harry time to recover from his weakness.

The company present is invited to make their way indoors, to dinner, but Hogarth and Hayman, with their fresh-faced assistant, are busy touching up a cow.

'Where I come from,' says the student, 'we call such beasts an Essex lion.'

'I'll join you, sure I will,' says Swiney, and Harry is grateful, for he will shield him from the excesses of Mr Tyers' good humour. Already his knees are shaking and the pain in his head is crushing his spirits.

As they return to the house, which is situated at the entrance to the gardens, Tyers greets everyone by name.

'John-Joe, I'm glad to see you are back with us, Seth, the stonework is coming up a treat, Matthew, we need new gravel here, Marcus, would you take a message to the glassworks in Vauxhall.' Harry finds his energy exhausting.

'My wife is most anxious to see you,' he explains. 'Dinner is all laid out, and it is our great pleasure to have you join us.'

The fare at the Tyers' dinner table is simple but there is plenty of it. It is served with weak beer for they are not in the habit, Harry suspects, of drinking wine. A large ham sits on the sideboard, also a plate of sliced duck and a side of beef. Several wooden platters of black bread are placed on the table, as are salvers of root vegetables with sour cream. It is too late in the season for anything leafy. The company includes Tyers' son, Jonathan, a younger, but more silent version of his father, and two young women, both sober in dress, one being the daughter-in-law, Dorothea. Mrs Tyers, overdressed in satin with a soft cleavage on full display and delightful dimples when she smiles, insists that Harry sits next to her. The name of the other young woman he misses.

'So you were a prisoner of King Louis, were you, Walsh? These gardens, you know, are most vulnerable to attack should the French ever decide to sail up the Thames.'

'My love, don't speak of such things.'

'Wife, I have to be practical, it is my job to think of such things.'

'Just imagine,' says Swiney, 'the place, full of people, enjoying their supper, the lights all lit, the waiters scurrying here and there, only to have blue coats rush in, brandishing their bayonets.' He takes a large helping of duck.

'Mr Swiney, do stop.' The dimples flash.

'You are giving me ideas, Swiney. As a businessman I have to ask myself, would a massacre in our gardens promote our interests?'

'How very messy,' says Dorothea.

'We have staff. That's what staff are for, daughter-in-law.'

'Clearing up dead bodies, picking up empty food wrappers, what's the difference?' The duck grease on Swiney's chin glistens.

'We'd have to lay on extra boats afterwards, have tours to show where the victims fell, and an exhibition of uniforms and weaponry.'

Harry looks up and makes eye contact with the unnamed girl. She smiles at him discreetly. He smiles back. All of a sudden he feels a little less shaky.

'The reason I spend so much time thinking of ways to promote ourselves is because I am what the Italians call an impresario.'

'I agree with Dorothea, though, a massacre sounds too messy,' says Swiney. 'Voices, singers, that's what you need, not just the orchestra.'

'Already in hand,' young Jonathan stammers, 'You are approaching Thomas Arne, are you not, Father?'

'I wish him to be my new Director of Music. Arne lacks the lofty grandeur of Handel, but that is of no matter, the ease and elegance of his melodies render his compositions attractive in the highest degree.'

'The hey nonny nonny brigade as I call them,' says Swiney.

Mrs Tyers giggles, the dimples appearing endearingly on each cheek. Harry smiles again across the table and is rewarded with a small play of the lips. The girl, she looks vaguely familiar.

'In honesty, do you not think that our wandering minstrel hankers after the past - all them milkmaids, rose hips, flowery meads and what-have-you, - simply because our countryside is changing so fast?' Swiney comments. Harry recalls the doleful face; it strikes him, that, had Arne been a medieval minstrel, the peasants would have locked themselves in their cabins on his approach.

'That's all the more reason for reminding people of what they're losing,' booms Tyers.

'Father-in-law, what do you know of the country?'

'Enough, Dorothea, I know enough, even though, unlike you, I don't come from Norfolk.'

'A very pleasing county, home to Mr Walpole, I gather.' Mrs Tyers is trying to counteract her husband's scorn. Young Jonathan looks pained, his father looks annoyed. It is not to his taste to have his authority questioned.

'I am hoping to sing with Arne, at a revival of one of his masques, Alfred.' These are the first words Harry has spoken. His voice sounds alien. A flash explodes in his head.

'Tell us more, Walsh.' He regrets having opened his mouth and looks down at his plate. Tears are welling up in his eyes.

'It is a fine piece, I have made fair copies of the music.' It is the girl across the table who speaks. He glances up and sees a look of concern aimed towards him. 'Yes, Thomas uses Johann Christoph's scriptorium at times. We, his devoted scribes, work all hours to clean up the autographs of his various composers, often at short notice. It is not in the way of musicians to plan, and once they are resolved to show their work to the world, they want it straight away.' Tyers roars.

'Artists, so impractical!'

'Hannah, my dear, Johann Christoph is lucky to have your services, and your dear brother, how is he?'

'He plays in Handel's orchestra now, just as my father used to.

How Philip loves to play with him, he says his greatness is unmatched.'

'He is not of the fashion but his oratorios, they are most pleasing,' says Dorothea.

'Edifying, like the sermons of Mr Wesley. And as to fashions, they change. Just wait, daughter-in-law, Handel's star is turning, and soon he will be very much the fashion again.'

'Then I for one will rejoice,' says Swiney.

The company has forgotten about Alfred, no-one is pressing Harry to say anything. He looks again at the face on the other side of the table. It is brown and wholesome, like a nut. Tawny hair catches the fading light. He hardly recognises her from all those years ago.

Hannah is staying at the Tyers' but before his coach comes round the front to collect Harry for the journey back, he finds that she is standing next to him. While Tyers issues forth like a trumpet she says quietly, 'That first time you came into our horrid cold room when Mother was so ill, you looked like a Greek God.'

'I remember it now.' He recalls the moment when Tyers, Peter and he had followed Philip to their miserable room, but the truth is that he hardly noticed her at the time.

'I will never forget the moment you entered with your flashing teeth and flowing hair.' She laughs. 'There was a peach-like bloom about your cheeks.' Said by anyone else, these words would seem forward, but coming from her they seem matter of fact.

'I'm sorry I did so little to help your family,' Harry stammers.

'But why should you have? Peter was so kind, he often visited. I'm afraid I would pester him with questions about you. Young John Christopher, he gave Philip lessons.'

'Yes, I know.'

It is time to say goodbye but, as Harry sits alone in Tyers' coach, swaying from side to side, he tells himself he is going to get better. He needs to because he has just met the woman he intends to marry.

58. St Bartholomew's Church

The choir at St Bartholomew's sits at the back of the church and the pews face inward towards the central aisle. It strikes Harry, as he looks round, lost in his thoughts, that when a grand abbey occupied the site, what is now the main body of the church must have simply been the chancel. There is a crowd this Sunday but Doctor Walsh, looking pale after sitting at his books for hours on end, sermonises for barely twenty minutes. Light from the high windows hits the ancient columns, with their bold Norman carvings, and the sound of the choir's chanting reverberates from arch to arch. When Harry sings, a great sense of peace settles on his soul. For the entirety of the service he has not been burdened by a single noise exploding in his head.

After a while he is conscious of two pairs of eyes looking across from the pews that sit immediately to the right of the choir stalls. They belong to his dear friend, Lucy, and to Hannah Krich, who, it appears, is a friend of hers as well.

'What brings you here?' Harry asks after the service.

'Your father's soup kitchen,' they laugh. 'We have been helping him for some time, did he not tell you?'

'He had no reason to. This is the first one he has held since my return.' What a fraternity these philanthropists run, why, Lucy must be involved in every good cause in London. Does the same apply to Hannah Krich? Harry is grateful that there is much to do and that, with the addition of Mrs Trebeck, who joins them shortly, the women form a group, cutting up vegetables and stirring the flummery. Hannah applies herself swiftly and quietly to her work. At one point she looks up and catches Harry's glance in her direction. She gives him a little smile. In the bitter cold, men and women come timorously through the gate, holding their bowls, pulling hungry children behind them. The sight of them makes Harry want to weep and, after he has lit the fires and piled enough wood next to them, he retreats indoors as the pains in his head make him dizzy.

His resolve to marry Hannah seems utterly futile. If he approached her, how could he tell her about his past? Not just his love for Peter, and his licentious ways, but the dreams he suffers which can only mean one thing, that he is a coward. If, instead, he lied, what sort of a marriage would that be? Further deceptions, like the ones he practiced for years with Peter, sicken him.

Quiet footsteps approach on the flags of the dining room where he is seated by the window, looking out.

'Harry, why have you not come to visit your friends? We are so relieved that you are back. I have been waiting for you to come to Hanover Square.' Lucy takes his hand and squeezes it.

'Because I am melancholy and beat about. My company is no good for anyone.' He leans over and kisses her dear, sweet face; her hand in his gives him so much comfort.

'There's a young lady who thinks very differently. She was more than usually keen to help out today.'

'I once asked you if it is best for someone you love to know everything about you, but you were not sure. I think I love Hannah Krich but I want her to know me, realise, I suppose, that I am full of flaws. That, surely, will drive her away.'

'Is one of those flaws the love you held for Peter?' she asks.

He looks at her with surprise.

'You know?'

'I was his pupil, remember. I told him about my hopes and fears. He told me about his. Forgive me, Harry, I am discreet. I do not understand it, that a man can love another, but Peter is my close friend.'

'Did he tell you how he hates me?'

'No, he didn't. I'm surprised you should think that because I don't think it's true.'

'Lucy, you know nothing.'

'Maybe not, but possibly Handel told him to stay away from you.'

'Yes, that's most certainly the case,' he says with bitterness. 'He used to come here when I was away. Checking up, I suppose, making sure I was gone.'

'Harry, please do not say such things, he is a good, wise person. Maybe he realised that one day you must find yourself a wife.'

Her words make him stop, fill him with confusion. After a pause she says quietly, 'Sometimes it is easier to write things down. Why don't you write Hannah a letter and try to explain the confusions in your mind, ask her to wait a while? She is a very determined young lady and has her sights firmly set in your direction.'

'I have no skill as a writer. I find it hard to express myself, I am slow.'

'Do you want me to help?'

Harry fetches Lucy paper, quill and ink and a blotter. She sits at the dining room table. He tries to start a sentence. He tells her not to write until he can work out in his head what he wants to say. He twists and turns and words get caught in his throat. Then he starts to dictate.

'Dear Miss Krich,

If I could I would beg you to marry me. Alas, I am a coward and a sinner who is not worthy of your attention. I feel compelled to tell you that when I was sixteen I fell in love. To me the feelings I had for the party in question seemed natural and uplifting but, to this day, I do not know if I loved this person for themselves or for the milieu they inhabited. They were gentle, quiet and sensitive and, in the end, I acted the betrayer because I discovered a taste for loose living and I thought it was possible to lead two separate lives, one that was based on consideration for others, another that consisted of instant pleasures and fleshly delights. I failed to appreciate the commodities of love and decency until they were taken away. Seeking escape, I went to war and I fought in a battle with neither courage nor bravery. God has seen fit to allow me to survive but now I am a broken string, a worthless tub, and I beg of you, forget me as soon as you can.

I am your most humble servant,

Harry Walsh.'

When Lucy stops writing, he says, 'I admit, it is not exactly what I planned to say but I think it will serve.'

'What do you want me to do with this?' she asks.

'Why, give it to her of course.'

'You are such a fool,' she says eventually. 'Hannah is a good person, Harry, she would have helped you. This is worse than saying nothing.'

'For the very first time, Lucy, I am thinking of someone other than myself. I beg you, once you both leave, let her read what I have to say.'

'Poof, it is pride. I know, Harry, because I too was rejected once by someone simply because they were too proud.'

She sighs, folds up the paper and slips it into a pocket in her skirt.

'You really are an absolute fool.'

He goes out with her then, to clean up the fire, but he does not look at the figure of Hannah for to do so pains him too much. Lucy does not look at him for she is angry.

59. Doctor Walsh is Ill

Doctor Walsh, who suffered so much when his son was away, collapses shortly after they have breakfasted. Samuel and Harry carry him upstairs. They light the fire in his bedroom, close the window because of the soot from the chimneys that sit all around them, and place his favourite Bible by his bed so that he can see it when he opens his eyes. Harry feels a sense of catastrophe enfolding him. It is several days since Lucy and Hannah were at the soup kitchen and now he regrets very strongly having driven them away. He thinks of Hannah's presence in every room of the house. Now his father, his foundation, the person who gives meaning to all he has striven to achieve, lies speechless in his bed. Harry is convinced that he will die, all because of the worry he has caused him, and that he will be left alone, not even with a place to live for the rectory goes with the living.

For twenty four hours he sits in the armchair facing his father's bed, sleeping fitfully. When the following day dawns, Samuel brings Harry a bowl of tea and shaves him. They hear knocking on the front door but Harry is too tired to go downstairs. The hall is too far away. Some poor wretch will be standing there begging for alms. But somehow Doctor Walsh has heard the knocking, and he opens his eyes and listens.

'Papa, it is Harry here, don't go to sleep again, I beg you.'

'The door,' he says. 'Someone must open the door.'

'It's a beggar. We cannot care for them just now.'

His eyes close, but the knocking continues and Harry calls down to Samuel. The house, mercifully, becomes silent again.

After some time she enters. She removes her cape, quietly and efficiently, for that is her way, wets a cloth in the bowl on the stand, and wipes Doctor Walsh's face. She taps his cheek, gently, and when he opens his eyes, she smiles.

'For a while we cannot allow you to sleep,' she says.

'It's Hannah,' he murmurs. 'The soup kitchen.'

'Good, you remember.'

'Now, Harry, help me to sit him up, we must keep him talking.'

They pat his hands, get him to answer questions and Harry even talks to him about the sounds in his head, the dreams that trouble him and make him morose. Once he starts to talk, he cannot stop; he wants to tell his father about the care that the men had for each other in the barn, the kindness of the farmer's red-faced wife. Doctor Walsh smiles and dozes and Harry is persuaded by Hannah to take himself off to rest. When he returns, his father is awake again, there is some colour to his cheeks and he is being fed, spoon by spoon, a nourishing gruel.

'The smell of that makes me hungry. I will ask Samuel to make us some soup.'

'But eat it up here, don't leave me.'

He exchanges a look with Hannah across the bed. The patient is becoming demanding.

That night, Hannah sleeps for five hours in his bed and he snoozes in the armchair. Then they swap places, so he can have a few hours' sleep, except that he cannot rest for he can feel her warmth in his bed. He is filled with a new panic, that his father will get better and that she will go.

'Do you know what I've always wished for?' Doctor Walsh asks when they are both at his bedside and he has finished eating.

'No, tell us, Doctor Walsh.'

'For a daughter as well as a son.'

'Am I not good enough?' Harry asks.

'Harry, you are a wonderful son, wonderful.' He seems to sink back into sleep.

'My mother died,' he explains. 'How I would have loved a sister as much as he wanted a daughter.'

'Maybe a single son is not enough because you are a sinner, isn't that so, Mr Walsh?' Hannah is smiling at him. 'That's why I came round, to return your letter.'

'I am a sinner, but a penitent one.'

'Yes, I think you are, penitent and sad. I would like to see you happy again.'

'I used to be happy, that was my disposition, but now, I don't know.'

'Your flaws, it seems, preoccupy you, why, you must be the most evil person in London, a veritable monster.'

'You think I am too taken up with my woes?'

'I do.'

'Would you help me to free myself of them?'

'Is that a proposal?'

'Of sorts.'

'It is an improvement on your letter.'

'If it is, would you be fool enough to accept it?'

'I would.'

They have forgotten the old man who lies between them and is now awake.

'Good, good,' he murmurs before closing his eyes again.

60. Timon's Jewels

A few days later Harry is rifling through his bedside drawer when he comes across the jewellery that once belonged to Timon's mother. Immediately he is struck by an idea. It seems obvious, all of a sudden, what he should do with it. Filled with a sense of resolution, he takes it out of its boxes and puts it in several hempen bags; the more valuable items he stuffs into the fob pocket of his belt, the less valuable ones into the side pockets of his coat. Apart from the little ring, the first gift that Timon gave him which he promised Tiberius he would place on someone's finger one day, there is the necklace of moonstones, a bracelet of jade, a full set of sapphires (earned after a particularly lustful night), a little diamond ring, a broach of opals, a string of pearls, with a broken clasp, and a number of gold chains. Timon's mother loved jewels.

Although his exertions have already made him tired, he leaves his father in Samuel's care and sets out for Covent Garden. Noises and flashes go off in his head but still he walks on. He goes across the Piazza to the tall pillars to the rear of St Paul's church and, to his surprise, sees that the peddler girl, who used to sell ribbons, is still there after all this time. This day, two children cling onto her. When she notices Harry, she advances.

'Buy a piece of dobbin, Guv, me dab's in the suds.'

He fishes around his pocket, pulls out the bag of gold chains, and places it in her hand.

'I have no coins but I think you will get something for these if you pawn them.'

'Where you git 'em?' she asks suspiciously.

'They're mine. I suggest you don't show them to your used-up, whip jack husband in case he's as suspicious as you are.' Sensing that he has taken offence, and that he might change his mind, she looks round slyly, grabs them and slips them into the recesses of her filthy clothing.

'Me dab's in quod, I won't be showing 'em to him, don't you worry.'

Harry thought he would feel buoyed by his act of charity, that he would be imagining the eager faces of her children as they looked at the square meal in front of them. Now he is convinced that the money won't get much further than the gin shop. Hoping to do better with his next act of charity, he makes his way to Mrs Gould's and hesitates for a moment at the front door. He enters it and asks the foggy dell who sits at the desk if Adele is in.

'She don't work here no longer. You the father then?'

Fancy being taken for Adele's father. He has no wish to rouse the bold wench's interest, by asking where she lives, and hastily takes his leave, feeling disappointed but also foolish. What to do next, he wonders. He has told Hannah that she must give him a few weeks, to straighten himself and get work, and she has agreed. But now all he wants is to see her. Despite his best intentions, he calls at the little house on Russell Street, opposite Button's, where she lives with her mother. Hannah looks surprised when she opens the door but welcomes him in. On seeing her, he instantly feels stronger. Can it really be that she has agreed to marry him?

'Would you come back to the rectory? I have something for you,' he says, thinking of the ring.

'Of course.' She giggles and puts his hand round her waist. 'I'm glad, you couldn't wait.'

As they walk back across the Piazza to the Long Acre, Hannah points to a woeful couple consisting of a small figure, swollen with child, with another, even smaller one, sobbing and straggling behind her.

'Why, that's Adele,' says Harry. 'I'm sure of it.'

'Who is Adele?' asks Hannah, but he is already hurrying away from her, shocked by the bump of Adele's belly and the blue rings under her eyes. When he addresses her she looks bewildered.

'Don mek me go Guv, I'm only twelve, I never lay wiv a man before,' says the smaller of the two. 'I wanna help Adele but me bruvver, he bounced me into this.'

'You're sick,' says Hannah to Adele. 'Who is this young girl?'

Adele has a coughing fit, the silt in her lungs gurgling as she does so, then whispers, 'Me sister. She's too young, that's what I tells me bruvver but the family, we're gut foundered, we need food.'

Harry's head is now throbbing but he realises that he cannot now walk away from Adele. The girl is really no more than a stranger but she has become his responsibility.

'Dearest one,' he says to Hannah, 'I will explain later but will you take Adele and her sister back home, to the barn at the rectory, she can rest there. I must go to Lombard Street, I have some jewellery, and it will raise money for a doctor.'

'I don't understand nuffing,' says Adele between coughs, looking suspicious and frightened, 'but I'll go wiv the lady, come Susan, you stay wiv me.'

Harry leaves Hannah to lead the two girls away, pleased at the fact that he has a task to do. When he returns from the jewellers he finds them in the barn in their courtyard. Samuel, on his employer's instruction, has already called for a doctor. Adele is barely conscious and lies, shivering, under a sheepskin rug. Susan has been given soup.

Harry's act of atonement, it transpires, has come too late.

Some of the coins he has for Adele are taken home to Southwark by Susan. Before she returns, Adele dies. The reverend struggles from his bed to say a prayer over Adele's puny body, then Harry takes it round to the gravedigger's house. He feels a great depth of sorrow. What are fair-minded people expected to do, he wonders. To ignore the poor because nothing can be done for them?

'Come, Susan, I will help you,' says Hannah to the weeping younger sister when she returns to the rectory the following day. 'The Hospital for Foundlings may offer you work in the kitchens. I will ask a friend of mine, Mrs Plunket, who runs them.'

As she leaves with her young charge Harry pulls Hannah to one side.

'I wanted to do good but I failed. I thought that if I did something noble I would deserve you more,' he says. His exertions, it seems, have simply made him more sensible to his own failings.

'Poverty and disease, how can one person hope to tackle those?'

'I've been a leather-head.'

'Not completely, you trusted me, I'm glad of that.'

'Trusted you?'

'Not to ask where the jewels came from or who Adele was. And don't worry, I won't.'

At this moment, he thinks, she must wonder if she has made a gross error in accepting him.

1745

61. Johann Christoph's Scriptorium

As Harry comes through the low door from Coventry Street he is nervous. To be back in Johann Christoph's scriptorium seems strange. Rows of tilted wooden desks line up against the windows, the better to catch the light, and large sheets of music lie across them and on the floor. It is the habit of the scribes to simply toss the finished sheets down to the ground once they have done with them. There is a smell about the place, of ink and paper and dust.

Hannah comes towards him, smiling. Despite the dismal manner of Harry's courting they have been married for several months. She blushes and lowers her eyes when she sees him. The freckles on her face stand out like the speckles of a thrush's breast. When they are alone he teases her. He does so because he knows he is almost better.

'What a pathetic creature you have married who depends on you to nurse him back to health.'

'That's right, you miserable addle pate, how do I tolerate you?'

He has met up with Arne again, with his dear Jonny and John Lampe, and has got to know their wives. The families rendezvous regularly, sometimes at the park, at Vauxhall Gardens, or at an ordinary on the outskirts, at Richmond or Kensington. Henrietta, Isabella and Cecilia have become Hannah's friends.

It is also their habit to walk up Saffron Hill to the Foundling Hospital to visit Lucy. Normally so calm, if they catch her when Mrs Trebeck takes it on herself to help out, she tends to look harassed. Little Susan, who is now Lucy's maid, always drops them a curtsy and blushes prettily when she sees them. Maybe Harry's attempt at philanthropy was more successful than he thought.

At table each night, when Harry is home, he stares across the table at Hannah in the candle light, for he can scarce believe that he has himself a wife. His father glows, for he loves her as much as Harry does. It is as if the rectory is made whole again to have a woman in it. Harry realises that his father is having to steel himself to the fact that they will move soon. They will share the tiny house in Russell Street with Hannah's mother, Friedal. Not only will it be convenient for Harry to be down the road from John Rich's theatre, but he wants Hannah to be close to her mother in the event of her conceiving. He promises the reverend that, when he has funds, they will all live together, for, to have one's family and old retainers under a single roof, is surely the natural state.

Now Harry is in the scriptorium, the old trouble with his nerves is reasserting itself. He is worried that if he encounters Peter, or Handel, he will not know how to act; the noises will start again in his head and make him stutter. True, the noises have eased, as have the dreams, but they come back every now and then. He is happiest on the stage; that's when he feels, at last, like the man he used to be. He digs his nails into the arm he is kneading in an effort not to come over cranky. He does not know that one of the scribes has run down to the theatre to find the composer. When he sees Handel hurry through the door, he wants to approach him, to greet him casually, but, despite his best intentions, is rooted, silent, to the spot where he is standing.

Handel is dark-clothed, like a bishop, and both his girth, and his long-bob wig, look too large for such a confined space. He looks round for Harry, then, when he sees him, walks up to him and throws his arms round his old singer. It is not Handel's habit to show emotion, but now he pats Harry on the back with almost Tyers-like vigour.

'Harry, how I pray for this moment. How is it that you have

not been round to Brook Street? Johann told me you were back. I hear you have nearly taken away one of his best copyists,' he turns and squeezes Hannah's hand, 'so each day I am expecting you but you do not come.' Surprised by the warmth of this greeting Harry makes a host of pointless gestures before managing to say, 'I wanted to come but I didn't know if it was right.' Handel ignores this.

'Hannah, you have a fine husband here. I am arranging for a set of linen to be sent to you. It is from Brussels.'

He begs Hannah to allow them a few moments together and pulls Harry up a set of decrepit steps, which look set to collapse under his weight, and bids Harry enter Johann Christoph's orderly office. He takes the only chair, tipping over a neatly folded pile of scores, then has Harry squat on a low stool looking up at him.

'You are only writing your oratorios now, so Jonny tells me, no more Italian operas?'

For a moment he looks thoughtful.

'Opera. What does it consist of but adapting music to vain and trivial words? That, at least is the view of some. Yes, I am done with it, too expensive, too difficult. Composing sacred music is, perhaps, an employment better suited to a man of advancing years.'

'I have missed singing in your oratorios, Maestro.'

'No longer, no longer. I've known you since you were a boy, do you realise that? You and John Beard, what a pair of pranksters you were at the Chapel Royal. I have always thought of you both as my creations.'

'It pleases me to hear you say that.'

'And now you are married. Plato once said that the human soul has three parts: libidinous, rational, spiritual. I am moving, I hope, towards the spiritual.' He chuckles. 'With your marriage I hope you are moving towards the rational.'

'To have chosen Hannah is probably the most rational thing I ever did.'

'My first real taste of the spiritual was writing Messiah.'

'I heard you wrote a fine aria especially for Susanna.'

'Susanna.' He pauses and looks dreamy. 'She have the most beautiful way of expressing herself. But when that actor fellow, Garrick, turned up in Dublin, I couldn't stand to be with them. He is a pretentious fop, how you say, a mere fribble, but the ladies, goodness knows why, they seem taken in by him. They were doing Shakespeare together at the Smock Alley Theatre. All his affected gestures: "Handel darlink, you simply must come and see mein Hamlet". I have no time for them.' Harry smiles at his attempt at impersonation.

'Dublin was a great success, was it not?' The sword flashes above his head; he hears the scream of an animal.

'Harry, it was wonderful to be free of the Goths and Visigoths of London who take delight only in contradiction and absurdity.'

'I am happy for you.'

'I do not pretend I welcomed the arrival of young Arne, I thought he was taking advantage of my success. But, for Susanna's sake, I was most gracious, I help him prepare a couple of concerts. I probably needed Arne to spur me to return, after all I was away ten months. Return and grapple with the contrary tastes of Polite Society. Then there was the letter from Nanette, that was a shock for us. So yes, another reason we return was to try and change your mind about going away.'

Harry can hear soft footsteps coming up the steps. Graceful footsteps. They pause outside then the door opens a crack. Before he can turn round the door closes again and the footsteps retreat. He decides to plunge in and ask Handel the question that plagues him still.

'Why was it you didn't invite me to Dublin?'

Handel thinks for a while.

'There were a number of reasons, there is never just one, but the main one was this, Harry. God placed into my care someone who was vulnerable. He needed me although after a time we needed each other in equal measure.' He pauses again. 'You hurt him. I'm sure you did not set out to do so. Some people it seems are destined to be hurt. I didn't want to lose you, of course I didn't, but I needed to take Peter away. It was in part to give you freedom, because I knew you should find yourself a wife. It was to calm you down if nothing else, and it was to protect Peter from the suffering he experienced. That you would take yourself off to war in Europe was most certainly not part of the plan.'

Harry finds himself amazed to be talking, openly, about what in the past was always secret and furtive. It makes him feel as if he has been released from a great burden.

'I thought you were jealous.'

'Not at all, just protective. I remember the very first time when he came to Brook Street. He was very young. He came up the stairs to the front parlour. Johann and I, we were making a little music, I think Rosengarve was there too. There was a pile of boxes to Peter's right, all higgledy-piggledy with the scores falling out of them. Discreetly, he leant over and he straightened them. Ah, I thought, this boy, he likes order, so do I.'

Handel didn't realise then that Peter was driven by some manner of compulsion to straighten things.

'Did you think once, as I always did, that you would marry one day?' Harry asks him.

'Some of us are not destined for the married state. Sadly, that can lead to...' he is looking for a word, 'complications.'

'Will Peter ever talk to me again? I want so much to be forgiven for what I did to him.'

'Give him time, Harry. Give him time. He is very fond of Hannah, that I know. For his own good he must forgive you one day.'

Harry thinks of the quietly closed door. When he goes downstairs Peter will have vanished like a wraith. Me and him, he sighs, if only we could put our conflicts behind us.

'What would make my life complete, make me better,' he says at last, 'is if he and I could be friends. And if I could sing for you again.'

'I can help you with one of those, but the other, it is not up to me.'

That night Harry tells Hannah everything about him and Peter. She weeps, for she does not understand. But her husband knows that she will find it in her heart to forgive him for she loves, not just him, but the man whom he still loves even though no longer with passion.

After their talk, once he goes to sleep, he soon finds he is on the battlefield again. As always, the wound on his head makes it so heavy that he cannot move. The contorted face with the raised sword stands above him. All of a sudden there is the sound of a shot and the face explodes into a hundred pieces. Just the body is left which falls across Harry, blood oozing out from the mess of torn flesh and bone above the collar.

When Harry wakes he feels calm. More than that, he feels relief at having managed, at last, to remember what happened. The next day, before he goes, as he does every day, to put a posy on Adele's grave, he digs up one of the lilac seedlings that grow in the garden at the rectory. He plants it in the graveyard of his father's church in memory of the unknown Frenchman who, out of fear, tried to kill him.

62. Paolo Rolli's Goodbye

His letter is handed to Harry by Attila at the stage door of the theatre.

'Harry, Mio Caro,' it starts. 'Paolo Rolli, you will be interested to hear, is staying with Farinelli in Madrid, for when I decided to leave Britain's shores it was too dangerous to cross the Continent and go back to Italy. I am sorry that I never said goodbye, properly, before I left for I wanted to tell you that I was very pleased to hear of your safe return.'

Did Harry misjudge the man? Did he have a heart after all?

'Farinelli, as you may have heard, is chamber musician to the Bourbon king, Philip of Spain, who is much afflicted by melancholy; he is so ill, in fact, that his physician has prescribed music as the cure. Each night Farinelli sings to him the same four arias. Whose soul could not be moved by that voice? He has become quite the centre of court life, putting on masques and entertainments a plenty. You will not be surprised to know that he is held in total adoration by their Royal Highnesses, particularly by the crown prince's wife, Barbara of Portugal. She is not unlike those aristocratic ladies who would swoon when they heard him at the King's.'

The times he talks about at the King's, they were nearly a decade ago. Much has changed.

'Senesino, meanwhile, is enjoying the delights of his palatial villa in Tuscany, all paid for by the proceeds of his sojourn in London. What a fruitful period that was for him. My sympathies go out to him just at present for he has Francesca Cuzzoni as his guest. I imagine that, now she has discovered the opulent style in which he lives, she will prove to be quite a sticker. She narrowly missed execution for trying to poison her worthless husband. Too bad that he survived. I always knew that she would never be able to hold onto her money, what a useless person she is and the voice, gone by now, I should imagine. Those sopranos never last long.'

That is closer to the Rolli he used to know.

'Before leaving I heard the Te Deum that Handel wrote after the battle of Dettingen - tell me, is it possible to have a public event without him setting it to music – then I attended the first London performance of the oratorio that was our undoing at the King's, his Messiah. I believe it is a piece that you will be singing in soon, I shall be sorry to miss hearing you. Although audiences in London have yet to fall in love with this work, one day they will. Handel's followers, to my eyes, consist now of merchants and Jews, not the fashionable crowd, but then, with all the talk of war, London, I am afraid, has lost its elegance. The audience notwithstanding, and the language as well, the Messiah is a fine piece of work. Your master is, without doubt, a genius and I would like to be remembered with forgiveness by you both.'

Forgiveness? Is this some deathbed conversion to guarantee his place in heaven? The letter ends simply with the following words.

'I will spend the next five days looking out at harsh sunlight and arid hills, for the journey from Madrid is a long and uncomfortable one and I must make my way home at last. Your good friend, Paolo Rolli, Bilbao.' The date, some months back, is July, 1745.

Harry pictures Rolli in his coach, disappearing into some Spanish haze. They were like a collection of exotic plants, the Italian singers and their entourage, briefly bursting into bloom on the London stage. With their vibrant colour and foreign scent they resembled those curiosities that are brought to these shores by the East India men. Our scenery-makers and aristocrats surrounded them with their fantasy creations, just as the Duke of Chandos surrounded his collection of artists with his Arcadian gardens. But somehow the native plant life proved too vigorous for these hot house blooms. Gay with his vulgar burlesques, Arne with his pastoral idylls, Handel with his personal blend of the sacred and profane. In the end it wasn't Handel, but the Italian opera, that became passé.

Paolo Rolli is right on one matter. All the talk is of war. Now that the Old Pretender's son, Charles Edward Stuart, is marching south from Scotland, panic is gripping the capital. Shops are closing, people are leaving, their carts or carriages filled to the brim, shutters are appearing across door fronts, there are shortages of food. It is, to Harry's mind, a passing hysteria. Besides, Charles Edward Stuart is a fool. The only person who truly believes that he will reach London within a matter of days is Jonathan Tyers.

Harry puts Rolli's letter aside, for he intends to show it to Handel. It is irony, indeed, that it has taken a battle, and exile in Dublin, for old enmities to subside. It reminds Harry that, for one person still, old enmities have not subsided. Peter talks to him civilly enough when they meet, he visits Hannah when Harry is not home, solicitous for her welfare now that she is sure she is with child, but he refuses to grant Harry what he really wishes for. The hand of friendship.

63. Revisiting Cavendish Square

Harry sees them one day, sitting in a box close to the stage while he sings the part of Jupiter in a revival of Semele. Handel is back, this season, at the King's, but his performances are on Saturdays only. Afterwards he seeks them out, the earl and his fubsey of old; the memory of both of them he holds dear, for the help they gave him when he first moved out from the rectory. They repair to a private dining club on Piccadilly, of which the earl is a member, and sup at his expense while the countess eats little and quaffs champagne. Harry tells them, as best he can, about his travails down the Main, and the earl gives the news he has of Douglas. Charles Edward Stuart's troop of 5,000 or so, mostly Highlanders, are encamped near Glasgow, but Douglas is disillusioned with his Stuart leader, he explains.

'He's a dreadful man, by the sounds of it, quite dreadful. Spoilt and petulant, says Douglas, I hope he will leave him well alone.'

'He's gone to ground it seems. The news sheets are telling people here to resume their normal lives,' Harry comments.

'That's because the threat from France has melted away. King Louis finds the Young Pretender as impossible as the rest of us,' says the earl.

'Harry, we go tomorrow to Cavendish Square. We are moving there.' The countess has drunk too much and she is slurring her words. 'Come and join us, look at our new apartment.'

'The square must be near finished now.'

'Oh yes, there are new streets aplenty, a church, many trades. Come, my dear, I am going to take you home now.' The earl gives her a concerned look.

'Can I bring my wife?' Harry asks.

'You have a wife? I knew you would.' The countess's face seems to crumble.

'Yes, do, we would love to meet her, wouldn't we, Bumbo?'

In the end, Hannah wishes to rest but Harry is keen to go, not so much to see the earl's new residence as to make enquiries of his own. His dearest wish is that they live as a family, Friedal, his dearest Papa, himself, Hannah, and the little one. Whether he can afford the rents is another matter.

The next day he makes tracks to the Fox's Paw. Marcel's welcome is ecstatic and unrestrained. He introduces him to grey Edmund who, to his surprise, has an apron on and is baking round the back. After he has imbibed one of Marcel's horribly strong coffees he makes his way to the offices of James Gibbs & Co and is delighted to see Timon. He makes no mention of the jewels but tells him about Hannah.

'I like the name and I'm glad you are settled. We both had a rum turn over Simeon. I am recovered now, I hope you are. Forget about the interest you owe me, I feel that I led you into your troubles.'

Harry asks him about the latest properties to be leased but quickly establishes that he does not earn enough, even with the help of Hannah's earnings and his father's stipend. The earl comes in to collect a key and Harry joins him and the countess; their apartment is one of the grander ones sitting directly on Cavendish Square. When he looks out of the back windows the clay pits and fields have gone, more streets now stretch out behind them.

'Bumbo would love you to be our neighbour. Would you ever

consider moving back here?' asks the earl.

He explains his position and why it is that he has no plans at present to move. The earl gently steers him out of earshot of his wife, to one of the windows.

'It's a fine view, don't you think?' He looks round, then lowers his voice. 'Harry, she is melancholy, I cannot rouse her spirits. If you and your wife wished to live near here, why, I would purchase a lease for you. There would be a quid pro quo, of course, but nothing that need disturb your family life.'

Harry looks out to the rooftops and thinks back to the nights that he and the countess enjoyed; the soft light, the silky sheets, waking up feeling sore but satiated. In his mind he thanks her for what she did for him but, on this matter, he is unable to oblige.

'Forgive me, My Lord, but I am leading a new life, free of temptation.'

'Dear dear, how virtuous. I am disappointed but I understand.'

1746

64. Birth

'Dearest Daughter, are you sure you do not wish me to stay with you?'

'Mama, please go to the theatre. I want you to hear Harry sing, there is only one performance left.'

What Hannah says to Friedal is true. Handel has been unwell, with his paralytic disorder, so only a short season has prevailed, this time at Covent Garden. His performers are singing in his Occasional Oratorio, a piece of military bombast designed to put backbone into the brave boys marching north to engage with Charles Edward Stuart. Harry's beautiful wife looks like an edible pudding, her condition makes her skin and hair glow, and he is immensely proud of her. He is also concerned, for her time is near.

Before he takes his leave for the theatre, her mother on his arm, he strokes her hard belly, gently pushes her hair behind her ears and rubs her darling, freckled nose against his.

'Go early to bed, my love, I will see you later.'

After the show there is a downpour, unusual for April; the coachmen sit hunched atop their carriages, their coats dripping, and the light boys look disconsolate because their flares have gone out. The rain releases a stench from the dank rags of the beggars that lurk in the darkness; theatre-goers, filled with uncertainty, are slow to disperse from the foyer. Harry looks for Friedal, whom he has forbidden to walk home without him, because the streets become dangerous late at night, and catches sight of her talking to Handel. He is cross, because Peter has disappeared, but he is rescued by the Reverend and Mrs Trebeck who insist that he join them in their hackney. Before Mrs Trebeck departs she implores Harry to give a concert in her house to help raise funds for the Foundling Hospital. Agreeing, he catches Handel raising his eyes to the ceiling behind her.

When they get home to Russell Street, and open the door, the first thing they hear is a scream from the upper room. The pair of them race up the stairs and there is Peter in the candlelight, his head and shoulders bent over Hannah's open knees. Her skirts are rucked up around the top of her belly, her face is distorted, sweat drenches her hair, her whole body writhes, and she screams again. Peter looks up.

'Thank goodness. Fetch rags, water, a knife; the baby is almost here.' Sure enough, something hard and slimy is emerging from the mess of bedclothes. In no time at all Peter is cradling a wriggling, crying infant, and Friedal is closing in with fresh wrappings and a knife. She tells him to put them round the baby while she deftly cuts the chord. Meanwhile, Harry moves to the top of the bed where he cradles his poor dear Hannah. Her face has gone the colour of ash, when he whispers that they have a daughter she makes no response. Friedal tells Peter to move and starts pushing rags under Hannah's legs. A damp, dark stain oozes out from beneath them.

'I can't seem to stop the flow,' she says.

Harry rocks her face in his arms and starts to moan although he knows that it is more than a moan, he is shouting.

'You mustn't leave me.' When he looks up, Peter and the baby are gone. Eventually he lies down beside her, putting his arm under her neck, and weeps until sleep hits him. When he wakes up, his arm numb, the grey of dawn seeps in through the window. His rumpled clothes are wet with the ooze that has come from between her legs. Friedal has covered her with a blanket. He checks immediately for a heartbeat. She is still alive. Friedal comes in, quietly.

'Go and change, I will watch over her now.'

'I'll go out and get bread and brew some tea,' he says. He can hear the hawkers begin their early morning calls out in the street.

When he goes downstairs, to the kitchen in the basement, still with his stained britches on, he finds a woman he recognises as the egg seller sitting in their Windsor chair. She keeps a cart on the corner of the Piazza and Russell Street. Peter is bending over her bare breast.

'Let us see now, will she suck? Oh you little pumpkin, of course you will, you are so hungry.' He fusses round the woman's teat while the baby sucks noisily. Two infants lie on a greasy blanket beside them on the floor; they belong to the egg seller Harry presumes. 'Your turn next, my little ones,' Peter says, picking one up and cradling it. He looks up at Harry and says, sharply, 'Hannah, what is her condition?'

'Awful, but she is alive.'

'Thanks be to God. Would you like to hold your daughter once she's fed?'

'No, not really. Thank you by the way. For being here, for what you have done. I wish I'd never left her.' He wants to ask him how it was that he came to the house. As if reading his thoughts, Peter says, 'Hannah sent a boy with a note to the theatre; he asked me to help him find you but you were on stage and Friedal was lost somewhere in the pit. That's when I raced across to Russell Street to see what I could do; once here I couldn't leave her, I was so thankful when you came back.'

For the next two days Peter and Friedal care for little Jessie who squirms and contorts her face in all manner of odd expressions. The milch-cow feeds the baby, under Peter's close supervision, then feeds her twin boys. Harry strokes his loved one's hair, washes her, feeds her, and nurses her. For much of the time she has a fever. When no-one else is in the room he goes down on his knees and prays. He senses that she is fighting for her life. On the third day after the birth she is able to pull herself up, painfully, to a seated position. When Harry accidentally brushes her breast she cries out. It looks swollen and sore. He goes downstairs to consult Peter.

'She needs to feed that child, that be it,' says the milch-cow, wisely. Peter lifts his bundle tenderly in his arms and takes her upstairs. He pulls back Hannah's shift and expertly props Jessie's head where she will smell the teat. He slowly massages Hannah's breast and she cries out in pain. In time her discomfort eases, and the baby sucks. There is so much milk that one of the twins has to be bought upstairs to drain the other breast. He is a trencherman, seizing on the teat so that Hannah cries out again. Harry watches as his ex-lover strokes and squeezes his wife's breast, for all the world as if milking an udder. Despite her ordeal, Hannah starts to look happier.

On the fourth day a chariot pulls up alongside the front door. It is Handel.

'So now, Peter, you are a midwife.'

He has bought a woven basinet and daintily knitted blankets, bottles of fruit in syrup, his best port, to build up Hannah's strength, he says, champagne and a side of cold beef which he loses no time in slicing and laying out on a platter. Anthony trudges from coach to kitchen with his arms laden.

'You be at the theatre times, me brother and I, we sees yer from the top gallery,' the egg seller says in her strong country accent.

'I am at the theatre,' says Handel, 'and this man here, he is too.' He points at Harry.

'Dun think I recognise 'im, singer be he?'

'Yes, a very famous one.' Handel is in excellent spirits.

The egg seller, emboldened by his bonhomie, says shyly, 'I sees a tin bath under that there table, always wanted to bathe me chitties, oi'ave.'

'And so you should,' pronounces the composer. 'In Germany we like our baths, it is good for us. Is that not right, Friedal? Come, Harry, make yourself useful, we bathe the kinder.'

Every one of the buckets, that a girl brings from the well down the street each day, is emptied into a large copper. The water is heated and the bath filled. Three naked babies, Harry's looking red and out of proportion, the egg seller's boys looking bonny, are laid out on blankets. She lowers a twin into the water and he screams then, as he kicks, he starts to relax and chuckle. Handel is delighted. The other boy is next, then Peter gently lowers Jessie. She does not even scream, she wriggles, arches, struggles to be free and smiles, making her cross little features look pretty for the first time. Then Peter wraps her tenderly in a new gown that Handel has brought with him, and ties a little bonnet round her head. The egg seller has lost no time in routing round the basinet and finding clean clothing for her boys. They look even more bonny now. Their dirty rags have been thrown, by Handel, into the fire. He looks up at Peter who is cradling Jessie.

'Now you must let Harry hold her,' he says quietly.

With reluctance and hesitation Peter hands Harry the bundle. He takes hold of her, she is warm and, despite the fact that she is sleeping now, so alive. He puts her face close up to his and smells the sweetness of her skin. Friedal, who is watching, wipes away a tear.

'I must take you home now,' says Handel. As he says this, Peter leans over the bundle in Harry's arms and kisses the little forehead. Then he puts his arms round Harry and they embrace.

'I'll be back soon,' he says.

'Godparents, have you decided Godparents?' asks Friedal.

'I would be honoured if you would both be her Godparents,' Harry says, looking at his guests.

Handel looks satisfied. Peter smiles and kisses Harry's cheek.

As they open the front door they hear church bells ringing. Not just the bells at St Paul's across the way, but the bells as far as St Clement Danes and St Mary le Strand, then after a while they realise that bells are peeling across the whole of London, their chimes echoing from as far away as St Paul's Cathedral and from across the river. A crowd is pouring out from the drinking den across the road next to Button's.

'Heard the news, guv'nors?'

'What news?'

'Cumberland's victory.'

'The Jacobites are routed.'

'We're saved.'

'There was a battle, up in Scotland. The Young Pretender, he's been defeated.'

'Where?'

'Don't reckon I care.'

'I can tell you, guv'nor.' A small boy, ragged and dirty, looks up at them. 'It was near the coast, up towards the Highlands, on the moors. There's a small town nearby. Culloden.'

65. Luncheon at the Vauxhall Gardens

The women fuss over the baby and Harry looks out of the window, admiring the sight of the Lambeth Palace, as they trot past it, but wishing that they did not have to celebrate the victory at Culloden. They are attending Tyers' grand luncheon that is being held in the Prince of Wales dining pavilion, in order to support Handel, the guest of honour. Young George is sitting on his lap, taking in every sight. Hannah smiles at the little boy.

'Look,' says George, then reads out the words 'Wright's-starch-manufactory,' written on a large sign.

'That means we're nearly at the gardens,' Harry tells Gorringe. 'I think you'll like them.'

'Better than I like your filthy streets, I hope.'

He and Gorringe have developed a friendly rivalry over the competing attractions of London and Haarlem. That is, when his Dutch guest is not looking, smitten and dog-eyed, at Lucy. Harry experiences a twinge of disappointment; ever since she made an appearance at their house, Gorringe, whose visit he'd been so excited about, has been very poor company.

Once they arrive, Mrs Tyers hastens the ladies away and Susan follows young George, for it is her unfortunate fate to keep an eye on him. A groom takes Lucy's smart new coach and four round the back to the stables. Since her father, the duke, died, and left her all his money, she has allowed herself certain luxuries. Gorringe and Harry are left with the expansive Tyers.

'Do you know what I see when I look out onto the river here, Mr Gorringe?'

They follow his eye along the empty expanse of water which offers little to see other than reflected clouds. Gorringe has already made a comment on the absence of crossings over the great river.

'I see history, the making of our great British nation,' Tyers continues. 'I remember when I first read that Charles Edward Stuart had got as far as Derby with his army of Highlanders. "Wife," I said, "I blame the new toll roads, it's too easy now to cross England".'

'The Jacobite threat took us all by surprise,' Harry explains to his friend.

'But there was one party who had been expecting it all along because he was the one behind it,' says Tyers. 'And that was King Louis.'

'He is troublesome, that French king, but no worse than King Fritz,' comments Gorringe.

'It was a near escape, my Dutch friend. Your nation by the way, a brave ally of ours, we thank you for that. But to return to the French, they had their fleet all set for an assault on Dover.'

'And possibly on these gardens,' Harry adds.

'We were in danger, Mr Gorringe, one step from being invaded.' Tyers looks satisfied and Gorringe winks behind his back. They are taken through the tunnel and, as the fantastic sight of the gardens, full of revellers, unfolds before them, Tyers waves an arm.

'Follow me, follow me, Peter has arrived already with Handel. You must meet my Director of Music, Mr Gorringe, Thomas Arne, he has arranged for some military music to be played later on today as befits our celebration.'

'Ah yes, the ever popular Rule Britannia,' Gorringe murmurs.

Every dining pavilion, it seems, is occupied, for it is June and the weather is fine. The Prince of Wales Pavilion has a long table in it laid with white linen cloths and large silver tureens of punch.

Harry introduces his friend to the assembled company. Tyers' son and daughter-in-law are already seated, and their children have whisked young George away. Handel is sitting between John and Henrietta Beard, while Peter topes near the bandstand with the flap-eared trumpeter, Valentine. Every now and then Handel's eyes look fleetingly in their direction. Arne is paying his respects to Hannah who is being looked after by Mrs Tyers. Lucy is listening intently to his young son, Michael.

'Papa is highly pleased with my progress on the cello and the harpsichord,' he boasts.

'And your singing,' his father adds.

'George, I'm afraid, is very behind,' laughs Lucy. Arne simpers. Harry pats the six year old prodigy on his back, exchanges a look with his wife and mouths the word 'brat'.

Gorringe looks expectant when a waiter comes forward, offering drink, and disappointed when he learns that the punch consists only of fruit juices. He takes a sip as if it was poison. He is settled near the ladies and intends to draw Lucy away when there is an opportunity.

'Do you remember where you were when you heard we had won at Culloden, Handel?' Tyers shouts across the table. 'I do. I was on the steps by Westminster Hall, waiting for my barge.'

'Ah so,' says Handel, slathering butter on a chunk of bread.

'I'll never forget that moment. Members of both Houses were swarming outside, the boatmen were standing in their boats banging their oars on the water. We are saved, that's all I could think of; we are saved.'

'Did you think that when the poor bedraggled prisoners were

brought south to be executed?' Dorothea interjects. 'Maybe you went to watch, father-in-law, it wasn't far from here. It was only then that we learnt about the cruelty of the king's son.' Handel nods and Tyers glowers.

'The excesses of war are a price that has to be paid in the interests of our safety, daughter-in-law.'

'The excesses were those of youth. The duke and his adversary were just twenty-five years old, remember. Both are contemptible; one is a butcher, the other a worthless coward.'

'Hush, dear, you will upset your Papa,' Mrs Tyers calls across the table. Dorothea looks unmoved by this prospect. Harry wonders about the friendship between Hannah and Dorothea. She's so very earnest, her braids have a Puritan look to them, and worst of all, not one corner of flesh is on show. He can picture the pair of them marching down Southwark High Street, exhorting the denizens to follow Mr Wesley. She is one of those types, he thinks, who listen to Handel's oratorios because she finds them uplifting.

Gorringe successfully entices Lucy away so she can show him the gardens. He will not be happy because Jonny and Henrietta follow them, trying to catch up. Peter comes back to Handel's side and wants to hear from Harry if Gorringe is a worthy man.

'I think he is,' pronounces Handel.

'I hope he is,' says Peter quietly. 'After all, she's had her heart broken once.'

'You exaggerate.' Handel looks uncomfortable.

'Do I?' He lowers his voice. 'You know she loved you. You thought that people would think you were after her money. But it would have given her pleasure to help you. It would have given her pleasure to be your wife.'

'It was you?' Harry gasps, 'who broke her heart?'

'I protest,' says the composer.

'I wasn't the only one running away to Dublin,' says Peter, then keeps his silence.

Hearing the word Dublin, Jonathan the Younger leans over.

'What were your impressions of Dublin, Sir? They love their poets do they not, the Irish? I envy them, it keeps their history alive.'

'It does more than that, it puts music in their soul,' says Handel. He is only too happy for the subject of conversation to change.

'Plenty of music here, in our souls,' Tyers interrupts. 'Handel, you always said that what we, the great British public, likes, is something that hits one right on the drum of the ear.' Tyers, Harry assumes, is the only person present who takes this comment as a compliment. Handel nods. He is looking longingly at the platters of meat being laid out on the table. A dish of venison in a red wine sauce is put right in front of him and he almost whimpers. When offered a refill of fruit punch, he says, 'Get some red wine for goodness sake, I'm not a monk.'

'Dublin has two cathedrals, does it not?' asks Jonathan.

'Yes. Remarkable, no? They are quite close to each other. Do you remember, Peter, how you and Maggie, you hand out alms near them, in the Liberties? You'd see much poverty there, more even than here.' Peter nods.

'Two cathedrals? Most odd,' says Dorothea as if an indecency has been committed. 'Did they have charities there, Mr Handel?'

'Oh many, all of them with their claws in me.' He laughs.

After lunch Harry wanders over to the furthest pavilion, arm in arm with the composer. Peter, who has been titivating him as if he was Roubiliac's statue, has returned to the company of the trumpeter. Their friend, Lord M, is there, talking to Lord and Lady Harlow. The daughter, Isabel, is in conversation with the Duke of Richmond and his young sister, Lady Sarah Lennox, one of Harry's pupils. Isabel's arm threads through her husband's as he approaches and she turns her back.

'Trouble is with Maria Theresa,' Lord M is explaining to Harlow, 'she's a Catholic zealot and don't like Jews.'

'Ridiculous,' yawns Harlow. 'How does business run without them? The card tables would be empty.'

'Seen the king lately?'

'No, he's gallivanting in Hanover, last heard of in a Turkish tent dressed as an Eastern potentate.'

'No doubt with Von Walmoden as a Turkish concubine.'

The two worldlings break off their conversation to greet Handel and his guide.

Handel bows elaborately to Lady Sarah, then to a fresh-faced lass who Lord M refers to as his niece. Harry remembers her from their afternoons at St Clement Danes.

'I am sorry about your wife,' says Harry.

'Yes, terribly sad,' sniffs his lordship.

'So, Handel, I saw your oratorio recently at Covent Garden,' says Lord Harlow, 'there was a lot of banging on the kettledrums and girding of loins for the battle.'

'Yes, that is what the public like at present,' says the maestro.

'You are right, the theatre was full.'

'I love all that military bombast,' says Lady Sarah. The composer smiles at her winningly. The marchioness still studiously ignores them; her passion for Handel, which she once boasted of, is clearly spent.

Because the composer tires easily, after a few more minutes of conversation they return to their table and Harry joins Hannah. She looks well, at last, and their little baby, with the screwed up face, has blossomed into a plump, pink, smiling cherub. Peter comes and sits with them and, as usual, cannot stop himself from fidgeting with her bonnet, wiping the dribble from her lips, and cooing and chuckling so that she is quite unable to remain asleep. Hannah looks on lovingly.

Six year old Michael Arne is ushered onto the bandstand by his proud parent and gives an underpowered rendition of Rule Britannia. Then one Thomas Lowe sings a new song by Handel about the victory over the rebels. Tyers looks pleased and leads the applause. Once the clapping dies down Valentine takes to the centre of the bandstand. A small choir shuffles onto the stage behind the trumpeter and the haunting trumpet solo of Handel's popular adaption, in honour of the Duke of Cumberland, of See the Conquering Hero Comes, rings out.

Gradually the talk and laughter amongst the crowd ceases as their attention is focussed on the bandstand. Arne slows the tempo of Handel's rousing chorus. The singing gets louder and louder, the choir members smile as the audience starts to join in. Arne then turns. He waves his baton in Handel's direction. The eyes of the audience follow him, as they realise that the composer is with them. The music continues, the trumpet sings out. The entire audience is now singing. Handel stands. There is an eruption of cheering and clapping. People shout out, joyfully; he waves.

'Yes,' says Tyers, 'his star has turned. I knew it would. Mr Handel, you are now a man of the people.'

Postscript

Writing historic fiction

Handel's career really was as vicissitudinous as it is depicted here; he really was the presiding genius of the Italian opera when it bloomed on the London stage, and the inventor of a new idiom, the English dramatic oratorio. His principal Italian singers are named in the book, as is one of the librettists at the Italian opera; Farinelli was indeed the Prince of the Opera of the Nobility as the rival company became known eventually. His English singers included John Beard and Thomas Reinhold and one of his favourite sopranos (turned mezzo-soprano) was Susanna Cibber, sister of Thomas Arne. Arne was most certainly overshadowed by his older rival but was an earnest promoter of English opera with his friends, John Lampe and Robert Carey. Jonathan Tyers was the founder of the Vauxhall Gardens, and a great populariser of Handel, and the artist, William Hogarth, was most certainly a Trustee of the Foundling Hospital and one of Tyers' artists. At a time period, later than the book, the annual performances of Messiah at the chapel of the Foundling Hospital was to become famous.

But the curious thing is that in a career so well recorded, so that we know where each of his entertainments was played and on what dates, Handel's private life, and his sexuality (for those who are interested in such things) remains something of a mystery. According to his will, his manservant living at the time of his death on April 14th, 1759, was a Huguenot and nephew to his original manservant. He had several close circles of friends, like the Harris brothers, cousins of the Shaftesburies, who he visited near Salisbury, also near neighbours, Mrs Pendarves, her brother Mr Granville, and her friend Anne Donnellan. And, of course, there was that most endearing of figures, his treasurer and copyist, Johann Christof Schmidt as well as the son, John

Christopher Smith, who was groomed to take Handel's place in the musical firmament.

Beyond that is a void which I have peopled with the characters you find in this book: Harry and Hannah Walsh, Peter, Nanette and Anthony, Mrs Pendleton, Anne Donovan, Lord M, John Swiney, Mrs Tyers, Rosengarve, Lucy, Gorringe, and Rachel Trebeck. Any resemblance to existing historic characters is incidental but all are props to this drama of a real life lived at an extraordinary time, the first two reigns of the Hanoverian kings. I apologise to Handel scholars and singers if this fictional depiction of the great composer is very different to the Handel they have composed in their own hearts and whom they hold dear.

Those familiar with Handel's biographies (he is served to this day by a body of scholarly and knowledgeable experts) will know that a few dates have been changed in order to serve the needs of the story. Semele, for example, is mentioned several years before it was written, and the organist of St George's makes his ignominious return to Dublin too early; the Arne's upholstery shop on the other hand had closed, in real life, by the time Nanette came to London, and Simpsons, in Candle Alley, had yet to open. There may be other inadvertent inaccuracies for which I apologise. I also say now that writing historic fiction is always a balancing act; rather than striving for authenticity, one is striving for believability and concerns that chime with those of the modern reader.

A Note on Handel's name. Scholars today usually refer to Handel as George Frideric because this is the spelling, translated from the German, Friedrich, used in his naturalisation papers of 1727 and at the bottom of all but one of his wills. However, the author has decided to use the current spelling of his name.

**TOP HAT
BOOKS**

Historical fiction that lives.

We publish fiction that captures the contrasts, the achievements, the optimism and the radicalism of ordinary and extraordinary times across the world.

We're open to all time periods and we strive to go beyond the narrow, foggy slums of Victorian London. Where are the tales of the people of fifteenth century Australasia? The stories of eighth century India? The voices from Africa, Arabia, cities and forests, deserts and towns? Our books thrill, excite, delight and inspire.

The genres will be broad but clear. Whether we're publishing romance, thrillers, crime, or something else entirely, the unifying themes are timescale and enthusiasm. These books will be a celebration of the chaotic power of the human spirit in difficult times. The reader, when they finish, will snap the book closed with a satisfied smile.